TAKING CHANCES

LAURA FARR

This book in intended for over 18s only.

ISBN-13 978-1542913225

IBSN-10 1542913225

Editing by Laura Hampton at Editing For You.

Cover by April Flowers Cover Designs

http://www.afcoverdesigns.wordpress.com

DEDICATION

This book is dedicated to Four Brits Book Fest (FBBF 2016). This was my first ever book signing. If I hadn't attended this signing, and met so many amazing authors, I can hand on heart say that this book would not exist. FBBF 16 gave me the courage and determination to pursue my dream of writing. Thank you xxx

Prologue

I sighed as I walked to the car. "Mitch, are you sure you're okay to drive?"

My best friend's boyfriend turned to me and scowled. "I've already said I'm fine to drive Libby, I've only had one drink, just get in!"

I fisted my hands at my sides before I opened the car door and slid into the back seat. Mitch and I had never seen eye to eye, he treated my best friend like shit, and for some reason, she put up with it. Mia was sitting in the front seat of Mitch's car; she'd stormed out of the club we were in after catching Mitch flirting with some girl at the bar. I squeezed her shoulder as I scooted along the seat, sitting behind Mitch.

It was meant to have been a girl's night out, we'd been having a great time dancing and enjoying ourselves until Mia had spotted Mitch at the bar with some girl draped all over him. He'd tried to say he was only talking to her while he waited for his drink, but we'd both seen what he was doing. Mia had walked out, and I had followed. Unfortunately, Mitch had also followed and convinced Mia to let him take us home. I would rather have caught a taxi, but it was 2am on a Sunday morning, and we all knew that getting a taxi at that time wouldn't have been easy.

Mia and Mitch had always had a fiery relationship, and I was dreading being a witness to the argument that was brewing. I dropped my head back against the seat, closing my eyes as Mitch pulled out of the carpark.

I must have fallen asleep, waking up to Mia screaming and the car skidding down the road. I looked out of the passenger side window to see a set of headlights coming straight towards us. The impact threw me sideways into the car door, smashing my head against the window. Everything was happening in slow motion, and it seemed an eternity until the car stopped moving. I could feel something warm running down my face, but I couldn't make my arms move to feel what it was. I tried to speak, but no sound came out, my whole body felt heavy, and I could feel myself losing consciousness. I struggled to stay awake, slowly moving my head to look into the front of the car, desperately searching for a glimpse of Mia. I saw her slouched forward in her seat before the blackness took me.

Chapter One

Libby
Four months later

I woke up screaming. My arms and legs were wrapped in the duvet, sweat covered my body and tears were running down my face. Suddenly the lights flicked on and my Mum rushed into the room.

"Libby, sweetheart." She said, pulling me into her arms and kissing me on the head. "Was it the same nightmare?" I nodded, shutting my eyes tight.

I'd been having nightmares two or three times a week for the past few months, it was always the same, Mia screaming and the sound of metal hitting metal as the van ploughed into us. Mia would be pleading with me to help her, but I was never able to reach her. In reality, I had never had the chance to help her, after losing consciousness in the back of the car, I woke up in the hospital three days later. I'd been placed into a medically induced coma, allowing the swelling on my brain to go down following my head hitting the car window.

It was after I woke up that I found out that my best friend of fifteen years had died, the van that hit us impacted directly onto

3

Mia's side of the car. She'd never stood a chance. Mitch had also died; he wasn't wearing his seatbelt and was thrown through the windscreen. For days, I sobbed, feeling guilty that I had survived while they had died. I later found out that Mitch had a blood alcohol level of 160, twice the legal limit at the time of the accident. He'd assured me that he'd only had one drink that night, when in reality, he must have had five or six at least. Maybe more. I should never have let us get in that car with him, I should have pushed for us to get a taxi home. My best friend would still be alive if I had.

I was pulled back to the present by my Dad's voice from my doorway, asking me if I wanted a cup of coffee. I might have been nineteen years old, but I was still my Dad's little girl.

"What time is it?" I asked, looking around for my phone to check the time. "You need to get back to bed, you've got work in the morning. I don't want to keep everyone awake." I told him feeling guilty.

My parents had been amazing since the accident, but I could see in their faces how tired they were and how worried about me they had become.

"Nonsense." My Dad replied, waving his arm. "It's 5 am, got to be up in an hour anyway. I'll go and put the kettle on."

"Thanks, Daddy, I'll be down in a few minutes." I smiled weakly at him. I turned to my Mum who was looking at me, worry etched on her face.

"Libby, I really think that you should talk to someone, it's been four months and these nightmares aren't going away, talking to someone can help you deal with things." She said gently.

"I'll think about it, Mum." I lied.

"You've been thinking about it for months Libby, that's your standard response when your Dad or I mention it. You can't carry on like this."

I gave her an irritated look, and she put her hands up as she backed out of my room. "Okay okay, just think about it, please!" She begged. "I'll go and help your Dad in the kitchen, come down when you're ready."

I flopped back down on my bed, my arm coming up over my head. I knew deep down that my parents were right, the nightmares weren't going away and something needed to change. However, the thought of sitting in a room with someone I didn't know, going over and over what had happened, filled me with dread. I just couldn't see how that would help me.

I made my way downstairs, stopping in the bathroom to splash some cold water on my face, my Dad was right, there was no point going back to bed, I had to be up for work in just over an hour anyway.

I had been studying English Literature at Manchester University before the accident, but had dropped out after missing so much work during my recovery. I had suffered with headaches following the head injury and found it difficult to concentrate for long periods, I'd moved back home with my parents for the time being. I wanted to finish my university course, but it just wasn't a priority at the moment.

I had started working at the village bakery about four weeks ago, while it wasn't something that I wanted to do forever, it got me out of the house for a few hours and took my mind off the accident and Mia. I think my parents were just grateful that I wasn't lying in bed all day.

As I walked into the kitchen my Mum and Dad were sat at the table talking in hushed voices, they stopped when I pulled a chair out to sit down, a sure sign they were talking about me.

"Here's your coffee sweetie." My Dad said, sliding the mug across the table to me.

"Thanks," I said, eyeing him warily.

"When you're home from work later we want to discuss

something with you, we'll talk about it over dinner. Okay?" He asked, smiling at me.

I gave him a tight smile back. Great, I thought to myself, they were joining forces in the hope that I would decide to go and speak to a counsellor, just what I needed.

"I'm going to get ready for work, thanks for the coffee," I replied, ignoring his comment and heading upstairs.

The walk to work was a short one, my parents lived in a small village in Shropshire, and everything was within walking distance of their house. They had moved to the village just before my older brother had been born. There were two years between me and Jack, he had left university last year with a degree in Finance and was currently travelling around America with some friends. He'd flown home after the accident and had stayed for a couple of weeks.

He'd never said anything to me, but I always thought that he had a soft spot for Mia, growing up she was always around our house and I saw the way he looked at her when he thought no one was looking. I'd told Mia numerous times that I thought my brother liked her, she had always brushed it off as nothing, though, saying that Jack was too nice for her, she always went for the bad boys, Mitch being no exception.

I sighed as I walked past the small village park, I'd spent hours here with Mia as a child playing on the swings, and then later as a teenager, flirting with boys and drinking cider on the roundabout. We had met on the first day at primary school, she had come bounding over to me, her long blonde pigtails bouncing around her shoulders. I'd been standing on my own in the playground, she had told me that her name was Mia and that we were going to be the very best of friends. She had been right, even at the age of four she had been outgoing and confident, the complete opposite to me, I was shy and awkward growing up. We were an unlikely pair but it worked for us, most of the time, we occasionally argued the older we got, normally over boys, specifically Mia's boyfriends who tended to treat her badly and break her heart. We never let anyone come between us, though, our friendship was too important for that, boyfriends came and went, but we were always there for each other.

I pulled my arms tight around myself as the wind whipped my hair around my face. It might have been early April and officially spring time, but in typical British fashion, it was freezing. I hurried along the pavement, as I reached the bakery I pulled the door open and the smell of fresh bread hit my nose, making my stomach rumble. It was then that I realised I hadn't had any breakfast in my rush to escape the kitchen and my parents.

"Morning Libby." Said my boss Sarah, "You look freezing, come and get warm before you start work."

"Thanks, Sarah," I replied as she handed me a mug of steaming coffee, my hands tightening around it in an attempt to thaw my freezing fingers.

Sarah had owned the bakery in the village square for as long as I could remember, she was a friend of my Mums and had offered me a job after seeing how worried my Mum was about me. Since the accident, I hadn't been out much, so my time at work was really the only time I spoke to people outside of my family. My friends from university had tried to stay in touch, but when I wasn't returning their calls and texts, they soon gave up.

I'd just finished my coffee and thawed out slightly when the first customer came through the door. A lot of the customers were regulars, and I was getting used to what they would order each day. "Morning Mrs Rogers, the usual?" I asked her, smiling.

"Yes, please dear, and can I also get a victoria sponge? I've got my sister and her husband coming over for lunch." She replied, frowning at me slightly. "You look so tired Libby dear, are you sleeping okay? It must be so hard for you, losing your friend the way you did, and for you to be in the accident as well, so terrible."

She cocked her head waiting for me to reply. Thankfully Sarah had heard the whole conversation and came to my rescue. "Libby, Leo could do with some help out the back if you don't mind? I can finish off serving Mrs Rogers."

I smiled at her gratefully and hurried out the back. People commenting about the accident and Mia happened a lot. Living your whole life in a small village, everyone knew your business, and most seemed to have an opinion on it. Leo looked up as I burst through the door.

"You okay, Libby?" He asked looking concerned. Leo was Sarah's son, and he ran things behind the scenes at the bakery.

"I'm fine, just escaping the village gossip. Your Mum has just saved me from Mrs Rogers," I told him rolling my eyes.

He nodded his head in understanding. Like myself, Leo had grown up in the village, he was the same age as my brother, although they hadn't been friends at school. He had asked me out before I went off to university, but I'd turned him down. It had made the first few days working at the bakery a little awkward, but we were both past that now and had become friends. I was just hoping that he wouldn't ask me out again. I wasn't at all interested, it wasn't that Leo was ugly, quite the opposite, in fact, he was tall with short blonde hair and bright blue eyes, but he just didn't give me that fluttery butterfly feeling I had read so much about in the romance books that I loved.

Mia had never understood my passion for reading, she had told me that the men in those books didn't exist, and that I would never find anyone if I was holding out for Mr Perfect. She thought that I should live in reality and not between the pages of some book. I wasn't holding out for Mr Perfect, but I was waiting to feel that connection with someone. I hadn't felt the need to sleep with lots of boys at university, unlike most of my friends. I'd been on the odd date, but it had never led to anything. This meant, however, that I was still a virgin at the age of nineteen, something else that Mia never understood. She was fifteen when she'd lost her virginity to an older boy in the back of his car since then she had never been without a boyfriend, even if they didn't stick around for long.

I heard Sarah shout that Mrs Rogers had left, and that it was safe to come out. I smiled at Leo and headed back to the counter. "Thanks," I told her, gratefully.

"Anytime sweetie. How are you doing?" She asked me, turning to wipe down the counter. "I know your Mum's worried about you." She paused and looked over at me. I dropped my eyes to the ground. I hated the 'how are you?' question.

"I'm okay I guess, just taking each day as it comes," I mumbled.

"I'm always here if you need to talk Libby, anything I can do to help, just ask."

"Thank you," I told her, giving her a small smile. It wasn't that I wasn't grateful, I just couldn't understand why everyone was so keen on getting me to talk about my problems. Talking about things made me remember, and right now remembering hurt. I was thankful when I heard the bell chime on the door, announcing the arrival of a customer and I greeted them eagerly, making myself busy to avoid any further personal chats.

The rest of the day passed by quickly, thankfully without any more awkward conversations. Before I knew it, it was closing time, and I was heading home to face what felt like the firing squad.

Chapter Two

I opened the front door to an empty house, breathing a sigh of relief I headed upstairs. My parents must have still been at work, my Dad worked as an IT Consultant, and my Mum worked part time as a receptionist at the local Doctors surgery. She would normally be home by now but often worked late if the Doctor was running behind.

I had a quick shower and headed downstairs, flopping on the sofa. As I did, I heard the key in the door and my Mum walked in. "Libby?" She called out.

"In here Mum," I shouted back. She popped her head around the living room door.

"How was work, honey?" She asked.

"Fine," I answered deciding not to tell her about Mrs Rogers, even though Sarah probably would when they next spoke. "How was your day?" I asked her, getting up off the sofa and following her into the kitchen.

"Good, busy, but good. Can you get the dinner on while I go and change?" She opened the fridge door and got out a cottage pie that she must have made this morning after her early wake- up call. "Your Dad should be home soon, can you set the table as well, please? Thanks, honey." She said making her way upstairs.

Ten minutes later my Dad arrived home, he called out hello as he entered the kitchen and headed over to my Mum, kissing her on the lips. My Mum was preparing the vegetables, and I was sitting at the kitchen table, fidgeting nervously while I waited to hear what they wanted to discuss with me.

I didn't have to wait long, as soon as we all sat down to eat they hit me with it.

"We've been talking to your Aunt Claire." My Mum said hesitantly. "We think that you should go and visit her for a few weeks, the weather will be lovely there, and Claire would love to see you, as well as Uncle Ryan and your cousins." She looked over at me nervously, obviously worried as to what my reaction would be.

"You want me to go and stay with Aunt Claire?" I asked, shocked. "But she lives in America!"

My Dad's sister had gone to study at the University of Texas in Austin, it was there that she had met Uncle Ryan. After university, they had married and had two children, apart from the odd visit to see us over the years she had never come home. We had been out to visit them twice when I was growing up, once when I was ten, and again when I was fifteen. They owned a huge horse ranch near to Austin in Texas, people could holiday there and learn how to ride the horses among other things. Uncle Ryan had inherited the ranch from his father a couple of years ago, and now he and my Aunt ran it together.

"Libby, we're worried about you, you're not sleeping, you're barely eating, you've lost a lot of weight sweetheart. You're not living you're just existing. Mia died, and that was tragic, but you're still here, and you need to start living again. We think that this will be good for you." I could hear her voice cracking with emotion as she spoke.

"It sounds like I don't have a choice, that you've already decided that I'm going, what about my job? I can't let Sarah down; I've only been working in the bakery a few weeks, and I hate flying!" I rushed out, panicked.

"Libby, you're nineteen years old, we can't make you go, but we really think that you should, and as for your job, I've already spoken to Sarah, this is only a holiday, you can go back to the bakery when you get home if that's what you want." Her eyes pleading with me.

"I need to think about it, I'm going up to my room," I said, quickly jumping up and making for the door.

"Libby?" My Mum called out.

"Leave her love, give her some time to think it through." I heard my Dad say quietly.

I went upstairs and lay on my bed, I couldn't go to America, could I? What would I do when I was there? I hadn't seen my cousins in over four years, would we even get on? Brody was twenty-two, and Savannah was a year older than me at twenty. As far as I knew Brody worked on the ranch and Savannah was at the University of Texas. The ranch was beautiful; it was just outside the town of Marble Falls and close to the Colorado river. I had loved visiting when I was a child, maybe my Mum was right, and I should go, what did I have to lose?

The more I thought about it, the more I liked the idea. I would need to speak to Sarah tomorrow, to check that she really was okay that I take time off so soon after starting to work for her, but the thought of escaping for a few weeks really appealed to me. What I'd said earlier to my parents was true though, I did hate to fly, but I'd done it before, I could do it again. I could even contact Jack and see if he would be able to visit for a week or so. I hadn't seen him in months, and I missed him. I rolled over and reached for my phone, Jack checked in every few days and the last I'd heard from him he was in Fort Lauderdale. I had no idea what time it was there, but I send him a quick text anyway.

Me: Hi Jack, hope ur ok?? Mum and Dad have suggested that I visit Aunt Claire and Uncle Ryan at the ranch for a holiday, they think it will be good for me to get away! If I decide to go do u think u could meet me there for a few days?? Xxx

My phone lit up almost immediately with a response.

Jack: Hey little sis, I'm good, how are u? I think it's a great idea to visit Aunt Claire! Why are you even thinking about it? It's a great opportunity, you should definitely go. I'm sure I can fit a trip to Texas into my busy schedule lol! Let me know your decision. Love ya xxx

I smiled at his response, I think we both knew that he didn't have a busy schedule! He was having a great time, his time to come home was creeping up on him, but I could tell when I spoke to him on the phone that he didn't want to come back.

Me: I feel guilty. Mia would have loved to visit the ranch but she can't, and it's my fault.

Jack was the only person I spoke to about how guilty I felt following the accident. I'm sure my parents knew how I felt, I just never spoke to them about it. It was somehow easier to talk to Jack; we weren't face to face, and I couldn't see the pity in his eyes. I knew that he was just as worried about me as my parents were. He had even offered to cut short his trip and come home permanently after the accident. There was no way I was going to let him do that, though, he had been planning this trip for ages, and I wasn't going to ruin it for him.

My phone rang in my hand. "Hello," I answered, as Jack's name flashed on the screen.

"Libby, you need to stop blaming yourself for the accident, you weren't driving, that arsehole was, he is responsible for Mia's death, not you! You can't not live your life; Mia wouldn't want that! If you had died in that accident would you have wanted Mia to blame herself and lock herself in her bedroom?" I could hear the frustration in his voice.

"I should have known that Mitch would have had more than one drink. I shouldn't have let him take us home! If we'd caught a taxi, she'd still be alive." I almost shouted, tears rolling down my face. "And I don't lock myself in my room!"

"You asked him if he'd been drinking, he made the decision to lie to you, he drove that car knowing that he would have been a danger on the road. You *cannot* be responsible for his decisions, please Libby, Mia wouldn't want you to feel like this." I could hear the pleading tone in his voice. "Go to Aunt Claire's. I agree with Mum and Dad that it will do you good to get away from there. You're allowed to be happy Libby." He said quietly.

"It's just so hard Jack, I miss her so much," I whispered.

"I know…but she would want you to be happy. Please, promise me you will seriously consider going?"

"I will, I promise."

"I'd better go; the boys are waiting for me. Let me know when you've decided. I love you."

"I love you too. Have a good day. I'll speak to you soon." I promised as I ended the call.

I stood up and looked out of my bedroom window, staring at the darkening sky, I could just make out the moon in between the clouds. I thought back to what Jack had said on the phone. I knew that Mia would hate that I was putting my life on hold because I felt guilty over her death. She would never have blamed me, but I still couldn't stop blaming myself.

She would want me to go to the ranch, I remember how jealous she was that I went when I was fifteen. She had made me tell her every detail when I'd returned. I smiled to myself as I thought back to the conversation we'd had that day. I'd gone straight over to her house when we'd got home from the airport.

"Thank god you're back Lib. It's been so boring here while you were gone. You have to tell me everything you did." She'd said, linking my arm and guiding me up to her bedroom. I'd followed her, laughing as she pulled me along. "Urgh, you're so brown, don't stand too close to me." She joked.

"It was great Mia, I wish you could have come. The ranch is amazing, they've got loads of horses, and I rode every day, as well as sunbathing and swimming in the river with Savannah and Brody. Next time we go, I'll ask if you can come too."

"How is that fine cousin of yours?" She'd asked, wiggling her eyebrows at me.

"Savannah's great thanks." I'd told her, smiling.

"I mean Brody!" She'd exclaimed.

"He's good too." I'd said laughing.

"I bet you met loads of gorgeous cowboys, didn't you?"

I squeezed my eyes shut as I was pulled from the memory and shook my head, smiling sadly. She really was boy mad even then.

I made my way downstairs to speak to my parents. They had

finished their dinner and were now relaxing in the lounge. They smiled at me when I walked in.

"We heard voices, were you on the phone honey?" Asked my Mum.

"Yeah, I was talking to Jack," I replied. "I asked him if he'd be able to meet me at Aunt Claire's for a few days."

My Mum jumped to her feet. "Does that mean that you'll go?" She squealed excitedly.

I laughed. "Yes, Mum I'll go, as long as Aunt Claire and Uncle Ryan don't mind having me there. I'm happy to help out around the ranch. I don't want to be in the way."

My Mum burst into tears as she flung her arms around me, pulling me in for a hug. "Of course they don't mind having you there, it was actually Claire's suggestion that you come. I'm so happy that you've decided to go. I really do think it will be the best thing for you." She gushed. "I'm going to call Claire now and tell her the news." She rushed out of the room in search of the phone.

I forced a smile, looking towards my Dad. While I had agreed to go, my Mum was giving the impression that a few weeks away was going to miraculously cure my nightmares and make me forget all about the accident. My Dad gave me a small smile. "She just wants to see you happy love." He must have known what I was thinking. "She's so worried about you, she's just hoping that a few weeks away will pull you out of your shell and somehow get you back to your old self."

"I can't promise that Dad; I can't imagine ever being how I was before the accident, but I'll do my best." I went over and planted a kiss on his cheek. "It's been a long day; I'm going to try and get some sleep. Tell Mum I'll see her in the morning. Night Daddy."

"You'll get there sweetheart; these things take time, and this is definitely a step in the right direction. Night night." He said.

I could hear my Mum on the phone, talking excitedly to Aunt

Claire as I went up to bed. I found my phone lying on the bed, and I sent a quick message to Jack.

Me: I've decided to go to Aunt Claire's. Mum is on the phone to her now, she's a bit excited! I'm sure Mum will be booking my flight tomorrow, so I'll let you know the details. Love you xxx

I put my phone on the side and got ready for bed, sliding under the duvet my eyes felt heavy. My early morning and a full day at work were catching up with me. I hoped that I would be able to avoid the nightmares tonight and get a decent night's sleep. Just as I was nodding off, I heard my phone beep with an incoming message. I reached over and grabbed it, seeing that I had a reply from Jack.

Jack: That's great Sis! It will be so good to see u, I miss your face! Will catch up tomorrow with the details xxx

I smiled as I fell into what I hoped would be a peaceful sleep.

Chapter Three

I woke up the next morning stretching my arms above my head. I reached over to pick up my phone and saw that it was nearly 9.30 am. I had slept for nearly twelve hours straight with no nightmares. I hadn't slept this well since before the accident.

I wasn't working today, but I wanted to head to the bakery to speak to Sarah. I wanted to make sure that she was okay with me going away for a few weeks. I still couldn't believe that I was going to be visiting Aunt Claire. I don't think it had really sunk in yet. I had been unsure last night when my parents had first mentioned it, I haven't really been out much other than to the bakery since I moved back home. I guess the idea of going half way around the world on my own was daunting.

I didn't want to live hiding away in my bedroom, though. Jack had been right last night when he accused me of locking myself away, I just wasn't ready to admit that to him yet. Moving back with my parents had been my only choice after the accident, but it was hard being here. There were memories of Mia and me everywhere I went in the village, and right now those memories hurt. Time away would be good.

I pulled myself out of bed and headed for the shower. After I dried my hair and got dressed, I went downstairs to find my Mum.

I found her in the kitchen taking a cake out of the oven. "Morning Mum," I said kissing her on the cheek. "That smells nice."

"Morning Libby, how did you sleep?" She asked smiling at me.

She must have known that I'd had no nightmares as I usually always woke her up with my screaming. "Really well actually, the best in a long time," I replied smiling back at her.

"It's so good to see you smile honey, I've missed it." She told me pulling me in for a hug, tears welling in her eyes. "So," She said, recovering quickly. "I spoke to Aunt Claire last night; she is so happy that you've decided to go and visit them. Savannah can't wait to see you. Your Dad and I had a quick look at some flights last night, we think we can get you on one on Friday afternoon." She said excitedly.

"Friday afternoon! But it's Wednesday today." I exclaimed.

"There's no reason to wait is there?"

"I guess not. It's all just happening a little quickly. I need to speak with Sarah to check that I'm okay to take some time off."

"I've already spoken to Sarah, I told you yesterday. There really is nothing stopping you."

I think my Mum was just desperate to get me on the plane in case I changed my mind. "I know you did Mum, but I'd really like to speak with her myself to check that she really is okay with it. It is *my* job after all." I said a little frustrated. I reached for the bread and put two slices in the toaster.

"Of course, sweetheart." She replied sheepishly. "But I promise you that Sarah is fine with it, she thinks that it's a great idea."

My toast popped up, and I sat at the table eating it. I looked down at the clothes I'd put on, an old pair of black joggers and a black t-shirt. It was what I usually wore unless I was at work. The joggers were baggy, and the t-shirt wasn't much better. I thought back to what my Mum had said last night about me having lost a lot of weight. I hadn't really noticed until now, but I was considerably thinner than before the accident, and I wasn't exactly big then, a size 12 at the most. I must have been an 8 or a 10 now.

"Mum, I think I'm going to need some new clothes to take with me. Everything I've got is baggy and black." I hesitated. "Do you think you could come with me to get some new ones? I'm guessing it's hot in Texas this time of year?" I asked.

"Yes definitely! I've been dying to take you shopping for ages." She clapped her hands together excitedly. Suddenly she stopped and turned to me, her face taking on a worried look. "Will you be okay in the car? We could take the train if you'd prefer?" She suggested.

The first time I travelled in a car after the accident I'd had a panic attack. It had been on the way home from the hospital after I was discharged. My Dad nearly had to turn the car around and take me back, but somehow, I managed to pull myself out of it and get home. I'd been in a car a couple of times since then. I'd never had another panic attack, but I had to concentrate on my breathing and count my breaths in and out to calm me down and get through the journey.

"No, we'll go in the car, I won't be able to avoid the trucks once I get to Aunt Claire's," I said, my stomach fluttering with nerves. The ranch was huge, and they used trucks to get around. I knew that I'd have to travel in those if I was going to help out while I was there.

I stood up. "I'll go and get ready, but I want to stop by the bakery on the way."

"Ok honey." My Mum replied smiling.

Fifteen minutes later and we were parked in the village. Mum had decided to wait in the car while I visited with Sarah. As I pushed open the door to the bakery, the bell chimed above me. "Be right with you." I heard Sarah shout from the back. She came into sight a few seconds later, wiping her hands on her apron. "Hi

Libby, I wasn't expecting to see you today. I thought you'd be getting ready for your trip?" She asked me, a smile on her lips.

"That's actually what I came to talk to you about," I replied.

"You haven't changed your mind, have you?" She asked, concern evident in her voice. "I really think you should go Libby, you could do with getting away from the village for a bit."

"No, I still want to go. I just wanted to make sure that I wasn't leaving you short staffed. I don't want to let you down." I told her quietly.

Making her way around the counter, she pulled me into a hug. "Of course, you're not letting me down. Leo can always help out if we get busy, please don't worry about anything here. There will always be a job here for you Libby, no matter how long you're gone."

"Thank you," I told her, hugging her back.

"I can see how lost you are sweetie, a break could be just what you need."

I nodded, stepping out of the hug. "Mum and Dad are looking at flights for Friday, I'm sorry I can't give you any more notice."

"Libby, it's fine. Don't come in tomorrow, use the time to get yourself sorted and I'll see you when you get back."

"Thank you," I told her again.

"Stop thanking me. Just promise me that you'll have an amazing time."

"I'll do my best," I told her, giving her a quick hug before leaving the shop and making my way towards the car. I felt a weight lifted off my shoulders knowing that I wasn't letting Sarah down, and that my job would still be waiting for me once I came home.

I was now sat in the passenger seat of my Mum's car with my hands clasped tightly together and my eyes shut. My Mum was trying to take my mind off my nervousness by talking nonstop. I, however, had zoned out and wasn't listening to what she was saying. I was counting my breaths in and out in an attempt to ward off a panic attack. We lived about twenty minutes from Shrewsbury, our local town, and we'd been in the car for about ten minutes, so I didn't have long left. Before I knew it, my Mum was parking the car, and I was breathing a sigh of relief.

Shrewsbury was a lovely market town packed with old fashioned black and white buildings and steep, narrow streets. The River Severn looped around the town, and there was even a castle in the centre. It had been well over a year since I'd been here, and I'd forgotten how much I liked it.

I pretty much needed a whole new wardrobe. Before we left, I had looked online at temperatures for Austin this time of year, and I was going to need summer clothes if it was going to be the 25 Celsius it said.

Several hours later and my feet were killing me. We had bags full of clothes, shoes and even the odd bikini which my Mum had insisted we buy. We were also pulling along a new suitcase to put it all in.

When we stopped for a well-earned food break, my Mum called my Dad and asked him to book the Friday flight that they had found the night before. He called back about ten minutes later to say that it was all booked. It was official. I was going to America. On my own. The nerves soon kicked in, and I suddenly couldn't finish my food. My Mum noticed my change in mood and reached over the table to squeeze my hand as I hung my head, my eyes on my lap.

"You will be fine Libby, I promise." She said, smiling encouragingly at me as I looked up. "I know that you don't like to fly and because of that, we've booked a direct flight to Austin from Heathrow. It will mean us getting up early on Friday morning to get you down there, but it will save you having to get a connecting flight like the last time we went." She paused. "And were going to take the train to Heathrow, so I don't want you worrying about the car journey down there either."

When we had visited Aunt Claire and Uncle Ryan when I was fifteen, we had flown from Manchester Airport. That had meant catching a connecting flight from O'Hare International Airport in Chicago, down to Austin. Not only had it taken forever to get there, it meant catching two flights and I really didn't like flying.

Tears filled my eyes. "Thank you for doing this for me." I paused wiping my eyes. "I know I haven't been easy to live with since I've moved home. I know how much you worry about me."

"Sweetheart you do not have to thank me. Your Dad and I would do anything for you. You have been through a terrible ordeal; we just want to see you happy again Libby. I really think that a trip to the ranch could be the start of you returning back to your old self." She stood up and pulled me in for a hug. "Come on, eat up, we can get home and get you packed then." She said smiling at me.

We got home about forty minutes later, and my Dad's car was on the drive as we pulled up. We headed inside to find him on the sofa eating fish and chips. He never was very good in the kitchen; my Mum was the cook of the house.

"Good day shopping ladies?" He asked taking in our huge haul of bags.

"Yep!" I replied as I flopped on the opposite sofa. "My feet are killing me."

"She's got everything she needs; we just need to get it all packed, and she'll be set to go." My Mum told him.

I think my Mum was more excited for this trip than I was. I knew after today that she was desperate to have me back to my usual self, I just hoped I didn't let her down. I had really enjoyed our shopping trip. It had been a while since we'd done something just the two of us. We'd had plenty of shopping trips before I went off to university, but once I'd moved to Manchester, trips home were few and far between, and after the accident, I hadn't wanted to go out and do anything. I realised then how tough the past few months must have been for both of my parents. I had been too busy drowning in my own grief to notice. The accident had impacted all of our lives.

I got up off the sofa and went over to hug my Dad. He hugged me back. "What was that for sweetie?" He asked.

"Just a thank you for all you've done for me, for this trip and putting up with me these past few months. I love you, You too Mum." I said looking over to her.

"We love you too Libby. Very Much." My Mum said coming to hug me.

"I'm going to go up to my room and sort through my clothes," I said walking out into the hall.

"Let me know if you need any help?" My Mum called after me.

"Will do," I replied back, climbing the stairs.

I emptied all of the bags onto my bed and started folding everything, placing it in my suitcase as I went. We had gone a little overboard with the shopping, but with the weight I had lost over the past few months none of my summer clothes from last year would have fit me. Even my current underwear was big, and I'd had to have new bras and knickers. I didn't want to think how much my Mum had spent.

An hour or so later I was all packed. My Mum had come upstairs to tell me that she had spoken to my Aunt and arranged for her to pick me up from the airport in Austin once my flight had landed. Aunt Claire knew about my nervousness when I was travelling in a car, so at least if I had a panic attack, she would know why. I really hoped that I wouldn't, but it was about an hour's car ride from the airport to the ranch, and that would be the longest journey I'd done in a car since before the accident. My stomach rolled at the thought, but I pushed my fears away. I had a ten-hour flight to get through first.

I brushed my teeth and got ready for bed. I remembered that I needed to text Jack to let him know that we'd booked my flight. I grabbed my phone and sent him a quick message.

Me: Hey Jack, my flight is booked. I land in Austin at 6.10pm on Friday! Let me know if u can manage to get a flight out xxx

Jack: Will definitely be getting a flight, will have a look and let u know xxx

Me: Great, I'll be seeing u soon then! Can't wait xxx

I reached for my Kindle to read for a bit. I was exhausted after today's shopping trip, but I loved to read, it was my escape from reality. It allowed me to get out of my head and live in someone else's world for a while. After everything that had happened, it felt like everyone else's life was better than mine at the moment. I was hopeful that things would soon change for the better, though.

Chapter Four

T he next day raced by. I spent most of the day getting the last few bits and pieces together, making sure I had everything I would need. My Mum sorted out some snacks for the flight, while I made sure my Kindle was stocked with plenty of books to read and that my iPod had plenty of songs downloaded onto it.

After lunch, I took a walk to the local Church. It wasn't raining when I'd left the house, but as I entered the Churchyard, it started to drizzle. I pulled my umbrella out of my bag and opened it, the wind blowing my hair in my face.

I made my way through the graveyard, past the old tombstones dating back to the 1800's towards the more recent plots. I hadn't been able to attend Mia's funeral as I had been in hospital for nearly three weeks after the accident. I had suffered with dizzy spells, and the Doctors were reluctant to let me go home until the dizzy spells had stopped.

I had been devastated that I hadn't been able to say a proper goodbye. I had come to Mia's grave daily in the weeks after my release from hospital, sometimes needing to talk to her and other times just to think. I hadn't been for a few weeks, finding it too hard to be here. I stood in front of her headstone and read the words written there.

Mia Eliza Green. Born 18 August 1997.
Died 13 December 2015. Loving Daughter, taken too soon.
Always in our hearts.

I traced my fingers over the letters of her name as I sat down on the wet grass, not caring that the rain was seeping through my jeans. There was a bunch of pink roses in the small vase in the front of her headstone. I'm guessing that her Mum had put them there.

Mrs Green came weekly, although I was ashamed to say, never at the same time that I had come. I had avoided Mia's parents since the accident. I just couldn't face them. They had been to see me at the hospital, and I will never forget the pain in their faces at seeing me alive while their daughter was dead.

They had tried several times to visit me at my parents' house, but I had always refused to see them. My parents had told me that Mr and Mrs Green didn't blame me for Mia's death, they just wanted to make sure that I was okay. I just couldn't believe that after seeing their faces that day at the hospital. Somehow, by some miracle, I had managed to avoid them in the village, but I knew that wouldn't last forever.

"Hey Mia," I said shakily. "Sorry I haven't stopped by in a while, it's just…hard. It doesn't mean I haven't been thinking about you, though. I think about you every day. I miss you so much." A tear fell down my cheek, and I reached my hand up to wipe it away. "I've started working at the bakery for a few hours a week. I'm working with Leo; it was a bit awkward to start with but were friends now." I paused, taking a deep breath. "I'm going to visit my Aunt Claire on the ranch in Austin. My parents think it will do me good to get away and have a break from things. I wasn't too sure to start with, but I think I'm actually looking forward to going. I wish you could come with me. I know you'd love it there. Well, you'd love the cowboys anyway." I said with a small smile. "Jack is going to see if he can get a flight out to Austin to spend a few days with me, I haven't seen him in a while, so it will be great to catch up with him for a bit," I told her.

I sat for a while longer telling Mia about my shopping trip yesterday with my Mum, and how many bags we'd had to carry around with us. Soon I began shivering, the rain coming down heavier now and the cold bleeding through my clothes. I stood up and again ran my fingers across her name. "I'll come and visit again, as soon as I get back, I promise…bye Mia," I whispered, backing away from the grave.

I made my way back home and went straight in the shower to try and warm up. I stood for a long time under the hot spray hoping the water would wash away all of the pain and hurt I was feeling. I got out a while later and went downstairs to find my parents. They had both been at work today, so I'd had the house to myself. I found my Mum in the kitchen making dinner.

"Hey Mum," I said giving her a hug.

"Hi sweetheart, how was your day? Have you just got out of the shower?" She asked taking in my damp hair.

"Yeah, I got wet at Mia's grave," I said quietly. "I went to tell her about my trip to Austin, and to say goodbye."

My Mum looked at me in surprise. "Oh okay." She said. "Are you alright?"

I didn't often talk to my Mum about Mia so I could tell that she was surprised. "Yeah, I'm okay. I haven't been in a while. I wanted to go before I left for Austin as I don't know exactly when I'll be back." My parents hadn't booked my return flight home. They had said they didn't want to put a timeframe on my trip.

Aunt Claire was happy for me to stay as long as I wanted, and we could book a flight pretty quickly once I decided I wanted to come home.

"Oh, honey." She said, wrapping her arms around me. "I'm so glad you're talking to me again about Mia, I know how hard it is for you to talk about her, but I'm always here for you, and will always listen when you want to talk."

"I know, thanks, Mum." I hugged her back hard. I was going to miss my parents while I was away. When I left to go to university I'd missed them, but Mia hadn't let me dwell on it, and university was so busy I didn't really have time to think about it. I imagined that I would have plenty of time to think while I was on the ranch. I just hoped that I wouldn't be too stuck in my head to enjoy it.

"Are you all ready to go? Any last-minute packing to do?" My Mum asked as she got back to peeling the potatoes.

"No, I'm all set. Nervous about the flight, but I've got my Kindle loaded with books and my iPod ready. I should be fine once we've taken off." I'm sure I was trying to convince myself more than my Mum.

I'd been abroad a total of three times. Twice to the ranch and when I was around twelve we'd gone to Spain for a week. I'd hated flying all three times. There was no logical reason for my fear, I just hated the take-off and landing. Providing the flight was smooth the rest of the way, I was generally okay, although I'd never flown on my own before.

"You'll be fine sweetheart." My Mum replied, trying to reassure me. I smiled at her and hoped that she was right.

After dinner, I spent a couple of hours with my parents watching television and chatting before we all headed off to bed. Tomorrow would be an early start. We needed to get up around 5 am to catch the train. Although I knew that I needed to get an early night, I had trouble falling asleep. The nerves had kicked in, and I was thinking of Mia and how much she would have loved to have come with me.

I must have fallen asleep at some point as I suddenly found myself awake and sitting up in bed crying. I wiped my eyes and reached for my phone on the bedside table. It was 4.30 am, I had been asleep for longer than I thought. I paused and listened for any movement from my parent's bedroom across the landing. Thankfully I was met with silence. My nightmares hadn't woken them this time.

I shut my eyes and pulled my duvet around me. I knew realistically that a trip to Austin wasn't going to suddenly stop my nightmares or make me stop missing Mia. I would always miss her, but I didn't want to feel like this anymore. I wanted to start living again, and I hoped that I could find a bit of my old self while I was away so that I could begin to heal.

There was no point trying to go back to sleep when I needed to be up in thirty minutes. I dried my eyes and reached for my Kindle, excited if a little nervous at what lay ahead.

Chapter Five

After a four-hour train journey and a ten-hour flight, I landed in Austin. I couldn't quite believe that I was here. Saying goodbye to my parents had been hard. They had been my rock for the past few months, and I was going to miss them like crazy. The flight that I had been dreading had actually been okay. It was long and tiring, but I had managed to read quite a bit, so that had been a bonus. I was glad it was over, though.

I switched my phone on as I waited for my luggage, sending my Mum a quick message to say that I had landed and that I would call her tomorrow. My phone chimed with a message. It was from my Aunt Claire.

Aunt Claire: Hi Libby, I'm waiting in arrivals can't wait to see you xx

I sent her a quick reply back, telling her that I would be out as soon as I had my suitcase and that I couldn't wait to see her either. If I was honest, I was a bit nervous. Although I'd spoken to Aunt Claire on the phone over the years, it had been four years since I'd actually seen her. They had planned to come and see us in the UK a couple of years ago, but Uncle Ryan's Dad had passed away and left them the ranch, so they had been too busy working to come.

About ten minutes later I walked into arrivals, looking around for her. She squealed and waved when she saw me, throwing her arms around me when I'd made my way through the crowds to her.

"Libby! It's so good to see you. How was your flight, honey?" She asked, grabbing my suitcase and leaving me with my hand luggage.

"Hi, my flight was good thanks. I'm glad it's over." I replied quietly.

"You must be exhausted, come on, we'll get you in the car and back home." She said, motioning for me to follow her. "Savannah is so excited to see you. She wanted to come with me to pick you up, but she wasn't home from college in time. She'll be home when we get back, though."

"I'm looking forward to seeing her too." I followed her through the airport. The humid air hit me as we went outside. "Wow, it's warm."

"This is nothing sweetie, it's cooling down a bit now, wait until tomorrow. You're going to need all those summer clothes your Mum said you'd brought. It's a bit different to April in the UK, isn't it?" She said laughing.

"Just a bit! It's freezing at home. I'm looking forward to some sun."

Claire came to a stop next to a large black pickup truck. She took my hand luggage case off me and put it, along with my suitcase, on the back seat.

"Climb in sweetie." She said.

I took a deep breath and climbed into the passenger seat, quickly putting my seatbelt on.

"Thank you for having me come and stay with you, Aunt Claire.

I didn't realise how much I needed a break until my parents suggested that I come."

She leaned across the console and squeezed my hand. "No need to thank me, Libby, you're welcome anytime. We know what a tough few months you've had, and we'll do anything we can to help. I'm a good listener if you ever feel that you want to talk about anything. No pressure, but the offer is there if you want it." She said smiling at me.

I gave her a small smile in response. "I should probably warn you." I paused, wringing my hands nervously. "I don't always sleep very well, and sometimes I have nightmares. I can be quite loud. I know how early you have to get up, so I really hope that I don't wake everyone."

"Oh, sweetie. Your Mum has told me about your nightmares, and I don't want you to worry about waking us up. If it happens it happens, please don't feel bad about it. She also reminded me how you can sometimes struggle in the car, were about an hour from home so if you want me to pull over at any point, just let me know."

I nodded in response, and Aunt Claire pulled out of the car park. I concentrated on my breathing and closed my eyes. I really wanted to look out of the window and see where we were going, but I didn't want to have a panic attack on my first day here. I must have fallen asleep as the next thing I knew Aunt Claire was nudging me awake.

"Libby, honey, we've just gone through Marble Falls, were about five minutes from the ranch," She said.

"I can't believe I fell asleep, I'm normally a nervous wreck in the car!" I told her, looking around at where we were.

"It must be my excellent driving." She said laughing. "It's the middle of the night at home, though, you must be exhausted from the travelling. Your Mum said you were getting up at 5 am to catch the train, it's been a long day for you."

"It has been a pretty long day..." I paused. "The last time I fell asleep in the car..." I trailed off, looking out of the window at the fields flying past the window.

"I know honey. That isn't going to happen again. You're safe." She reached over and patted her hand on my knee. "Look we're here now." She said motioning with her hand for me to look.

I turned and saw a sign that read 'Wild Oak Ranch and Retreat.' We turned off the main road and drove up a winding driveway that led to the house. Oak trees lined the way, and it was easy to see where the name for the ranch had come from.

We must have been driving up the dusty driveway for about half a mile before it opened out and I saw the huge ranch house where my Aunt and Uncle lived. Their house was incredible. It was two stories and had an amazing wraparound porch. I could see a porch swing off to the left of the steps that led to the front door. I was looking forward to sitting on that swing curled up with a book. There were flower beds on either side of the steps that were filled with colourful wildflowers, and a white picket fence that went all the way around the lawn.

I looked to my left and saw the barns and stables where they kept the horses. In the distance, I could see a smaller, but equally impressive house along with log cabins where guests holidaying at the ranch stayed. A group of about ten people were just coming out of the barn talking and laughing.

"They've just got back from horseback riding down by the river." I heard Aunt Claire say. "It's one of the activities we offer to guests. We haven't got many guests staying at the moment, about fifteen or so. April is a quiet time for us, but numbers will pick up the closer we get to the summer months. Come on, let's get you settled in your room and then I'll show you around."

She jumped out of the car and grabbed my suitcases from the

back, suddenly the front door flung open, and Savannah flew down the steps towards me.

"Libby! You're here" She screeched throwing her arms around me.

I hugged her back, laughing. "Hey Sav. It's so good to see you." I told her, squeezing her tight. After our visit to the ranch when I was fifteen, Savannah and I had regularly chatted via text, and occasionally on the phone, so although we hadn't seen each other in four years, we'd remained close. After the accident, I'd shut nearly everyone out of my life, but she had never given up on me, regularly sending me messages, even if I didn't reply for weeks.

"Come on, I'll show you your room, you're just across the hall from me. I can't wait to show you around, and for you to meet everyone. A lot has changed since the last time you were here." She gushed, pulling me along with her.

"Wait!" I said laughing. "I need to help your Mum with my bags." I turned around to make my way back to Aunt Claire, but she shook her head at me.

"Don't worry Libby, I'm fine. You go on in with Savannah, she's been dying for you to get here. I'll bring your bags up."

"Thank you."

I followed Savannah as she went into the house. I'd forgotten just how gorgeous this house was. The front door opened onto a huge hall, the walls lined with family pictures of Brody and Savannah, pictures from when they were babies right up to their proms. There were pictures of my Dad's parents and what I'm guessing were Uncle Ryan's parents. I even spotted one of Jack and me from the last time we visited.

Savannah grabbed my hand and pulled me up the stairs. The upstairs was just as stunning as the downstairs. There were five bedrooms, each with its own bathroom. I got a quick glimpse in each room as Savannah pulled me from one room to the next.

"This one is yours." She told me, stopping in a room twice the size of my bedroom at home. "We went out and got you all new bedding when we knew you were coming."

"It's gorgeous," I told her, looking around in awe. There was a king size bed against one wall, with a chest of drawers and a dressing table on the other wall. A door to the left led into a bathroom, and another door opened into a walk-in wardrobe. I walked over to the window and took in the view of the barn and stables, as well as what looked like hundreds of acres of land. "What a view! This room is amazing!"

"Here are your bags honey." Aunt Claire said, coming into the room and dropping them on the bed. "Savannah why don't you help Libby unpack, I'll get dinner started. Dad and Brody will be back soon. I'm sure Libby will want an early night; it's been a long day." She smiled at me. "I'll call you when dinner is ready."

Twenty minutes later and I was all unpacked. My clothes nowhere near filled the huge walk in wardrobe in my room. I think even if I'd brought all of my clothes from home it still wouldn't be full. I dropped down on the bed. I was shattered. Aunt Claire was right, it had been a long day.

"Come on Libby, lets go downstairs before you fall asleep," Savannah said, pulling me up by my hand. "Mom's making your favourite."

"My favourite?" I asked looking at her confused.

"Yep. Wait and see." She replied cryptically.

As we made our way downstairs the most amazing smell reached my nose. My stomach rumbled in response. "Frito pie!" I screeched rushing into the kitchen. "You remembered," I said in amazement.

Aunt Claire turned to me laughing. "Of course I remembered. How could I forget? You made me make this six times the last time you were here."

Aunt Claire's Frito pie was incredible. It was basically chili con carne, Fritos, which were corn chips, and cheese and she put salsa and sour cream on top. I loved it. My Mum had tried to make it at home, we'd even taken a load of Frito's home with us, but it somehow was never the same. "Thank you for making my favourite meal," I said walking over and kissing her on the cheek.

"No problem honey. I made sure I was stocked up on Fritos when I knew you were coming." She laughed, winking at me. "It's not quite ready yet, won't be long. Are you all unpacked?"

"Yep. She's all done." Savannah answered for me. "I'll take Libby and show her the new horses while we wait."

"Okay, don't be long; Dad and Brody will be back soon."

As we made our way outside Uncle Ryan and Brody were heading up the path towards the house. "Hi, Uncle Ryan. Hi, Brody." I said to them quietly. It had been a while since I'd spoken to my Uncle and cousin and I felt a bit shy. I needn't have worried, though, Uncle Ryan scooped me up into a hug as soon as he saw me.

"Hey Lib. Great to see you." He said swinging me round.

I laughed. "Great to see you too. Thanks for having me."

"Our pleasure sweetheart." He responded in his southern drawl.

"Hi, Libby. Long-time no see. How are you?" Brody asked.

I turned to look at Brody. He was even more well-built than the last time I'd seen him. I guess working on a ranch will do that to you. He was tall with dark hair and brown eyes. His white t-shirt was smeared with dirt, but you could clearly see his muscles through it. Even though he was my cousin, I could see that he was incredibly good looking. I'm sure he had all the girls falling over him. Mia would have been drooling if she'd been here. "It has been a while, hasn't it? I'm okay thanks, looking forward to spending some time on the ranch. I love it here. Savannah is just taking me to the stables to see the horses."

"Okay, well we're heading in to shower, we'll see you at dinner." Uncle Ryan said, walking past us and pushing the front door open. Brody smiled and followed him.

I heard Aunt Claire shouting at them both to remember to take off their boots. I smiled at Savannah before she skipped through the garden and out towards the stables.

"We've got twenty horses now; the ranch is getting busier with guests, so we needed more horses."

Savannah loved the horses. The last time I was here we rode nearly every day. She'd had her own horse that wasn't used by the people holidaying here, but he stayed in the stables with all the working horses. "Do you still have Marley?" I asked her as she pulled open the stable door.

"Yeah he's in here, I'll show you."

I loved the stables, the smells, well most of them, the sounds and the calmness I always felt when I was in there. As I walked in now the sweet smell of the hay hit me, and I inhaled deeply. There were rows of stalls on either side, each with a horse inside. Savannah walked past me and down to the other end of the stable, stopping at the last but one stall.

"Hello boy." She said to Marley, scratching his nose. "You remember Libby, don't you?" She asked the horse. "She's back to stay with us for a while."

Marley seemed to respond to Savannah by snorting and rubbing his nose into her hand. She laughed and reached into her pocket pulling out a couple of sugar cubes which she offered to him. I patted Marley on the neck as he ate his treat. Savannah walked me up and down the stable telling me the names of all the horses and which were the new ones.

"We can go riding tomorrow if you like?" She asked me.

It had been four years since I'd been on a horse, but I was eager to get back on one. "I'd love that, if you're sure you've got time," I told her. I didn't want to take up her time if she wanted to see her friends. I was pretty sure she didn't have a boyfriend. She didn't the last time we spoke properly, but that would have been before the accident. "If you want to see your friends, or your boyfriend, I can find something to do on my own. I don't mind."

"I can see my friends anytime Lib, and there is no boyfriend." She paused, then I heard her mutter. "Not for want of trying!"

I started to ask her what she meant, but Brody suddenly appeared at the stable door.

"Dinner's ready you two, come on."

I looked over to Savannah, and she quickly shook her head, her eyes pleading with me to not say anything in front of Brody. I gave her a reassuring smile, and linked my arm through hers as we followed Brody back to the house. I would speak to her about it when we were alone, maybe tomorrow if we took the horses out.

Aunt Claire's Fritos pie was as incredible as I remembered. I didn't realise how hungry I was until I started eating. Sitting at the dining table with everyone brought back memories of the last time I was here, and how much fun I'd had with Jack, Savannah, and Brody. We'd spent hours swimming in the lake, and exploring every inch of the ranch on horseback. I'd barely seen my parents during that holiday, as soon as the sun was up we were out and didn't return until we were hungry. Being away for a few years the memories had faded, but they were flooding back now, and I could only hope that I could enjoy this visit as much as the last one.

We all chatted easily over dinner with Aunt Claire and Uncle Ryan asking after my parents and Jack. I mentioned that Jack was looking into getting a flight to Austin to meet up with me, but I was waiting to hear back from him. Everyone seemed excited that he was going to be visiting.

"So girls, what are the plans for tomorrow?" Uncle Ryan asked, smiling at Savannah and me.

"We're going to go riding in the morning. I thought I'd take Lib down to the river and show her around the new log cabins." Savannah replied excitedly. "Then tomorrow night we're going out with the girls."

This was news to me. I looked at Savannah. "I don't have to come, Savannah, if you want to go out with your friends," I said repeating my comments from earlier.

"I want you to come. Some of those dresses you've brought with you are perfect for the bars in town. We just need to get you some cowboy boots tomorrow afternoon, and you'll be all set for a night of dancing." She smiled at me.

I frowned. I hadn't been out dancing since the night of the accident. "I'm not sure Savannah, it's been a while…" I hesitated.

She reached across the table and took my hand. "Even more of a reason for you to come." She said quietly. "I know you've been through a really tough time, but this is a fresh start. Please come Lib everyone is dying to meet you."

I took a deep breath. I did want this to be a fresh start, I wanted to start living again, be happy again. I closed my eyes "Okay." I whispered. "I don't drink though, so please don't make me," I begged. I hadn't wanted to drink since Mia had died. It didn't hold the same appeal as it did before.

"You're not old enough to drink here honey, neither is Savannah. Isn't that right Savannah?" Aunt Claire said, raising her eyebrows at Savannah.

"No, no drinking," Savannah smirked at her Mum. "They check your ID at the door Libby, if you're under 21 you get your hand stamped then they know at the bar not to serve you alcohol." She paused. "So, you'll come?"

"Yes, I'll come...but I'm not sure about cowboy boots," I replied with a smile. "What's wrong with my flip flops?"

"You're in Texas now Lib, you *have* to have cowboy boots, isn't that right Daddy?" I looked over to Uncle Ryan who rolled his eyes at Savannah.

"Well you would know sweetheart; you have about twenty pairs." He told her laughing.

Brody burst out laughing, along with Aunt Claire.

"I do not have twenty pairs; I've got like, six." She pouted. "And what are you laughing at Brody! You have more pairs than me!"

"Mine are working boots Sav. I actually wear them to work in, they aren't a fashion accessory." Brody replied.

Savannah stuck her tongue out at Brody across the table. I laughed "Okay, okay, I'll get some cowboy boots." I turned to Aunt Claire. "I'm going to turn in. I'm whacked. Thanks for dinner, it was amazing." I gushed.

"No problem. I'll make it again next week, maybe when Jack gets here." She suggested. "Sleep well, honey. If you need anything, you know where we are." She smiled reassuringly at me.

"Thank you. Night everyone." I made my way upstairs as everyone said goodnight. I hoped that my nightmares wouldn't make an appearance tonight, I was too tired to deal with them.

I had a quick shower before crawling into bed, falling asleep almost immediately, my head barely hitting the pillow.

Chapter Six

I padded downstairs and into the kitchen. I'd managed to get through the night without any issues, which I was grateful for. I knew that my Aunt and Uncle were aware of my nightmares, but I was still anxious about disturbing everyone and them realising how screwed up I really was.

"Morning sleepy head, or should I say afternoon," Savannah said laughing.

She was sat at the kitchen table studying, books and papers spread across the whole table.

"Afternoon?" I asked puzzled. "What time is it?" I hadn't looked at my phone when I'd woken up, I'd just come straight downstairs. My stomach was telling me it was breakfast time, though. I never normally ate breakfast; it must have been the country air making me hungry.

"It's nearly twelve. You must have been exhausted from the flight yesterday."

I picked up the coffee pot and found a mug. I held it up to Savannah. "You want one?"

"I'm good thanks. I've had one not too long ago."

"Sorry I've slept so long. You're right I must have been tired."

"No worries. I've caught up with some assignments. Help

yourself to some food. I'm just going to pack all this away." She said gesturing to the messy table.

I opened a few cupboards looking for the cereal. I pulled out the Cheerios and found a bowl. "Do you think we'll have time for a ride today if were heading into Marble Falls?" I asked Savannah, opening the fridge to grab the milk.

"Probably not, but we'll have plenty of time for riding while you're here. We need to get you those cowboy boots for tonight." She said wiggling her eyebrows at me.

I laughed rolling my eyes at her. I was secretly looking forward to getting some. My parents had bought me a pair the last time we were here, but I'd grown out of them. The ones you could get at home weren't as good, so I'd never replaced them.

"I'll be quick then, I'll just eat this," I said holding up my bowl. "It won't take me long to get ready." Savannah nodded as she packed her things away.

I sat down at the breakfast bar looking out of the window as I ate my cereal. The sun was shining, and there wasn't a cloud in the sky. It really was beautiful. I couldn't wait to get out and explore. It looked like a lot had changed since the last time I was here. The retreat side of the ranch was much bigger. Uncle Ryan had expanded after he had taken over, and it looked like they could accommodate more guests than before. I'd noticed the extra log cabins last night.

I was guessing that Aunt Claire, Uncle Ryan, and Brody were somewhere on the ranch, doing whatever it was that they did. I knew that they employed staff, but all three of them were heavily involved with the day to day running of things.

I hopped down from the breakfast bar and quickly washed my bowl and spoon in the sink. "I'll just run and get ready Sav, I won't be long," I called out as I ran upstairs.

"No rush Lib. I'll be waiting." Savannah called after me.

Twenty minutes later I was back downstairs. I'd had a quick shower, throwing my hair up into a messy bun and pulling on some denim shorts and a top. I'd called my parents while I was upstairs to let them know that I was okay. I'd told them that Savannah was waiting on me and promised to call them later.

"I'm ready," I said finding Savannah waiting in the hall for me.

"Great. Let's get going.' She said to me holding up her car keys.

I followed her outside feeling anxious about having to go in the car again. She stopped in front of a red Volkswagen Beetle.

"You okay Lib? You've gone a bit pale." She asked me looking concerned.

"I'm fine." I lied, trying to brush away my nerves. "Just a bit hot I think."

"Jump in, I've got air con, that should cool you down."

I climbed into the passenger seat and quickly put on my seatbelt. I concentrated on my breathing, counting my breaths in and out in my head. Savannah got in and looked over at me.

"Are you sure you're okay, Libby? Savannah asked, looking at me.

"I can get a bit anxious when I'm in a car, since… since the accident," I told her quietly.

"Oh Lib, you should have said. Is there anything I can do to help?"

"Not really; I'll be okay. I thought you knew, I know my Mum told your Mum so…" I trailed off embarrassed.

"She probably didn't want to say anything in case you didn't want people to know. Do you want to stay here and go for that horse ride instead?"

"No!" I almost shouted. "I want to go be able to go in a car without having a panic attack. I'll be okay. I'm better than I was just after the accident. The more I do it, the better I'll be, I hope.

Anyway, we have to go, I want my cowboy boots." I said with a small smile.

"I knew you wanted some cowboy boots!" She exclaimed hitting the steering wheel with her hand. "Well, it's not a long way to town, only about ten minutes." She gave me a small smile, and I could sense that she wanted to ask me something. "How are you really doing after the accident?" She paused. "I know you've come here to get away from everything at home, but I want you to know, if you need to talk about Mia, or the accident, or anything, then I'm happy to listen. I know I never met Mia, but you talked so much about her last time you were here, I feel like I knew her a little bit."

I decided then that I wasn't going to give my normal response when someone asked me how I was. I wasn't going to put on a brave face and pretend everything was okay. Savannah was my friend, and I needed a friend right now.

"I'm not okay, not really. I pretend I am when people ask me, but that's more for their benefit. It's easier to say yes, I'm fine. I miss her Savannah, so much. We did everything together, and now I've dropped out of university I'm just a little lost and lonely. My parents are great, but I can tell they don't really know what to say to me to help. They are hoping this trip will somehow get me back to my old self."

"I can't even begin to understand what you've been through Libby, but one thing I do know is that you don't have to pretend with me. If you feel like crying, then cry, if you feel like laughing then laugh. Hell, if you feel like skinny dipping in the lake then I'm with you! I'll be here for you whatever."

Tears filled my eyes. I'd missed having a friend. I'd shut everyone out at home, even my parents. No one could replace Mia, but it was nice to have someone my own age to talk to and do things with.

"Thank you. You don't realise how much that means to me, Savannah." I leaned across the centre console and gave her a hug.

"You don't need to thank me Lib." She said hugging me back. "Come on, let's go and get those boots!"

I laughed as we pulled away from the house and down the driveway. Savannah was right, the journey into Marble Falls wasn't a long one, and I counted my breaths in and out all the way. We parked outside a row of shops, and I got out of the car, relieved that we were here.

Marble Falls was beautiful; the town was set around the stunning Lake Marble Falls and amid green rolling hills. I glanced up and down the road we'd parked on. There were various shops ranging from coffee shops with tables and chairs out on the pavement, to shops selling furniture and handmade fudge. I made a mental note to visit the one selling the homemade fudge. American flags hung above the shops, and bunting was strung all along the street, as if there had been a recent street party or town fair.

Savannah grabbed my hand and pulled me along, pointing out her favourite coffee shop and clothes shop along the way. We came to a stop outside a shop called Blair's Western Wear.

"Come on, this is the best place in town for cowboy boots. Most of mine are from here." She said excitedly.

I let her lead me inside passing racks of jeans and shirts. At the back of the shop, there were rows and rows of cowboy boots. I'd never seen so many. How was I ever going to choose? I could see now why Savannah had so many pairs!

"Hey, Rose." I heard Savannah call out.

I turned to see Savannah talking to a very pretty girl with long blonde hair.

"Hi Savannah, you're not here for more boots, are you?" Rose asked, surprise evident in her voice. "You bought a pair about two weeks ago."

Savannah laughed. "No, not for me, for my cousin. Rose this is Libby, Libby, Rose." Savannah gestured between us with her hand. "Rose is one of my friends from school, she's coming out with us tonight."

"Hi Rose," I said. "Nice to meet you."

"Nice to meet you too Libby. You're from England?" She asked.

"Yeah. I'm over visiting for a few weeks." I replied smiling at her.

"So, you're after some cowboy boots then. I'm guessing someone here is forcing their cowboy boot obsession onto you." She said laughing.

"Hey!" Savannah shouted. "I'm standing right here. I can hear you." She pouted.

I laughed. I liked Rose already. "Well, it did start out with Sav insisting I have a pair for our night out. I must admit though I'm quite excited to get some."

"Have a look and see what you like, then give me a shout, and I'll fetch your size," Rose said, disappearing to serve a young couple while we had a look.

There were so many pairs I didn't really know where to start. "Savannah help! There's too many to choose from." I walked over to where she was looking at a pair of red and black boots.

"Aren't these gorgeous Lib." She held the boot out for me to see.

"They are, but I think they are a bit bright for me." I looked around spying a tan pair that I thought would go with a lot of my dresses and shorts. "What about these?" I held them up so she could see them.

"Oooo I like those." She gushed. "Try them on!"

I laughed, I'd never seen anyone get so excited over cowboy boots before. "Okay, I'll go and grab Rose."

When I tried them on they were perfect. They were tan on the foot and then a slightly lighter tan colour up my leg. Tan and blonde according to the sales label. I loved them.

"Libby those are the ones, you have to get them," Savannah told me. "I'm getting the red and black pair."

"You're getting another pair? How many is that you've got now? Uncle Ryan will kill you." I laughed.

"He'll never know; I'll just tell him I've had them ages. Come on, let's pay and then we can go and grab a coffee. I'm thinking I might need a new dress to go with these boots." She said grinning.

We paid for our boots and said goodbye to Rose, arranging to meet her later tonight. As we walked up the street, Savannah pointed out the bar where we had arranged to meet everyone. The Brass Hall was a big red brick building at the end of the high street. The sign outside was advertising live music and dancing. Savannah told me that it was the best bar in Marble Falls, and would probably be packed later on. Fortunately, a friend of Savannah's was a waitress there, and she was reserving a table for us.

After a quick stop for coffee and a piece of pecan pie, we headed to Savannah's favourite clothes shop. She tried on what seemed like a million dresses before eventually finding one to match her new boots. Savannah definitely liked to shop that was for sure.

On the way back, I used the breathing techniques I'd taught myself in an attempt to keep calm, and I managed to get back to the ranch without having a meltdown. As we pulled up the long driveway and parked the car, I saw Brody and another man going into the barn. I felt Savannah tense beside me, and I watched as her knuckles turned white as she gripped the steering wheel.

"Everything okay Sav?" I asked her. "Who was that with Brody? Does he work here?" I looked back over to the barn, but they'd disappeared inside.

She took a deep breath and let it out slowly. "That's Josh, Brody's friend. He doesn't work here, he must be here to see Brody."

"I remember Josh; he was here at the ranch a lot the last time I was here. You had the biggest crush on him back then." I turned to look at her and saw the look on her face. "You still like him, don't you? Does he know?"

She sighed. "I don't just like him Lib. I love him. I've loved him since I was fifteen, he knows how I feel, he's just not interested."

I looked over at her and saw the sadness on her face. I couldn't believe that Josh wasn't interested, Savannah was gorgeous. She had long wavy brown hair and green eyes freckled with blue. She had a figure I was envious of with legs that seemed to go on forever. If Josh wasn't interested, he must have been blind. Not only was Savannah gorgeous she was an amazing person as well.

"Oh Sav, are you sure he knows how you feel? How do you know he's not interested?" I asked her hoping she had it all wrong.

"I'm sure. It's kind of an embarrassing story." She cringed. "I basically threw myself at him a few months ago, at a party. I was drunk and decided I'd waited long enough to tell him how I felt. I pulled him to one side and told him I'd been in love with him for years. Then I tried to kiss him."

She went silent and stared out of the car window. "What happened?" I prompted her.

"He pushed me away, told me that he saw me as a sister and that nothing could ever happen between us." She wiped a tear away and turned to face me. "We've barely spoken since. I hate it Lib, but I can't make him want me." She whispered.

I was no relationship expert, having never been in one, but I'd been Mia's shoulder to cry on more times than I could count. Mia's disastrous relationships had shown me that you should be with someone who thought the sun rose and set with you, and that you shouldn't settle for anything less. If Josh really wasn't interested in Savannah, then there had to be plenty of guys that were.

"Savannah, you shouldn't have to make someone want you. You should be someone's everything, and you will find that I'm sure of it. If Josh can't see how amazing you are, then he doesn't deserve you."

"Thanks, Lib. I know you're right, but it doesn't make it hurt any less." She wiped her eyes and checked her makeup in the mirror. "Come on, let's go and get ready for tonight. I'm sure I can find some cowboy to dance with to take my mind off him."

She jumped out of the car, grabbed the shopping bags and headed for the house. As she did, Brody and Josh came out of the barn.

"Hey, Savannah," Brody shouted from the door of the barn. I saw Savannah take a deep breath before she turned around.

"Me and Josh thought we'd meet up with you and Lib for a drink tonight. Are you heading to the Brass Hall?"

"Erm… Yeah." She hesitated. "We're meeting the girls there at eight."

"Great, we'll see you there then. Save us a seat."

"Okay. See you later then." She told him, her shoulders slumping as she walked up the porch steps.

"I'm guessing Brody doesn't know you feel about Josh?" I asked.

"No. He's got no idea. Thankfully Josh never told him what happened, I just pray he never finds out. He's always made it clear that he doesn't want me dating his friends. I dread to think how he'd react if he knew I was in love with one of them."

I followed her into the house, my heart breaking for her. I'd never been in love, not even close. I could only imagine how it must feel to be in love with someone who didn't love you back. I was starting to think that my first night out in months could turn out to be a disaster.

Chapter Seven

I stared into the mirror, blinking rapidly. The reflection I saw wasn't what I'd been used to seeing over the past few months. Savannah had insisted that I let her style my hair. I didn't usually bother doing much to it. It was fairly long, midway down my back, and a mousy brown colour. I normally just threw it up on top of my head in a messy bun, but looking in the mirror now, it hung around my shoulders in loose waves.

"Thank you, Savannah. I can't believe how different I look, and how different I feel. I love it. I haven't felt this good in months." I told her truthfully.

"I'm glad you like it. Are you sure I can't do your makeup?" She asked smiling sweetly at me.

"I'm sure," I told her laughing. I didn't wear much makeup and was happy to just wear my usual mascara and lip gloss.

I'd chosen a strappy dress with tiny flowers all over it. It fell midway down my thighs, and my boots looked amazing with it. Savannah had lent me a bag that matched my dress perfectly. I twirled in front of the mirror and smiled. I'd been a bit apprehensive about going out tonight, but now I was looking forward to it. Aside from the possibility of Brody and Josh turning up of course.

I looked over at Savannah. She looked incredible. She was wearing her new dress; it was black and strapless with small red poppies on it. Her new boots looked great with it, and she had curled her hair like mine.

"Savannah, you look amazing. You'll be fighting those cowboys off with a stick." I joked.

"I could say the same for you." She said raising her eyebrows at me. "Come on, let's go."

Uncle Ryan gave us a lift into town and dropped us off outside the Brass Hall. We were meeting Rose and a few of Savannah's other friends inside. There was already a small queue to get in, and when we reached the front, we showed our ID's to the doorman who stamped our hand with a bright red stamp that read UNDER 21.

The inside of the bar was impressive. Loud music filled the room and tables were scattered around where people sat drinking and chatting. In the centre of the room, there was a large dance floor with the bar along the back wall. There were a few people dancing, but most were standing around the bar with drinks in their hands. In the corner of the room, there was a small stage where a band was setting up ready to play.

Savannah tugged on my arm. "This way Lib." She shouted in my ear, gesturing with her head to a table right on the edge of the dance floor. I looked over and saw three girls waving in our direction. As we got nearer I recognised one of the girls as Rose, who I'd met earlier.

"Hey, guys," Savannah said as we sat down. "This is my cousin Libby. She's over from England for a few weeks. Libby this is Harper and Ava, and you've already met Rose."

"Hi," I said shyly.

"Nice to meet you, Libby," Harper said smiling at me.

"Hi, Libby. I'm just headed to the bar. Do you want a drink?" Ava asked me.

"Ava and Harper are twenty-one. They can get you a proper drink if you want one." Rose said looking over to me.

"Oh, no thanks. A diet coke will be fine." I told her. "Thanks, Ava."

"Can I get a vodka and coke please Ava," Savannah asked winking at me.

"I'll help you with the drinks." Harper offered, standing and following Ava to the bar.

Just as the girls returned with our drinks, the live band began to play. "Thanks for the drink Ava," I told her taking a sip.

"No problem hun."

We spent the next hour chatting and drinking. The girls had been asking me all about England and what it was like to live there. I told them that it was rainy and cold most of the time, and nothing like living in Texas! They seemed nice, and we all got on really well.

All of Savannah's friends were beautiful, and it seemed most of the guys in the bar thought so too. There was a constant stream of men coming up to the table and trying to either buy them a drink or get them to dance. The girls were having none of it though and soon sent them on their way.

Suddenly Savannah jumped up, pulling on my arm. "Let's dance." She shouted in my ear.

While we had been chatting, the bar had gotten busier and was now packed. We fought our way through the crowds to the middle of the dance floor. I didn't recognise the music playing, it seemed a great song to dance to, though, so I closed my eyes and started moving my body to the music. I'd forgotten just how much I loved to dance. Mia had taught me everything I knew about dancing. I smiled to myself thinking that she would have loved it here. I realised that this was the first time I'd thought about her and not felt incredibly sad.

I opened my eyes and smiled at Savannah, she too was swaying her hips, her hands up in the air. I looked around and saw that she was getting plenty of admiring glances from the many guys on the dance floor.

After dancing for about ten minutes, I felt a pair of arms snake around my waist and I was pulled backward onto a hard chest. I tried to turn around and pull away, but the grip they had on me was too tight. I made eye contact with Savannah who must have seen how uncomfortable I was. She made her way over to me, her face a picture of anger.

"Hey!!" She shouted. "Get your hands off her, she doesn't want to dance with you." She pushed against the man's shoulder, and he reluctantly let me go.

"Is there a problem here Savannah?" I heard a voice say from behind us.

We spun around to see Brody standing there, his arms crossed over his chest. His eyes were fixed on the man standing next to me.

"Brody, am I glad to see you," Savannah said with a sigh of relief. "This jackass here had his hands all over Libby." She flung her arms towards the mystery man who was now backing away with his arms up. He'd taken one look at the size of Brody and obviously decided he didn't want to dance after all.

"She's taken. I get it, man. I'm out of here." He said turning quickly and disappearing into the crowd.

"You okay Lib?" Brody asked me moving closer.

"I'm fine, thanks, Brody, he just took me by surprise that's all."

"Let's get a drink," Brody said, grabbing my hand and leading me off the dance floor. I turned to check that Savannah was following and saw that she was looking straight past me towards the bar. I followed where she was looking and saw Josh leaning up against the bar waiting to be served.

I tugged on Brody's hand, and he turned to look at me. "I'm just going to head to the loo with Savannah," I told him. "We'll meet you at the bar in a minute." He nodded his head and walked into the crowd towards Josh.

"Looks like you need five minutes. Where are the toilets?" I asked Savannah who finally took her eyes of Josh and looked at me.

She took a deep breath, looking at me gratefully. "Thanks. They're over there." She gestured to the corner of the room.

We fought our way off the dance floor passing the bar as we made our way to the toilets. I looked over at Josh and saw that his eyes were fixed on Savannah. He wasn't looking at her like he wasn't interested. In fact, he was looking at her like he wanted to devour her. I smiled to myself as we entered the toilet.

"Urgh, I hate how good he looks in those jeans and boots," Savannah said exasperatedly. "I'll no doubt have to watch some girl hanging all over him later!"

"You're looking pretty good yourself Savannah. Why don't you show him what he's missing?" I told her fluffing my hair in the mirror.

"What do you mean? He's not missing anything Lib. He's not interested remember."

"I'm not so sure Sav," I said cautiously. I didn't want to get her hopes up if I was wrong. "Maybe if he sees you flirting with someone else, it might make him realise he is interested, and if not you might meet your Prince Charming instead," I told her winking.

"Prince Charming Libby. Really? There is no such thing. I really doubt he'd care if I was flirting with someone else. He never has before." She scoffed.

"You sound just like Mia," I told her smiling. "Let's go back out, more drinks and dancing is needed I think!"

She smiled and followed me out. As the bar came into sight, I saw that there was now someone else standing with Brody and Josh. He was tall, at least six foot two with dark brown hair. It was fairly messy but in a sexy way, and it was styled to look like he'd spent the day running his fingers through it. On his legs were dark denim jeans and he was wearing cowboy boots underneath them. His light blue t-shirt was stretched tight across his chest, his arms bulging out of the sleeves. I could make out the bottom of a tattoo that was just visible on his right arm. He was stunning. I stopped walking, and Savannah ploughed into the back of me.

"Lib, what's wrong? Why did you stop?"

"Savannah, who is that with Brody and Josh," I asked. I couldn't seem to pull my eyes off him.

"That's Mason, he works on the ranch. You know you're staring don't you Lib?" She said laughing.

"I'm not staring!" I exclaimed feeling my cheeks flush.

"Why are you blushing then." She teased. "He's been working at the ranch for about three months. No one really knows much about him other than he's been in prison. My Dad knows what for but he won't tell us, he says it's Mason's business. I do know he's older than Brody and Josh, though, twenty-six I think." She paused. "He's a bit of a player though Lib. He lives on the ranch, and I quite often see women leaving his place early in the morning…." She took a deep breath, looking over to Josh. "Let's get this over with."

I followed Savannah to the bar. Brody, Josh, and Mason were chatting and didn't see us coming. Savannah tapped Brody on the shoulder, and he turned around, kissing her on the cheek.

"Hey, you're back. What do you want to drink?" He asked looking between Savannah and me.

"Vodka and coke for me, please. Diet Coke Lib?" She asked me.

"Yes please," I responded looking up to Brody. I looked across to Mason and saw that he was looking at me with a smirk on his face.

"And who do we have here, Savannah? I don't think I've had the pleasure of meeting your friend before?" Mason spoke to Savannah but never took his eyes off me. As gorgeous as he was I was starting to feel a bit uncomfortable, but God was he gorgeous. Now I was up close I could see that he had the most amazing green eyes and just the right amount of stubble on his face.

"This is our cousin, Libby," Savannah told him. "She's staying with us on the ranch for a few weeks. Libby this is Mason."

"Hi," I said, holding out my hand for him to shake. He didn't shake it, though. Instead, he pulled it to his mouth, his lips brushing my skin. "Hi, sweetheart." He whispered. Goosebumps travelled up my arm, and I felt my face flush again. He must have noticed my reaction as I heard him chuckle. I quickly pulled my hand away and dropped my head.

Brody turned from the bar and handed me my drink. "Thanks," I muttered feeling like an idiot.

"Hey! Don't I get an introduction?" I heard a voice say.

"Erm sure," Savannah said. It was her turn to blush this time. "Josh, this is Libby, our cousin from England. Libby this is Josh, Brody's best friend."

Again, I put my hand out for him to shake. He too pulled it to his mouth and kissed it. Maybe it was a southern thing, and all the men here did it. I'd have to ask Savannah later. What I did know was that my body didn't react to Josh kissing my hand like it had when Mason had kissed it. Savannah had told me that Mason was a player and after all the heartbreak I'd seen Mia go through, someone like Mason was the last person I should be attracted too.

I turned my attention to Savannah who was sipping her drink and stealing glances at Josh. I put my hand on her shoulder and spoke in her ear. "Shall we dance?" I asked her. She nodded her head as she finished her drink, reaching between Josh and Brody to put her glass on the bar.

"We're going to dance Brody. Thanks for the drinks." She told him.

"We'll be keeping an eye on you." He told us. "Stay where we can see you."

"Brody we're not twelve, we'll be fine." She dismissed his request rolling her eyes.

"Savannah." He said sternly.

"Fine!" She threw her hands up in the air. "We'll be right there then." She pointed to the edge of the dance floor which was in full view of the three of them.

She pulled on my arm, and I turned to follow her, catching Mason's eyes which were still on me. My stomach fluttered, and I gave him a small smile as I headed to the dance floor.

"God, Brody is so annoying!" Savannah moaned to me. "I swear he still thinks I'm a child!"

"Jack's the same," I told her laughing.

"What was that back there with Mason?" Savannah asked me smiling. "I saw how he was looking at you."

"Nothing, he was just saying hi. I'm not interested if he's a player. That's the last thing I need."

"You like him, though don't you?" She pushed.

"I'm not blind Savannah, he's gorgeous, but if he's a player like you say, then he won't be interested in me. I can't give him what he wants." I shrugged my shoulders swaying my hips to the music.

"Well, he hasn't taken his eyes off you since he kissed your hand." She smirked at me looking over my shoulder towards the bar.

"What?" I asked spinning around. I looked over towards the bar, Savannah was right, Mason was still watching me. He lifted his drink in the air and smiled at me. My stomach fluttered again and I found myself smiling back at him. I'd waited a long time to feel this kind of attraction to someone, and there was no way I could deny the pull I felt towards him. I'd spent hours trying to convince Mia not to fall for the bad boy type. If what Savannah had told me was right, I was doing the exact thing I'd told Mia not to do. I wouldn't let anything happen between us, though. I couldn't get hurt. I didn't think my heart could stand it.

I spun back around to face Savannah. "Like I said, he's probably only after one thing, he won't be getting it from me." I wasn't sure if I was trying to convince myself or Savannah.

"Enough about Mason, didn't you see Josh staring at you while we stood at the bar?" I asked her, guiding the subject away from me.

"He wasn't staring at me. He barely spoke to me..." She trailed off. "And he's definitely not staring at me now." She said turning her back to the bar.

I glanced over my shoulder to see Josh talking to a pretty blonde girl. There was also a girl hanging off Mason, and he didn't look like he minded. I turned back to Savannah not wanting to watch, hating the jealousy bubbling in my stomach. I had no right to feel jealous. I'd only just met him. I didn't even want to like him.

Savannah had moved further into the centre of the dance floor, and I went over to join her. It wasn't long before we'd caught the attention of two guys who began dancing closely with us. I saw Savannah look back towards the bar before she flung her arms around the shoulders of one of the men, slow dancing with him. His friend made his way over to me.

"Hi, darlin. You want to dance?" He asked.

"Sure, why not," I replied linking my arms around his neck. "I'm Libby," I told him.

"Chase." He said in my ear. "You're a long way from home? What are you doing here in Marble Falls?"

I didn't get a chance to reply as I felt someone tapping my shoulder. I turned to see Mason standing behind me.

"Mind if I cut in?" I heard him ask Chase.

"Actually, I do," Chase replied.

"Tough. She's with me." Mason told him, pulling me out of Chase's arms and into his own. His arms looped my waist, and I instinctively reached up and put my arms around his neck. My head came level with his chest, and I rested my forehead there. He smelt incredible, a mixture of aftershave and soap. "I think the lady's made her choice." I heard him tell Chase, dismissing him.

I looked over to Savannah to see that she too was being taken out of her dance partner's arms by Josh. I couldn't tell what they were saying, but I could tell the conversation between them was heated.

I looked up to Mason, his eyes sparkling under the lights of the dance floor. He licked his lips, and my eyes instinctively dropped to his mouth, the corner lifting in a cocky smile as he watched me. That smile pulled me out of my Mason haze. I tried to push myself out of his arms, but he held me tightly. "What was that?" I asked him annoyed.

"What was what sweetheart?" He asked smiling at me.

"That!!" I gestured in the direction that Chase had gone. "I was dancing with Chase and then suddenly you turn up!" He'd let me pull away from him, and I crossed my arms across my chest glaring at him. "Well?"

He leaned in towards me, his face in my hair and his breath tickling my ear. "I decided I didn't like seeing you in another man's arms." I shivered as I felt his lips on my ear.

Angry at my body's reaction to him I tried to push him away. "Well don't look then!" I screeched at him. "It's not your decision to make, I don't belong to you, Mason. We've only just met."

He laughed, twirling a piece of my hair around his finger. "God, you're beautiful when your angry baby."

"I'm not your baby!" I turned and stormed off the dance floor. I was angry but turned on at the same time. I was frustrated by my reaction to him. I heard Savannah calling my name, and I stopped and turned, expecting to find her. Instead, I saw Mason right behind me with that cocky smile on his face again.

Savannah suddenly appeared beside me. "Libby, do you mind if we go? I think I've had my fill for tonight!" She asked me seemingly as angry as I was.

"With pleasure," I told her linking her arm. "We haven't spent much time with your friends. Let's go and say goodbye before we go."

We headed to the other side of the bar where the girls were still sitting at the same table. They had been joined by a few guys, and they looked like they were having a good time. We told them we were leaving and made our way outside. It was just after 11 pm, but it was still warm.

"Are we getting a taxi home, Savannah?" I asked. Before she could respond Brody and Mason had joined us outside the bar.

"No one is getting a taxi. I'll drive you home. We're all going to the same place" Brody announced.

Great! The last thing I wanted was to be stuck in a car with Mason. If I had a panic attack in front of him, I would be so embarrassed. I tried to get Savannah's attention to let her know how uncomfortable I was. I soon realised I couldn't get her attention without Mason and Brody knowing something was wrong.

"Can I sit in the front Brody?" I asked, ignoring Mason. "I get car sick in the back." I didn't, but I was able to control my anxiety better in the front. Being in the back brought back too many bad memories.

"Of course, Lib, the car is just down here." Brody replied motioning down the street with his hand.

"Where's Josh, Brody?" Savannah asked quietly.

"He's gone home, he was mad about something. Couldn't get him to tell me what, though."

I grabbed Savannah's hand, and she gave me a sad smile in response. I'd have to speak to her when we were alone and find out what had happened with Josh.

The ride home was thankfully uneventful, and I managed to control my breathing and avoid a panic attack. I'd noticed Mason giving me a funny look once or twice in the car. He'd sat behind Brody so could probably see my hands clasped tightly on my lap and my deep breaths in and out.

Savannah had fallen asleep on the way home, and Brody had carried her into the house leaving me alone with Mason. As he made his way over to me, I started to walk backward not stopping until my back hit one of the pillars holding up the porch. He stopped right in front of me, reaching up to tuck a loose piece of hair behind my ear. He leaned down and kissed me on the cheek. "Night sweetheart." He whispered in my ear. "Sleep tight." He turned and walked away leaving me standing by the porch, heart racing and palms sweating. I had a feeling it would take me a long time to fall asleep tonight.

Chapter Eight

I woke early the next morning despite it taking me ages to fall asleep. My mind drifted to Mason and how good it had felt to be in his arms last night. I needed to get my attraction towards him under control. He seemed to have me under some sort of spell, and I'd only met him once. If he lived on the ranch, I could hardly avoid him.

I reached for my phone and saw that I had a text from Jack. He was flying into Austin next Friday. I couldn't wait to see him. I sent him a quick reply telling him how excited I was to be seeing him, and that I would arrange for someone to pick him up from the airport. Maybe Savannah would be around; she'd told me yesterday that she's only got a couple of classes left at university and a few exams before the term ended for the summer. I'd have to check if she was free.

I needed to talk to Savannah about what had happened last night with Josh, maybe we could take the horses out this morning and talk. I got out of bed and opened the curtains, looking out over the ranch. It was a beautiful morning, not a cloud in sight. My eyes drifted to the barn where I saw Mason leading a horse out into the exercise area. I quickly moved back from the window not wanting him to see me. I stole another look outside and my breath caught in my throat. He looked incredible. He had on a worn pair of jeans that were tucked into a pair of cowboy boots and a tight black t-shirt. A cowboy hat sat on his head. I could see the tattoo that I'd spotted last night. It covered the top of his arm and shoulder before disappearing under his shirt. I couldn't make out from here the exact design, but it looked sexy as hell.

Mason turned towards the house and I quickly moved back from the window. I wasn't quite quick enough, though, and he tipped his hat to me before turning and heading back into the barn. I felt my face flush at the thought that he'd seen me watching him. Just then a knock sounded on my bedroom door. "Come in," I called out. I looked up and Savannah walked in.

"Morning Lib." She said giving me a funny look. "What's got you all flushed?" She crossed the room to where I was standing. "Oh! Checking out the view from your window I see." She smirked, seeing Mason bringing another horse out of the barn.

"Don't know what you're talking about," I replied, making a quick escape into the bathroom and locking the door. I could hear Savannah laughing on the other side of the door.

"You're allowed to like him Lib." I heard her say. "He obviously likes you, if last night was anything to go by. Have some fun with him while you're here, you deserve some fun after everything you've been through."

"Not going to happen Savannah." I opened the bathroom door. "Enough about me. What happened with you and Josh last night? I saw you two arguing on the dance floor."

"Urgh!! He's such a jerk!" She threw herself down on my bed. "He basically called me a slut for dancing with someone!" Her voice was angry, but I could see the pain and hurt in her eyes.

"What?! He actually said that?" I asked incredulously.

"Well, not in so many words…" She trailed off and then sighed. "He said I shouldn't let some random guy have his hands all over me... I was only dancing and why should he care anyway! He doesn't want me." She looked at me sadly. "I wish I could just get over him, but I've tried. He's all I see."

"Oh Sav," I said to her, grabbing her hand and pulling her off the bed. "Come on, let's go for that ride we talked about. We can bitch about men while we ride." I suggested giving her a hug.

I had already suspected that Josh liked Savannah after I saw how he was looking at her last night. Now that Savannah had told me how he'd reacted to her dancing with another guy, I was even more convinced. I needed to let them figure it out themselves, though. Josh was obviously struggling, for whatever reason, with his attraction to Savannah and he needed to deal with it. I didn't want to get her hopes up by continuing to tell her what I thought.

Savannah gave me a small smile. "That sounds like a great idea. Let's get ready and meet downstairs in a bit."

"Okay," I told her as she headed to her room. I had a quick shower, got dressed and thirty minutes later I was waiting in the kitchen for Savannah. Aunt Claire was making us some pancakes before we left.

"How was your night out Libby?" Aunt Claire asked, flipping a pancake at the stove.

"Eventful. Southern boys are a bit different to the boys at home." I laughed.

"Why? What happened."

"Oh, nothing." I brushed off my comment. I didn't know if Aunt Claire knew about Savannah's feelings for Josh and I didn't want to explain what had happened with Mason. "Savannah introduced me to Josh and Mason, and they both kissed my hand. Is that something all guys around here do? I thought stuff like that only happened in books" I laughed.

"If they've been brought up right, then yes, they'll even open your car door for you too." Aunt Claire smiled at me. "It's just how they are honey. Swoon worthy, right?"

"I guess so."

Aunt Claire laughed. "You'll get used to it. It's one of the reasons I never made it back home to England after university. Ryan swept me off my feet. Swooned the hell out of me and wouldn't take no for an answer!" She paused. "Some of these southern boys can be quite persistent when they see something they want, and once they've got you, God help any other man who comes near you." She put a plate of pancakes in front of me and slid a jar of maple syrup towards me.

"Yeah, I can imagine!" I rolled my eyes thinking back to last night and Mason's reaction to me dancing with Chase. "Aunt Claire, how much do you know about Mason?" I asked shyly.

"Not a lot honey, he's been working on the ranch for about three months. He had some sort of falling out with his parents. A friend of your Uncle Ryan's knew his Dad and asked if we could find him some work. He's had it tough as far as I know. I've probably said too much…" She trailed off. "Why are you asking Libby?" She turned to me eyeing me warily.

"Savannah mentioned that he's been in prison?" I asked, avoiding her question. I didn't know why I was asking about Mason, I just had a need to know more about him, I couldn't explain it.

"Yes, he has. I don't know all the details, Uncle Ryan does, though, and I trust his judgment, but Savannah, he's a lot older than you. Too old." She raised her eyebrows at me. "Did something happen with Mason last night at the bar?"

"No. No of course not. Nothing's happened. I'm just being nosey." I lied, my eyes on the pancakes in front of me. I started eating to avoid any further questions.

"Morning Savannah, pancakes?" I heard Aunt Claire ask. I

looked up to see Savannah entering the kitchen and Aunt Claire eyeing her suspiciously.

Savannah looked between her Mum and me. "Erm, yes please. Is everything ok?"

"Yes fine. I was just telling your Mum how different Southern boys are compared to the boys back home, you know all the hand-kissing and stuff." I said quickly, jumping in before Aunt Claire could quiz her.

"Oh right." Savannah looked at me confused. "On second thought Mum, I'm not that hungry. I'll just grab something when we're back from our ride. Come on Lib, let's get the horses ready."

I smiled at Aunt Claire and followed Savannah outside.

"What was all that about?" Savannah asked, hands on her hips.

I sighed, knowing I'd have to tell her. "I was asking Aunt Claire about Mason," I said quietly. "She got suspicious, wanting to know why I was asking about him, then she warned me off him, saying he was too old for me." I looked down to the ground.

"Libby, why *were* you asking? You do like him, don't you?"

I looked at her, taking a deep breath and letting it out slowly. "Yes. I'm attracted to him. He's gorgeous."

She smiled widely at me. "I knew it!"

"I don't want to be attracted to him, though. He's the complete opposite of what I want or need."

"What do you mean?" She asked me looking confused.

"I've spent the last four years watching Mia have her heart broken over and over again by guys who treated her badly and messed around on her. I swore to myself that I'd never get involved with a guy like that. I don't know Mason, but from what you've told me he's a player and a lady's man. I can't risk falling for him, my already broken heart couldn't stand it." I told her truthfully.

"You're not Mia though Libby, you're you and a guy who isn't a player can break your heart. Sometimes you've just got to take a chance and hope for the best. It won't always work out but what if it does? You just have to have the courage to try." She smiled sadly at me. I knew that she was thinking about her and Josh.

"I know Sav, but it's easier said than done."

She took my arm and gave me a small smile. "Come on let's saddle up the horses."

Chapter Nine

W e got the horses ready and thankfully managed to avoid Mason. He must have been busy elsewhere on the ranch. We rode away from the stables and out towards the many acres that made up Wild Oak Ranch and Retreat. It was a beautiful day, and the ranch was more incredible than I remembered. Green fields as far as the eye could see.

It had been a while since I'd been on a horse, and I was a little nervous. I was riding one of the new horses named Cookie. She was a stunning chestnut colour and fairly new to the ranch. Savannah was just ahead of me on Marley. We took it steady to start with, riding past the log cabins and the smaller ranch house. Savannah pointed out the newer cabins, there were around twenty cabins now, and there were only ten or so the last time I was here. They had expanded the retreat quite a bit since taking over from Uncle Ryan's Dad about two years ago. Once we'd got past the guest accommodations, I felt confident enough to follow Savannah in a trot. I decided not to mention Josh again unless Savannah did and we rode in a comfortable silence for about fifteen minutes until we reached the river.

There was a group of about eight people from the ranch fly

fishing in the river. I saw Savannah wave to the guy overseeing the group, and he responded with a quick wave back.

"Jump down, we'll stop here for a bit," Savannah said winking at me.

"Why are you winking at me?" I asked her as I got off Cookie.

"No reason." She laughed. "Come on let's get our feet wet."

I followed her down towards the water's edge. There was a small section between rocks that were jutting out into the water where we could paddle. It was almost like a small pebble beach sloping off into the shallow water. I kicked my cowboy boots off, leaving them on the shiny stones and dipped my foot into the water. It was freezing, but I welcomed it after the hour long ride we'd just done. It was a baking hot day, and the cool water was refreshing. I looked over to the group who were fishing. There was a mixture of both men and women having a go, all of them wearing long waterproof trousers up to their waists with braces over their shoulders. Savannah came up beside me. "They must be so hot in those long trouser things," I remarked.

Savannah laughed. "They're called waders Lib."

I screwed my nose up at her. "I'm not a big fishing fan, it's never really appealed to me." I actually couldn't think of anything worse. Having to bait your hook with a maggot to then catch a slimy fish! Yuk! I looked back towards the small group. "They've got a lot of equipment, how have they got down here, it's too far to walk?" I asked Savannah turning to look at her. She cocked her head to the right smirking at me and biting her lip. It was the opposite direction from where we had come, and I turned to look past her, that's when I saw him. Mason. He looked incredible, leaning up against one of the two jeeps parked a little way up from the river. He flashed that trademark cocky smile and raised his hand in a wave. I whipped my head back around to face Savannah.

I glared at her. "Oh my god!! You knew he'd be here, didn't

you?" I whisper shouted. Not being able to resist looking at him again, I glanced back over. He was pushing himself off the jeep and walking towards us. "He's coming over!! I'm going to kill you, Savannah."

Savannah laughed. "No, you're not." She whispered. "Hi, Mason." She chirped in a sugary sweet voice. "Nice to see you again."

"Hi, Savannah." He responded winking at her. He turned to look at me, dragging his eyes down past my chest to my bare legs. I squirmed, feeling my whole body erupt in goosebumps at his inspection of me. I watched his face as his eyes made their way back up to mine, his cocky grin in place as if he knew how my body was reacting to him. As our eyes met his cocky grin turned into a breath-taking smile reaching his eyes and making them sparkle. It was the first genuine smile I'd seen from him, and I found myself grinning back.

"Hey, Libby." He whispered, leaning closer towards me, kissing me on the cheek.

"Hi, Mason." I lifted my hand and touched my cheek where he'd kissed it. He watched my hand and smiled again at me.

"What brings you two down here?"

"Just showing Lib around. She's keen to get in the water and have a go at fishing." Savannah joked nudging me in the shoulder.

"I'm really not!" I laughed pushing Savannah back.

"Not a big lover of fishing then Libby?" Mason asked me chuckling. He had the best laugh, it sent a tremor through my body as I heard it.

"Well, I've never actually tried it..." I told him sheepishly. "But the thought of it puts me off. Slippery fish and maggots. Burgh!" I shuddered at the thought.

Mason let out another laugh. "Well, fish are definitely slippery darlin', can't really get away from that, but we don't use maggots.

I'll take you while you're here and show you. This your first time on a horse Libby?" Mason asked gesturing up to where the two horses were grazing and changing the subject before I could tell him no.

"Erm, no but it's been a while," I told him, thrown by his change of topic. "I haven't ridden since the last time I was here, about four years ago, so I'm a bit rusty."

"Well, it's my day off on Thursday if you fancy practising your riding skills." He said, raising his eyebrows, the double meaning not lost on me.

I narrowed my eyes at him and folded my arms across my chest.

"Whoa!" He put his hands up, took a step back and laughed. "I was offering to take one of the horses out with you. I can see where your mind went though and I'm totally up for that kind of riding too." He winked at me, his cocky smile returning.

"I think I'll pass thanks," I told him scrunching up my nose.

"Actually, Lib it might be a good idea." Savannah cut in.

I looked at her, stunned. How could she think it was a good idea!

"I've got classes all day on Thursday. You should take him up on his offer." She glared at Mason. "And I'm talking about the offer of a horse ride Mason. Nothing else!"

"Of course," Mason laughed.

"I'm fine, really. There's a book I'm dying to read, and your parent's porch swing has my name on it." I rushed out desperate not to be alone with him. As much as I told myself, and Savannah, that I wouldn't let myself be attracted to him, it was a battle I was most definitely losing. I felt a connection between us and from the way Mason looked at me I think he felt it too. I just needed to stay away from him, and I'd be fine. I had a feeling though that staying away would be harder than I thought.

"Well, now I know where you'll be, I might have to come and

steal you away from your book." He said it straight faced, but I could see the amusement in his eyes.

I shook my head and rolled my eyes at him. I didn't answer; I didn't trust myself that I wouldn't agree right now. I was sure that I wouldn't need much forcing if he did turn up.

"We'll see." I heard him murmur. I looked at Savannah who was grinning from ear to ear while looking between us. I scowled at her when her eyes caught mine, and she laughed.

"Shall we head back Lib, maybe get some lunch?" She asked me.

"Yeah, I'm pretty hungry now you mention it."

"Hey, before you go, are you planning on going to the county fair in Burnet on Saturday? There's a rodeo that night. I think Brody and Josh are going." Mason asked us.

I turned to Savannah. "A rodeo! Can we go?" I asked excitedly.

"Sure, why not. We can go with the boys but do our own thing when we get there." She said obviously not wanting to be around Josh all night.

"Oh, that reminds me Sav," I said, glancing at Mason who was smiling widely at me. "Jack's flying in on Friday for a few days. I can't wait to see him. Will you be able to pick him up from the airport with me? He gets in at lunchtime I think." I looked back towards Mason and saw that the smile had slipped from his face.

"Oh Lib, I can't I'm at university on Friday. I bet Mason could take you, though?" She looked over to Mason expectantly.

"Who's Jack?" He asked quietly, looking straight at me.

Savannah burst out laughing. "Don't worry Romeo, he's not competition. Jack is Libby's older brother."

I thought I saw him breathe out sharply as if relieved before the gorgeous smile that made my knees weak appeared on his face again. "In that case, I'd be happy to pick him up. You're coming too, right?" He asked me.

"Erm…" I hesitated. "I can ask Aunt Claire. I'm sure you have stuff to do." I said, not looking him in the eye. I couldn't let him drive me, what if I had a panic attack in the car?

"Nope, no plans for Friday lunch time. We've got a riding tour that afternoon but Colt and Taylor, the other ranch hands, can manage without me. Friday is normally a busy day on the ranch for Claire. I better get back, looks like they're finishing up with the fishing. See you soon ladies." He said the cocky smirk returning.

I didn't get a chance to tell him no before he jogged off to join the group. I couldn't help my eyes drifting down to his incredible ass as I watched him leave.

"It's a nice view from behind, isn't it?" Savannah kicked her foot at me, water splattering my legs.

"Hey!" I kicked my foot back at her spraying her with water too. I stepped out of the water and made my way back to the grass flopping on the ground. Savannah followed me. "I can't let Mason take me to the airport, what if I have a panic attack? He'll think I'm crazy." I closed my eyes, feeling the sun beating down on my face. When Savannah didn't answer me, I opened my eyes, shading my face with my hand, to see her looking down at me.

"So what if you have a panic attack Lib, you've got to let someone in at some point. You're not crazy, and there is no way Mason would think you are."

"If I have a panic attack I'd have to tell him about Mia and what happened."

"Would it be all that bad to tell him?"

"Then he'd know it was my fault she died," I whispered, tears falling down my cheeks.

"Oh Lib, it isn't your fault she died. I had no idea that's how you felt. Her boyfriend was drunk; he should never have been driving. You are in no way responsible. You could have been killed as well." She pulled me up by the hand and hugged me. I just nodded. I knew from my conversations with Jack that I couldn't make her understand. "It might help you to talk about Mia. He might just surprise you Lib."

I took a deep breath thinking about what Savannah had said. If I let Mason in, I risked my heart, and I didn't think I was strong enough for it to be broken. "Well it looks like Mason is my only option, it's not like I can pick Jack up myself. I'll just have to hope I can stay calm."

My thoughts were full of Mia as we headed back to the stables. Savannah must have known that I needed some time to think as we rode in silence until we reached the barn.

"Come on let's eat!" She said. I smiled, her enthusiasm infectious. I didn't want to be down and depressed. I was in the most amazing place; Jack was arriving in a few short days, and I was going to my first ever rodeo this weekend. I definitely had a lot to look forward to, and that was aside from the brown haired, green-eyed cowboy who took my breath away.

Chapter Ten

The next few days were quiet and laid-back. I spent hours sunbathing, reading and taking walks around the ranch. I needed a couple of chilled days as the nightmares had returned the night after Savannah and I rode to the river. I was exhausted. I had woken up screaming, the same nightmare invading my sleep. Savannah and Aunt Claire had come rushing into my room to check if I was okay. I was embarrassed that they had seen me like that but appreciated the hugs and support both of them gave me. Fortunately, I hadn't woken Brody or Uncle Ryan so I hadn't had to face them.

I'd spoken to my parents on the phone yesterday, excitedly telling them all about what I'd seen and done since I'd been here, and how much I was looking forward to the rodeo this weekend. They already knew that Jack was flying out at the end of the week, and were glad that we would be able to spend some time together. I'd decided not to tell them about the nightmares, and I'd made Aunt Claire promise she wouldn't tell them either. I didn't want them to worry when I was so far away from them. I must have sounded so enthusiastic on the phone that they never asked me about them anyway, I certainly wasn't going to bring it up.

It was late morning on Thursday, and I was curled up on the

porch swing trying to read. Savannah was at university, and Aunt Claire had gone to the shops in Marble Falls, she had asked me if I'd wanted to go, but I'd decided to stay at the ranch. I was wishing now that I had gone with her. I couldn't concentrate on my book. I was reading one of the few paperbacks I'd brought with me, but I'd read the same page about five times! My stomach was fluttering with nervous butterflies. It was Mason's day off, and I didn't know if he would turn up like he'd said he might. Part of me was terrified that he would while the other part was terrified that he wouldn't.

"Hey Lib." I heard a voice shout from just outside the barn.

I looked up to see Mason making his way over to me. My heart began racing, and the butterflies were well and truly taking flight in my stomach. As usual, he looked gorgeous, he was only wearing jeans and a simple t-shirt, but he couldn't have looked better.

"Hi." I squeaked out as he climbed the stairs and sat down next to me on the swing.

"Good book?" He asked gesturing to the book in my hand.

Flustered I looked down. "Erm, I can't really get into it at the moment." I looked up to see him smiling at me.

"So, I'm not interrupting you then?"

"No…" I said slowly.

"Come on then." He jumped up, the swing flying back. I grabbed onto the sides to stop myself from falling off. He stood in front of me, his hand stretched out for me to take. I looked at his hand, frowning. "Take a chance Libby, come with me."

I dropped my head, my eyes on my lap. "Come where?" I whispered nervously.

He reached forward with the hand he'd wanted me to take and used his forefinger to lift my chin so that I was looking into his beautiful eyes. "It's a surprise." He paused. "A good one, I promise. Please?"

His eyes were pleading with me, and although I was nervous

about being alone with him, I couldn't deny that I wanted to go. I took a deep breath. It was decision time. I could do what both he and Savannah had said to me and take a chance, or tell him no and most likely regret it later. "Okay," I told him making my decision. The smile spread across his face, and he grabbed my hand pulling me down the steps. "Mason! Wait I've got no shoes on." I said laughing, pulling back on his hand.

"Oh, well put your cowboy boots on we're taking the horses. I'll wait here for you."

I went back inside the house closing the door behind me. I slumped back against it and closed my eyes needing a minute to calm down. *Take a deep breath,* I told myself, *nothing's going to happen you're just hanging out as friends.* I must have been there freaking out longer than I thought as I heard a knock at the door and Mason shout. "You're not standing me up are you, Libby?"

"No…I'll be right out." I quickly ran upstairs and pulled my boots on. I caught a glimpse of myself in the mirror, my hair was a mess. I grabbed my hairbrush and threw my hair up in a ponytail. I wondered if I was dressed okay in my shorts and t-shirt, I had no idea where we were going. There wasn't time to worry about it now. I went downstairs and left a note for Aunt Claire telling her that I had taken one of the horses for a ride. I left out that I was with Mason as I knew she thought he was too old for me.

I opened the door, and Mason was sat on the porch swing reading my book. I paused to look at him, there was nothing sexier than seeing a man reading. He looked up and caught me watching him. "This book is filthy!" He told me with a smirk.

"What! No, it isn't!" I reached over and plucked the book from his hands feeling my face flush. "It's just a romance book."

"Why are you blushing if it's just a romance book Libby." He teased. "I've only flicked through it for a few minutes, and there is sex on every other page."

I felt my face flush, even more, when he started talking about the steamy scenes. Yes, there was sex in the book, but it was just part of the story. I didn't read it because of those scenes. I read it for the romance. "Whatever Mason, you seemed to be enjoying it when I came out anyway. Maybe you want to borrow it when I'm done?" It was my turn to give him a cocky smile.

Laughing, he said to me. "I might just take you up on that offer sweetheart. Come on let's go."

I followed him down the path and over to the barn. I was going to be riding Cookie again, and Mason was on a bigger horse named Titan. The name suited him, he was huge with a glossy midnight black coat. He was absolutely stunning. Mason helped me mount Cookie, his hands gripping my waist. He let his hands linger on my waist a fraction longer than needed and I shivered under his touch.

"You cold Lib?" He asked, his eyes twinkling with amusement knowing full well that I wasn't cold.

"I'm fine." I brushed him off. "Where are we going anyway?" I asked changing the subject.

"I've told you it's a surprise. Let's go, it's about a fifteen-minute ride."

I pouted at him. "Fine." I watched his eyes focus on my pouting lips. He shook his head.

"You might want to stop poking those lips at me darlin', unless you want me to come on over there and poke them back."

My eyes widened in surprise, and he laughed at my reaction. We headed away from the barn and over the fields in the opposite direction to the way Savannah and I had ridden a few days ago. "It's so beautiful here, I can't get over just how stunning it is," I commented.

"Yeah, I know what you mean. I'm having the same problem." I heard him mutter. I turned to look at him only to find him staring at me. He couldn't possibly be talking about me, could he? "How long are you staying at the ranch for Lib?" He asked me, changing the subject as we rode side by side.

"A few weeks I think, I haven't got a return flight booked yet, so it's pretty open-ended."

He nodded and gestured down to Cookie. "You're pretty good on a horse for someone who doesn't ride very often."

"Thanks. I was fifteen the last time I was here, and we rode every day, I loved it. I don't get the chance at home, but I seem to have picked it up again pretty quickly." I leaned forward and patted Cookie on the neck.

"You're nineteen then?" Mason asked me, his eyes finding mine as I looked over to him.

"How do you know that?" I was curious to see if he'd been asking Brody or Savannah about me.

"When we met at the lake the other day you said you hadn't ridden in four years, if you were fifteen when you last came that would make you nineteen now." He smiled. "I listen to what you say, sweetheart."

"I'm twenty soon, you're twenty-six right?"

"Yep, you've been asking Savannah about me?" He teased, his eyes dancing with amusement. "I like that you're asking about me Lib." He said quietly. My face heated and I heard him chuckle.

We fell silent heading further away from the barn and house. We rode across what felt like acres of land, the sun beating down on us. There was no sound other than the constant chirping of crickets, and the occasional snort from the horses. I chanced a look over at Mason. His strong thighs were gripping Titan, and one of his tanned arms rested on his leg while the other held the reins. He wore a cowboy hat that covered most of his dark, messy hair, but I could still see some of it poking out. He looked gorgeous, like he should be on the cover of a magazine or something. He turned and caught me looking at him, and I quickly looked away.

"We're here." I heard him say.

I turned to look, and due to my gawking, I had completely missed that the field we were in had quite a few big trees and a small lake. "Wow, this is beautiful. I never knew this was here." I'm sure I would have remembered if Savannah had shown me this the last time I was here. Mason had jumped off Titan and was at my side waiting to help me down. "I can manage," I told him, secretly wishing I couldn't so he could help me down like he'd helped me up. I swung my leg over not realising that he hadn't moved out of the way, I felt my boot crash into him.

"Ooomph," I heard him moan.

"Oh my god Mason! I'm so sorry! I thought you'd moved! Are you okay?" I jumped down spinning around to see him bent double and groaning. "Let me see where you're hurt?"

"I don't think you want to see sweetheart." He squeaked out. "This is our first date after all."

"This is not a date Mason," I told him, taken aback by what he'd said. "And why wouldn't I want to see?"

Mason attempted a laugh, but it came out like a strangled cry. "You've kicked me in the balls Libby, so unless you want to kiss them better, I think I can manage."

"Oh," I replied my face flushing for about the fifth time today. I don't know what it was about him, but he managed to make me blush nearly every time he opened his mouth. "I'm sorry."

"I'll be okay in a minute." He reassured me, standing up straight and taking a deep breath.

After a few minutes, he seemed to have recovered. He led the horses over to a shaded area where he left them to graze. He grabbed my hand again, which I had to admit I was beginning to like and pulled me towards a large oak tree. He sat me down in the shade of the tree and went off in the opposite direction. He returned a few seconds later with a picnic basket and a blanket.

"You hungry?" He asked, spreading the blanket on the ground and motioning for me to sit on it. I scooted over so that I was on the blanket and he sat down next to me.

"Starving." My eyes met his. "Mason this is amazing, when did you set all his up?"

He shrugged his shoulders. "Just before I came to get you. I didn't know what you liked so I brought a few different things. I hope you like it."

He looked nervous, not at all like the cocky Mason I'd met at the bar the other night. I kneeled up and leaned over, kissing him on the cheek. "I'm sure I'll love it. Thank you." I told him. No man had ever done anything like this for me. I was genuinely shocked by how much trouble he'd gone to. He looked up at me obviously surprised that I'd kissed him, albeit only on the cheek. I think I'd surprised myself a bit as well. "Mason, what would you have done if I'd said no to coming with you? Or if I'd gone out?" Thinking how Aunt Claire had asked me to go to Marble Falls with her.

"I wasn't going to take no for an answer. I saw Claire leave and I knew you weren't in the car with her. I figured you must be somewhere on the ranch. I must admit I didn't expect to find you exactly where you'd said I'd find you. You looked terrified the other day at the river when I said I was going to come and steal you away from your book. I was sure you'd have been somewhere else hiding." He grinned at me. "Maybe you wanted me to find you?" He raised his eyebrows at me in question.

"Maybe," I whispered.

"I like you, Libby. I like you a lot. There's this thing between us. I can't explain it. I know you feel it too. I've seen how your body reacts to me. What are you so afraid of?"

I couldn't tell him the truth, so I went for the obvious reason instead. "Mason I live in England. I'm only here on holiday. What would be the point of starting something? One or both of us would only get hurt." I sighed. "I do like you Mason, and I feel the connection too, but it wouldn't work."

His face lit up with a smile. "Why are you smiling? Did you not hear, what I just said?" I looked at him confused.

"I heard you. You like me; you feel what I feel. That's all that matters right now." He was still grinning from ear to ear.

I shook my head. "You're not listening though Mason."

He cut me off. "Let's eat before the food gets spoiled in the heat."

He completely ignored what I'd said and began to empty out the picnic basket. Despite being annoyed with him for not listening to me I couldn't help but laugh when I saw how much food he had brought, and he was still getting more out. There were pulled pork sandwiches, pieces of breaded chicken, two different sorts of coleslaw, potato salad, a pasta salad, crisps, fresh strawberries and a fresh fruit salad. "Are you expecting more people? We're never going to be able to eat all this." I told him giggling.

"Nope. Just us. I can pack away a fair amount. Being a ranch hand is hungry work." He pulled up his t-shirt and patted his flat, toned stomach.

My eyes were immediately drawn to his tanned stomach, and I couldn't seem to tear them away. It was an impressive sight. He easily had a six pack, and there was a trail of dark hair starting below his belly button and disappearing down into his jeans. He dropped his t-shirt and cleared his throat. My eyes snapped up to meet his, and he smiled. Heat once again flooded my face.

"I love seeing you blush. It makes you look even more beautiful than you normally do." He said quietly, reaching up and brushing my cheek with the back of his hand.

My face tingled where he'd touched me, and my stomach fluttered with nervous excitement. Had Savannah been wrong about him when she'd said he was a player or was he playing me? I couldn't decide. He seemed to have gone to a lot of trouble setting all this up when he didn't even know if I'd go with him.

"So," I began, eager to take the attention away from me. "Savannah tells me you've been at the ranch about three months, do you like it here?"

"I love it. Ryan and Claire gave me a chance when no one else would, and I owe them a lot for that." He said mysteriously. "They are great people, but I don't have to tell you that."

"No, they're the best."

"Libby, I'm guessing Savannah's told you that I've been in prison." He looked up at me with a frown. "I understand if that's the reason you're being cautious with me."

"It's not." And it really wasn't. I admit I was a little taken aback when Savannah had first told me, but I figured if Uncle Ryan had given him a job and a place to live then he must trust him. "Savannah doesn't know the reasons why and I'm not asking you to tell me," I added quickly. I didn't want him to feel he had to tell me. I had my own demons and would hate to feel forced to talk about them. For reasons, I couldn't explain, as I hardly knew him, I was sure that I wasn't in any danger of being physically hurt by him. I just wasn't sure I could say the same for my heart.

"I will tell you what happened, just not today. What I will say is that you're not in any danger with me. I would never hurt you, Libby." His eyes shone with sincerity. "Come on let's eat. I've got plans for you after lunch."

My mouth dropped open, and my eyebrows shot up in surprise. I heard Mason laugh out loud.

"Not those sorts of plans! God, you've got a dirty mind. That's twice you've jumped to that conclusion. I blame those dirty books of yours." He shook his head still laughing.

"I… I…" I stammered not knowing what to say. "My books aren't dirty, and I do not have a dirty mind. I just thought…"

"I know exactly what you thought. I'm a gentleman I'll have you know." He raised his eyebrows at me, and I laughed.

"That's not what Savannah tells me." I joked. I watched as the smile fell from his face.

"What has Savannah been telling you?" He asked me quietly.

"Just that you like the ladies," I told him not meeting his eyes. I paused. "She told me that she'd seen some women leaving your place early in the morning." I heard him sigh deeply.

"So, that's the reason you've been wary of me." He nodded his head as if it all made sense to him now.

"Mason…" I trailed off, not wanting to tell him about Mia but needing to tell him part of why I'd been pushing him away. "I was my best friend's shoulder to cry on more times than I can count when boys hurt her, she always chose the cocky, self-assured guys who had an eye for anything female. I swore that I'd never let myself get hurt like that. I'm sorry."

"You haven't even given me a chance though Libby." His eyes bore into mine. "Yes, I've been with a lot of women in the past few months, but I'm single. When I make someone mine, I'm committed to that person one hundred percent, and I would show that person every day how much I loved them. They would be the most important person in my life."

The idea that I could be the most important person in Mason's life caused my stomach to flutter with the familiar feeling of butterflies that seemed to be ever-present when I was around him. "You're right, I haven't given you a chance, and I'm sorry for judging you on what Savannah told me. That was wrong of me. Who you choose to date is none of my business, but as I said before I'm only here on holiday, and I know if I were to allow myself to fall for you I would fall hard Mason. I don't think my heart could take that right now." I gave him a small smile.

"Has someone hurt you, Libby?" He asked concern etched on his face.

"You could say that," I told him dropping my eyes from his. "I can't talk about it, I'm sorry. I can offer you friendship, though? I could certainly do with one more friend right now." I asked him, wishing things could be different between us.

"Ahh, the friend zone." He said with a small smile. "Of course, Lib, if that's all your offering at the moment then I'll take it. I hope we'll be good enough friends soon for you to be able open up to me." He paused. "Just so you know, though, I can't promise that I won't try and change your mind." He winked at me lightening the mood, and I couldn't help giving him a smile.

He passed me a sandwich, and I bit into it hungrily. "Mmmm Mason this is amazing; did you make it yourself?"

He looked at me sheepishly. "I wish I could tell you I did, but no, I'm no cook. I drove into Marble Falls first thing and bought everything."

I looked at him, impressed with the efforts he'd gone too. "Well homemade or not it's delicious." We chatted comfortably while we ate, I asked questions about his job and what it entailed, and he asked me what England was like as he'd never been. We both avoided any personal questions, sensing that today wasn't the time to be asking. After we'd finished eating, I flopped down on my back not able to move after all the wonderful food. "I'm stuffed," I told him. "Everything was lovely. Thank you."

"You're welcome darlin'." He lay down next to me, our shoulders touching. I turned my head towards him and saw that he was looking straight at me.

"You've got the most gorgeous eyes Lib; I could stare into them for hours." Our hands were resting on the blanket between us, and I could feel his fingers brush mine.

I closed my eyes embarrassed by his compliment, my fingers

tingling where he had touched. "Friends remember," I whispered. God, I wanted him to kiss me. I was so confused by my feelings for him. I shook my head. "Maybe we should head back. I bet Aunt Claire is home by now."

"Not yet Lib. I did say I couldn't promise not to try and change your mind." He winked again at me. "I haven't shown you your other surprise yet. Wait here and I'll get it." He jumped up before I had a chance to respond. I had a feeling resisting Mason was going to be harder than I thought. We'd only agreed twenty minutes ago to be friends, and he was already pushing the boundaries. I was just worried that he wouldn't have to push all that hard for me to fall.

He disappeared off to where he'd gotten the picnic basket from and came back with two fishing rods. "Oh, god Mason, we're not fishing, are we?" I asked horrified.

He burst out laughing. "Well, you did say you'd never done it."

"I also said I didn't want to do it and couldn't think of anything worse!"

"I promise you won't have to touch any maggots or fish, I'll do all the things you don't like. Just give it a try okay?"

"Okay," I told him reluctantly. He reached his hand out to me and pulled me up off the blanket. He kept my hand firmly entwined with his and led me the short distance down to the lake. "We're not actually going into the lake, are we? In those wader things?" I asked him scrunching my nose up.

"We only use the waders for fly fishing, we're just doing regular fishing. We don't have to go into the lake, but it might be nice just to go in a few feet to keep us cool."

It was a baking hot day again, and Mason was right it would be nice to cool off a bit by getting our feet wet. I pulled my hand free from his and reached down to pull off my cowboy boots. "Come on then let's get this over with." I took off, running ahead of him and straight into the lake. The water was freezing, and I squealed in shock. "Argh, it's freezing." I hopped around trying to get used to the chilly water. Mason came and stood beside me chuckling.

"Having fun there Lib." He asked me.

"Yeah, can't you tell?" I rolled my eyes sarcastically at him. "Go on then show me how amazing fishing is."

Mason stuck to his word, and I didn't have to touch anything slimy or wriggling. I must admit every time I got a tug on my line I got a little bit excited to see what I'd caught. Mason found my excitement amusing after I'd protested so much about doing it. After about an hour we decided to head back. I didn't want Aunt Claire to worry. "How will you get the fishing stuff back?" I asked him as we packed everything away.

"I'll head back up later with the truck, the sunset from this spot is amazing. Maybe I can bring you back sometime to watch it?" He turned to look at me with a hopeful expression on his face. "As friends, obviously." He added sheepishly.

"I'd like that," I told him truthfully. "Thank you for today, I've had a really great time."

"Me too Lib."

We made our way back to the stables chatting occasionally. We had no idea how long we'd been out, neither of us had taken a watch, but I guessed that we'd been gone a few hours at least. Mason put the horses away, and I watched him, feeling apprehensive on how we'd say goodbye. Although Mason had agreed to be friends, I had a feeling he was going to keep pushing the boundaries of that friendship. "Thanks again for today," I told him as he headed over to me, the horses safely back in their stalls.

"You're welcome." He bent down and kissed my cheek. "See you tomorrow sweetheart."

We'd arranged on the ride back that we'd head to the airport around eleven to meet Jack off his flight. "See you tomorrow Mason."

I made my way back to the house to find Savannah stood on the porch grinning at me.

"Had a good day?" She asked excitedly.

"The best," I said grinning back at her. She clapped her hands in delight.

"Come on. I want to hear every detail." She dragged me into the house and I followed her laughing.

Chapter Eleven

I woke up the following morning exhausted. After arriving back from my afternoon out with Mason, Savannah and I had sat talking for hours. It was after midnight when I'd finally gone to bed, only then to be plagued by nightmares. I'd been awake on and off all night, terrified to fall asleep again in case the nightmares returned. Fortunately, I hadn't woken anyone up this time. I rolled over and reached for my phone, it had just gone eight o clock, and I saw a text from Jack.

Jack: Hey Lib, I'm at the airport just checking in. Should be landing at 12.30. Can't wait to see you. Xx

I sent him a quick reply.

Me: Can't wait to see you either. Safe flight. Will wait for you in arrivals Xx

I dragged myself out of bed and into the shower in the hope that it would wake me up. After spending far too much time under the hot water, I forced myself to get out and get dressed. I made my way downstairs just as Savannah was leaving for university.

"Hey Lib, say hi to Jack for me. I should be back at lunch time, can't wait to see him. Got to run, see you later." She rushed out of the door waving her hand at me.

"Bye Savannah," I called after her smiling to myself, she was like a whirlwind. I ate breakfast alone in the kitchen, Aunt Claire must have already left for the day, and Uncle Ryan and Brody were long gone.

I had a few hours to kill before Mason was due to pick me up, so I decided to take a walk over to the stables to see the horses. I wasn't worried about bumping into Mason, I knew from talking to him yesterday that he was leading an early morning hike to watch the sunrise. As I headed over, I caught sight of a small wooden cabin tucked behind the stables that I hadn't noticed before. It was similar to the log cabins that the guests stayed in but much older and smaller.

As I walked closer to it, I could see that although it was old, it had obviously been well looked after. There was a small light attached to the wall by the front door and curtains hung at the windows. A bench sat to the right of the front door on a small porch, and there were wildflowers surrounding the cottage. It was beautiful.

I was eager to see if the inside was as beautiful as the outside. I quickly looked over my shoulder, there was no one around, so I walked onto the small porch and looked through the little window next to the front door. There was a tiny kitchen area to the left of the window with a sink unit and a couple of cupboards, a microwave and toaster sat on the work surface. Across from the kitchen was a small sitting area with a sofa and television. There was a closed door off to the right, which I assumed led to a bathroom. A wooden staircase behind the sofa led to a mezzanine level where a large double bed stood. Large rugs covered the floors, and a couple of pictures hung on the wall. It was small but perfect. There were personal things in the cabin, and I wondered who lived here, I'd have to remember to ask Savannah later.

After spending far too much time being nosey, I finally made it into the stables fussing over the other horses. I stayed for about half an hour, brushing Cookie and Marley before heading back to the house. The nerves were bubbling as I thought about the car journey to the airport. I prayed I could control my emotions.

I checked the time, Mason would be here in half an hour. I opened the kindle app on my phone and sat on the porch swing. Reading was my escape, and I hoped to get lost in the book I was reading until Mason showed up. I was so engrossed I didn't hear him and jumped a mile when he sat down next to me. "Arghhh," I screamed clutching my hand to my chest. "You scared me, I didn't hear you coming," I told him, my heart pounding.

"Sorry Lib." He said laughing. "I did shout hello as I came up the path, but your nose was buried in your cell. What's so interesting on there anyway?" He leaned in closer to me looking at my phone. I took a deep breath, my nose filled with the now familiar smell of Mason, aftershave, and soap. He smelt delicious. He must have showered recently too as I noticed that his hair was still damp.

"Oh, I'm just reading," I told him turning the app off and tucking my phone into my shorts pocket.

"Ahhh, no wonder you were so captivated, you were reading your *naughty* book." He winked at me and wiggled his eyebrows suggestively.

I rolled my eyes and jumped up off the swing. "Whatever

Mason. You're just jealous that it's not you turning me on." I watched his mouth drop open, and I realised what I'd said, my face flushing with heat. "I can't believe I said that. I'm so sorry" I cringed unable to look at him.

"Sweetheart, my moves are ten times better than anything you'll ever find in a book. Trust me!" He said, a cocky grin forming on his face.

"We should go," I said changing the subject, my face still flushed. "I don't want to be late for Jack."

He laughed, grabbed my hand and pulled me along behind him down the garden path and towards his truck. I couldn't believe I'd said that to him. I wasn't exactly giving off the friend vibe when I said things like that!

"Lib, I can hear your mind working overtime. Don't worry about it."

He opened the truck door for me, and I climbed in. "Thank you," I whispered as he closed the door. We headed down the long driveway, and I began my breathing exercises, counting my breaths in and out. My hands were clasped tightly on my lap, and my eyes were fixed on the dashboard in front of me. Mason seemed to be concentrating on driving, and I was glad I didn't have to make conversation. About ten minutes into the journey I realised that Mason was watching me out of the corner of his eye. I was struggling to control my breathing and losing count of my breaths as the panic began to set in, my heart was racing, and my hands trembled in my lap. There was a loud ringing in my ears, and I felt dizzy. I could hear Mason speaking to me, but it sounded muffled like he was far away. I felt the warm air hit me as he opened my door, I hadn't even realised he'd stopped the truck. I felt him lifting me from the truck, sitting me down on the grass verge, he kneeled in front of me.

"Libby breath sweetheart, breath." I heard him say to me. He took my hand and rested it on his chest over his heart. "Feel my heartbeat, Libby, count the beats, one, two, three, four, one, two, three, four. Come on Libby count with me."

We must have sat there for a few minutes, my hand on his chest and Mason counting aloud. After a while I could feel that the worst of the panic attack was over, the ringing in my ears had lessened, and my breathing was calming down. I could feel Mason's heartbeat under my hand. He may have seemed calm, but his heart was pounding beneath my fingers. I was quietly counting the beats along with him, and when I felt like I wasn't going to pass out, I raised my head and looked into his worried eyes.

"Thank God." He said the relief evident in his voice.

I burst into tears, the realisation of what had happened hitting me. I felt Mason reach for me and pull me into his lap, his arms tight around me. I sobbed into his chest, soaking his t-shirt. He let me cry, never releasing his hold on me. After a few minutes, the sobs had stopped, and I'd manage to calm down. "I'm sorry," I whispered into his chest, embarrassed.

"Don't apologise." I felt his fingers push my sweaty hair off my face and his lips brushed the top of my head. "Are you okay? What happened?" He pulled back slightly so he could look into my eyes.

I took a deep breath. I had to tell him, he looked so worried. I dropped my eyes from his. "I was involved in a car accident a few months ago. I've only been in a car a handful of times since then, and I struggle to stay calm. That's the second panic attack I've had, I can normally control them if I concentrate on my breathing, but it didn't work today..." I trailed off, feeling his arms wrap even tighter around me.

"Why didn't you tell me? I noticed you seemed on edge in the truck the other night on the way back from the bar, I just thought you were mad at me." He paused, and I lifted my head to look at him. His eyes were closed, and he whispered. "Were you hurt in the accident?" He opened his eyes and saw me looking at him.

"I hit my head on the window. I was in a coma for a few days, some dizzy spells. I'm okay now. I was lucky...others weren't." I looked away from him as a tear rolled down my cheek. He reached down and wiped the tear from my face.

"Please don't cry. Talk to me, Libby."

I didn't want to tell him about Mia like this, sat on his lap, crying on the side of the road. "I will, just not now, we'd better go, we're going to be late," I told him trying to get up.

"Sweetheart, wait." He said tightening his hold on me. "Are you okay? I can take you back to the ranch and go on my own to meet Jack?" He offered, stroking his fingers up and down my arm.

"I'm okay. I want to go and meet Jack. I need to do this. Please, Mason." I begged.

He sighed. "Okay but I'm stopping the minute it looks like it might happen again."

"Okay. Thank you." I gave him a small smile. He reached down and kissed me on the forehead.

"No need to thank me, sweetheart. Come on let's go and get your brother."

He stood up with me in his arms, carrying me back to the truck as if I weighed nothing at all. He managed to open the truck door without having to put me down, gently placing me in my seat and reaching across me to put on my seatbelt. "Okay?" He asked me, brushing my cheek with the back of his hand.

"Yeah," I whispered. He shut my door, and I took in a shaky breath, watching him go around the front of the truck and get in on the driver's side. I was so embarrassed that he'd seen me like that. There wasn't much I could do about it now, though, and it didn't seem like he was freaked out about what had happened. I focused my eyes on the dashboard again, counting my breaths again as Mason pulled out into the traffic. We'd been on the side of the road for about twenty minutes which meant we were probably going to be late.

"Does your brother know about your panic attacks," Mason asked breaking into my thoughts.

"He knows that I struggle in the car. The only other attack I've had happened on the way back from the hospital after I was discharged. I've always managed to control them other than today." He reached over and plucked my hand from my lap, entwining his fingers with mine. I looked down at our hands in surprise. "What are you doing?" I asked him quietly.

"Just thought it might help if the drive was still bothering you." He looked at me sheepishly. "I'm sorry."

He went to pull his hand out of mine, but I stopped him gripping his hand tight. "No, don't. It is helping. Thank you." I looked up to meet his eyes briefly before he focused back on the road, a small smile tugging at his mouth. His thumb gently stroked the back of my hand, and my head dropped back against the seat. I was exhausted after what had just happened, and I closed my eyes enjoying the feeling of Mason's hand in mine.

"Libby sweetheart, wake up, we're here." I opened my eyes to see that we'd arrived at the airport. I shook my head in an attempt to wake myself up.

"Sorry I fell asleep. I'll text Jack to see if he's landed." I said looking around for my phone.

Mason held my phone up. "He's landed; he text about five minutes ago. I replied, hope that's ok? He'll be out in a few minutes he's just getting his luggage."

"Oh okay."

"I didn't want to wake you until I knew Jack was here. I figured you could use the sleep."

"Thank you. I hope I wasn't snoring." I joked, smiling at him.

"Nah, think you were dreaming about me, though." He laughed. "You were saying, *Mason don't stop, that feels sooooo good.*" His voice high pitched and squeaky.

"I was not!" I laughed, reaching over to smack him. My hand connected with the rock-hard abs of his stomach and I quickly pulled my hand back hugging it to my chest. "Ouch! God whose stomach is that hard!" I whined, rubbing my hand which was now pounding.

"Me, darling that's who, and that serves you right for hitting me." He said playfully his eyes sparkling. "Let me see your hand." He held his hand out wanting me to show him mine.

"It's fine," I told him. "Come on let's go and wait in arrivals."

Ten minutes later and I was bouncing around, excitedly waiting for Jack to come through the arrival doors. "There he is. Jack," I shouted waving my arms in the air. I could hear Mason chuckling beside me. I pushed my way through the crowds and flung myself into Jack's arms. "You're here!" I exclaimed.

"Hi Libby, how you doing?" Jack asked me spinning me round in a circle, his bags dropped to the floor by our feet.

"It's so good to see you," I told him. "I've missed you so much."

"I've missed you too Lib." He said putting me down and kissing me on the cheek.

Mason had made his way over to us and had picked up Jack's bags. I turned to look at him and saw him grinning at me with that heart-stopping smile of his. I saw Jack looking between the two of us. "Jack, this is Mason, Mason my brother Jack." I gestured between the two of them.

Mason put his hand out, and Jack shook it. "Nice to meet you, Jack."

"Yeah, you too," Jack told him.

"Mason works on the ranch. Savannah is at university, and everyone else is busy, so Mason offered to drive me to get you."

"Thanks. I appreciate it." Jack said to Mason.

"No problem. Come on the truck's outside."

We all headed outside to the truck where Mason put Jack's bags on the backseat and held the passenger door open for me while I climbed in. As he went around the front of the truck to get in the driver's side, Jack quickly said to me.

"Are you okay in the car Libby? Does Mason know about your panic attacks?"

I nodded. "He does. First hand, unfortunately." I quickly shook my head as Mason got in the car hopefully signalling to Jack that I didn't want to talk about it.

"So, Mason, you work on the ranch? What do you do?" Jack asked. I turned and smiled at him grateful that he'd changed the subject.

"I organise and lead the trips for the guests staying at the ranch. They can choose from, hiking, horse riding, fly fishing, activities like that. It's quiet at the moment, but it gets busier during the summer months."

"I'm looking forward to getting back on the ranch, it's been a while."

I sensed Mason looking over at me, I'd been counting my breaths and wringing my hands in my lap while they were chatting. The last thing I wanted was another panic attack. I felt him take my hand and lace his fingers through mine his thumb stroking the back of my hand again. I smiled over at him, the small gesture of having him hold my hand really was calming me down.

"Is there something I should know Libby? Is something going on with you two?" Jack asked from the back seat.

I tried to pull my hand free from Mason's, but he gripped it tight and shook his head at me. "Nothing's going on Jack, me and your sister are just friends. Holding her hand just seems to keeps her calm in the truck." Mason told him.

I looked back to Jack who was looking sceptically at me.

"Lib, is that right?" Jack asked me.

"Yes, Jack. You don't have to go all big brother on me." I sighed, knowing I had to tell him what had happened on the way here. "I had a panic attack on the way to the airport. Mason had to pull over and calm me down. Holding his hand is helping me." I admitted. I heard Jack take a deep breath and exhale slowly.

"Thanks for looking out for her Mason."

"Anytime." Mason squeezed my hand and smiled at me.

Mason and Jack chatted on and off on the drive back. I was still anxious in the truck, so I didn't say much, I was happy to listen to them talk. Mason was telling Jack about the plans for the rodeo tomorrow. We would be heading over to Burnet early afternoon, Mason had said that there were fairground rides, live music, and stalls selling everything from food to cowboy boots with the bull riding starting around 7.30 pm. I couldn't wait.

As we arrived back at the ranch, I could see Savannah and Aunt Claire waiting on the porch swing for us. All three of us headed up to the house to meet them. Aunt Claire pulled Jack into a hug.

"It's great to see you, Jack. God, you've grown since I last saw you." She chuckled leaning back to look up at him. He must have stood a good foot taller than her.

"Great to see you, Aunt Claire, you too Savannah." He smiled over at her. "Thanks for having me, and trouble over there." He said motioning to me with his hand.

"Hey!" I protested.

"Behave Jack." Aunt Claire said laughing. "Libby's no trouble at all." She smiled over at me. "Mason." She turned to look at him. "Thanks for picking Jack up, that was a big help."

"No problem Claire. Happy to help." Mason told her.

"Hey, Mason why don't you join us for dinner tonight as a thank you? That's okay, right Mom?" Savannah asked.

Aunt Claire hesitated. "Erm, yeah sure. We'll be eating about six."

"Thanks, Claire, that would be great. I won't turn down a home cooked meal. I'll get back to work then. See you later everyone, nice to meet you, Jack." He stuck his hand out, and Jack reached out to shake it.

"Nice to meet you too Mason," Jack replied. "Thanks for all your help." His eyes drifted to me, and I knew he was thanking him for helping me in the truck earlier. Fortunately, no one else seemed to pick up on what Jack was saying. Aunt Claire and Savannah were heading inside, and Jack followed with his bags. Mason walked over to me.

"Are you sure you okay, after earlier?" He asked, concern showing on his face.

"I'm fine Mason, as embarrassed as I am about you seeing me like that, I'm glad you were there. I'm not sure how I would have managed if you hadn't calmed me down."

"There is no need to be embarrassed sweetheart, you never have to feel like that with me. I'm just glad I could help you, although I hope I never have to see you like that again. You scared the hell out of me." He wrapped his arms around me, and I rested my head on his chest. "I'm not too good at this friends only thing, am I?" He whispered, tucking a strand of my loose hair behind my ear. "I can't seem to stay away."

"Me neither," I admitted, sighing. I loved being in his arms, I felt safe there, and safe was something I hadn't felt in a long time. Every time we were together he managed to touch me in some way, be it, holding my hand, hugging me or touching my face. He was making it very hard for me to resist him and I think he knew it.

"I'd better go sweetheart. I'll see you later at dinner?" He asked pulling back from me slightly so he could see my face.

"I'll be there. Thanks again… for everything."

He smiled at me and leaned down to kiss my cheek "Bye."

I watched him go, and as I turned to head into the house, I saw Jack on the porch watching me.

"You sure there's nothing going on Lib?" He asked sceptically. "You can tell me."

"There's nothing going on. He'd like there to be but what's the point. I'm only here on holiday." I didn't want to tell him what was really holding me back. I was seeing no signs of his player ways, maybe Savannah had him all wrong, and my first impressions of him had been unfair.

"I see the way he looks at you Lib. I think he really likes you."

"I like him too, but there is no point opening myself up to more hurt. It can't go anywhere."

"Lib you've got to open yourself up to someone at some point. What would Mia say if she were here?"

I burst out laughing. "Mia would be telling me to jump his bones! You know what she was like."

"Eww Lib, that's not a visual I want in my head!" He grimaced.

"Well, you did ask!" I paused. "I really like him Jack, but I can't get hurt, I already hurt too much. And I would end up hurt when the time came to go home." I told him a little irritated that he was pushing me.

He put his hands up in defeat. "Okay Lib, but he seems a really nice guy."

"Where has all this come from Jack? I can't believe that you, my overprotective big brother, is encouraging me to pursue a guy I've known for less than a week."

"I can see the chemistry between you two, I'm not blind, and I just want to see you happy that's all."

"I know, and I want to be happy. I'm just not sure that Mason is the answer."

Aunt Claire appeared outside. "Come on you two, I've got cake and cold drinks inside."

Jack linked his arm with hers, and I followed them inside, confused even more over my feelings for Mason.

Chapter Twelve

L ater that night I climbed into bed exhausted. Dinner had been great. Jack had been telling everyone stories of his travels, places he'd visited and where was next on his list to go. He had been away from home for a while now and was planning to be back home for the summer. Seeing him tonight and catching up with him had made me realise just how much I'd missed him. I was looking forward to having him home.

Mason, Jack, and Brody had all got on really well, it was like they had all been friends for years, they had even arranged to go fishing on Mason's next day off. After dinner, we sat on the porch chatting, Aunt Claire and Uncle Ryan had turned in early, and Savannah had talked Brody into letting her have a couple of bottles of beer. Brody had found a pack of cards, and we had played poker for a couple of hours. I had never played, and Mason had offered to play with me until I got the hang of it. He had sat close to me all night, brushing is fingers against mine as he helped me with the cards, and flashing me his real smile, the one that made my stomach flutter and my body tingle.

We had all agreed to meet up at 1.30 pm tomorrow to head over to Burnet for the rodeo. Josh was going to be coming with us which I knew Savannah was stressing about. We would need to take the seven-seater jeep that they used on the ranch so that we could all go together. Savannah, knowing that I would need to sit in the front of the jeep would be stuck in the back with Josh. I just prayed they didn't argue the whole way.

Mason had left after we'd lost our fifth poker hand in a row, I definitely didn't have beginners luck. After quickly tidying up we had all come to bed. Jack was in the bedroom at the end of the hall which I was grateful for. I didn't want to wake him if I had a nightmare.

Now, I was lying in bed hoping that the nightmares would stay away so that I, and everyone else, could get a good night's sleep. I must have fallen asleep quickly, my dreams full of Mason and the memory of being in his arms, him kissing my hair and stroking my face. They quickly changed to memories of the panic attack earlier, my breathing accelerating and my heart pounding. I was suddenly back in Mitch's car, hearing Mia screaming and the metal of the car crunching as the van hit us. I woke up to my own screaming, tears running down my cheeks. I sat up in bed, clamping my hand over my mouth, my body shaking. As my breathing slowed down, I looked to the door waiting for someone to burst in, but no one did. Reaching for my phone I saw that it was 3.20 am, I had been asleep for longer than I thought. I flopped back down on the bed, afraid to fall back to sleep in case the nightmares returned.

It was warm in my room, and I was hot and bothered after my nightmare. I decided to take a walk out to the barn, it was always quiet in there, and it had become one of my favourite places to go. Spending time with the horses somehow calmed me down and cleared my head.

I pulled my hair off my neck and tied it up in a bobble. I picked up my kindle, creeping out of my room and down the stairs. I stopped in the kitchen and grabbed a bottle of water from the fridge, taking a swig before heading out of the front door. It was cooler outside, and I welcomed the cool breeze around my bare legs. I wandered over to the stables and pulled on the heavy door, hearing it creak slightly as it opened. The horses were asleep, but a few stirred as I came in, poking their noses over the stalls to see who had woken them up. I made my way along, stroking the ones who were awake until I reached the tack room at the other end of the stable. I'd noticed a small chair in the corner of the tack room the last time I'd been in there, and I intended to curl up on it and read for a bit. I inhaled deeply as I walked in, loving the smell of the leather saddles and riding crops. Just as I was heading to the chair in the corner, I heard the creak of the stable door.

"Is someone in here?" A familiar voice called out.

Oh god, it was Mason! I looked down at what I was wearing, suddenly conscious that it wasn't very much at all. A tiny pair of sleeping shorts and a sleeveless top. I hadn't bothered putting a bra on. I hadn't thought that I would be bumping into anyone at this time of the morning. I took a deep breath and walked out of the tack room. "It's me, Mason."

"Libby." He said surprised. "Are you okay? I thought someone was stealing the horses." He made his way down past the stalls towards me. His chest was bare, and he wore a pair of jogging shorts that hung low on his hips, his perfect v disappearing below the waist of his shorts. His hair was messy, and his eyes were hooded as he looked me up and down.

"I... I... I'm sorry." I stuttered, flustered at seeing him with barely anything on. "I didn't mean to worry you. I hope I haven't woken you up. I'm fine, I just couldn't sleep." I said quickly, feeling embarrassed.

I watched his eyes travel the length of my body, taking in what little clothes I had on. His eyes paused on my chest, and I saw them widen slightly when he realised I had no bra on. Watching him watch me made my body tingle and I felt my nipples harden. I quickly folded my arms over my chest, my face flushing. I could tell from the small smile on his face that he had seen my body's reaction to him. I watched the smile slip from his face as his eyes met mine.

"Libby, you've been crying." He said worry clear on his face. He came closer towards me. "I thought I heard someone screaming earlier, was that you?" He asked me gently.

I dropped my eyes, embarrassed that he had heard me. "I had a bad dream. I'm sorry I woke you." I told him quietly. I wondered how close to the house Mason must live for him to have heard me.

"This isn't the first time, is it? I heard you a few days ago, as well. Please talk to me Lib." He reached for me, unfolding my arms from across my chest and taking my hands in his.

I shivered suddenly feeling cold. Mason must have noticed, and he pulled me into his warm chest, wrapping his arms around me. I sighed, I'd told him about the accident yesterday, and now he knew about the nightmares, he might as well know about Mia.

"You're cold, come with me." He took my hand and led me out of the stables and around the back of the building.

"Mason, where are we going?"

"To my place."

"I don't think that's a very good idea." I protested.

He stopped walking and turned to look at me. "It's the middle of the night, you're cold and upset, we're just going to talk Libby, nothing else. I'll behave I promise." His eyes shone with sincerity.

"Okay," I whispered. He smiled at me and carried on walking, never letting go of my hand. I suddenly realised that we were heading for the old log cabin I had seen yesterday. When it came into view, I could see the pale glow from the porch light along with a light coming from the small window next to the door.

"You live here?" I asked him, a little taken aback that I'd been snooping through his window less than twenty-four hours ago, "It's beautiful."

"It is, isn't it. Ryan and Claire offered me one of the new log cabins to stay in, but I noticed this cabin on my first day here and fell in love with it. It was a bit run down, but I've done it up little by little, and it's almost finished now." He turned to look at me. "You seem surprised, have you been here before?" He asked.

I burst out laughing. "I actually came across the cabin yesterday morning when I went for a walk, I'm a bit embarrassed to say I was peering through your windows being nosey!"

"Good thing I wasn't walking around naked then." He laughed, turning back towards the log cabin and pulling me along behind him.

I let him pull me along, my heart pounding in my chest at the thought of sneaking a look through his window and catching sight of him naked.

"Now you can have a proper look around rather than a sneaky look through the window." He winked at me. He opened the front door and stood to the side motioning with his hand for me to go in.

I stepped inside, it looked even better than it did yesterday. There were a couple of small lamps dotted around giving off a warm, cosy glow. The cabin was tiny but perfectly formed, and it looked like it had all the essentials to live comfortably.

"Would you like a drink?" Mason asked me.

I turned to see him watching me from the small kitchen area. "Water would be great, thanks. I must have left my bottle in the tack room." I told him realising that I no longer had it with me.

Mason grabbed two bottles of water and handed me one as he flopped down onto the sofa pulling a t-shirt on that was thrown over the arm, he patted the space next to him, and I sat down. "So... do you want to tell me what happened tonight?" He asked quietly.

I took a long swig of my water, slowly putting the lid back on before looking up to meet his eyes. "I had a nightmare, I've suffered with them on and off since the accident. I needed some fresh air once I'd woken up, so I went to the stables. I'm sorry if I woke you up." I dropped my eyes from his, fidgeting on the sofa and picking at the label on my water bottle.

"Libby, stop apologising, you didn't wake me, I was already awake, and even if you had woken me, I wouldn't have minded." He reached out and took the bottle from my hands putting it on the small coffee table in front of the sofa. He took my now empty hands in his.

"When you told me about the car accident yesterday, what did you mean when you said that others hadn't been so lucky?" He asked me gently. His thumbs stroked circles on the inside of my wrists sending goosebumps up my arms.

I shivered again, not from the cold this time but from his touch. Not realising that I wasn't cold, he reached for the throw on the back of the sofa and wrapped it around my shoulders. "Thank you," I whispered. He looked at me expectantly, waiting for me to open up to him. I sighed. "The night of the car accident, I'd been out with my best friend, Mia. We were having a great time until she saw her boyfriend all over some other girl. Mia stormed out, and Mitch followed, he talked us into letting him drive us home." I paused, taking a deep breath and concentrating on the feeling of Mason's fingers circling my wrist. I felt him squeeze my hands in silent support. "He promised me that he'd only had one drink…turns out that he lied, he was over the limit, and he lost control of the car…" I closed my eyes. "They both died" I whispered. "Mia had been my best friend since we were four."

I heard Mason take a deep breath. "And your nightmares are of the accident?"

I nodded, silent tears running down my face.

"Libby," Mason said, pulling me onto his lap. "I'm so sorry that happened to you. Let it all out, sweetheart." He stroked my hair as my sobs grew louder.

I cried in his lap for what felt like forever. He didn't question me or say anything to try and make me feel better, he just held me, and I didn't realise it before, but it was exactly what I needed. I could feel the steady beating of his heart as I lay on his chest, and that, along with the feeling of being wrapped in his arms slowly calmed me down. Although it felt like I had been crying forever, it must only have been about ten minutes. Once the sobs had stopped I lifted my head off his now soaking t-shirt to look up at him. He was staring down at me, his eyes worried. "That's twice I've cried all over you. You must think I'm a nervous wreck!" I only half joked trying to lighten the mood.

"Libby, I think you're incredible. You're the most beautiful girl I've ever seen. You're funny and kind. I hate to see you cry and now I know the reason for those tears I would do anything to take your pain away."

I looked at him shocked, not knowing how to respond to him.

"I know you want to be just friends, but I'm struggling with that sweetheart. I don't want to be just your friend. I want to be your everything. I want you to take a chance on me, a chance on us. I know you're only here short term, but I want to see what this thing between us is."

I wasn't sure what to say to him. I dropped my head to his chest, and his arms wrapped tightly around me. My head and heart were in conflict, my heart was screaming yes, my head screaming no. It felt right to be in his arms, though, I felt safe and protected and dare I say it, loved. I knew Mason wasn't in love with me, we'd only known each other a week, but I knew he cared about me. I caught myself thinking about him when I wasn't with him, wondering what he was doing and when I would bump into him again. The connection I felt with him, I'd never felt with anyone else but could

I really take that chance and risk getting hurt? I suddenly smiled to myself, I could almost hear Mia in my head *"Libby what are you waiting for? You're sat in the lap of a gorgeous cowboy just go for it. Jump his bones!!"*

I lifted my head. "Okay," I whispered. I felt Mason's fingers under my chin, lifting my face to look into his eyes.

"Okay?" He asked, his face breaking into a breath-taking smile.

I smiled back at him. "Yes, okay, we'll give whatever this is, a go, but Mason." I paused, the smile slipping off my face. "We need to take this slowly, I'm not like the other girls you've been with. I've never... never had a boyfriend." I told him embarrassed.

Mason jumped off the sofa with me still in his arms and spun me around. "Sweetheart, we'll go as slow as you want." I laughed as he put me down. "Come on." He took my hand and led me to the foot of the staircase. I pulled back on his arm.

"Mason..." I started to protest.

"Libby, I heard you when you said you said you wanted to take things slowly. I just want to hold you... and sleep, it's nearly 4 am. We'll talk things through properly tomorrow, but for now, I want to fall asleep with you in my arms."

"Okay," I said, smiling shyly at him. He seemed to know exactly what to say. I was still a little apprehensive though as I followed him upstairs. I'd never shared a bed with a man before, and the nerves were building up in my stomach.

When we reached the top of the stairs it opened out into a small bedroom, there was a double bed against one wall with a small bedside table on one side. A chest of drawers lined the other wall. As I looked around Mason was rushing around the room picking up clothes that were strewn everywhere. He looked at me sheepishly. "Sorry about the mess. I wasn't expecting anyone."

"Mason, it's fine." I yawned, suddenly realising how tired I was.

He must have seen me yawning and came over, pulling me down to sit on the bed with him.

"Come on let's get some sleep."

I kicked my flip flops off and pulled the bobble out of my hair, my hair tumbling around my shoulders. I wrung my hands nervously in my lap. I felt Mason kneel behind me and wrap his arms around my waist, he brushed his lips across my shoulder. "Lie down Lib." He whispered as he moved back. I swung my legs onto the bed and lay on my side, my head on his pillow. I felt him lie behind me and he pulled me into his hard, warm chest, one arm going around my waist and the other under my head. I stiffened in his arms. "Relax sweetheart." He whispered in my ear, his breath tickling my neck. I turned in his arms and rested my head on his chest breathing in his scent. I slowly felt myself relaxing, loving the feeling of him holding me.

"Would it be alright if I kissed you, Libby?" I heard Mason ask after a few minutes.

He was running his fingers up and down my arm, my body tingling under his touch. Nerves swirled in my stomach. I'd kissed the odd guy before, but I knew this would be different due to feelings I already had for him. "Okay." I squeaked out.

He rolled me onto my back and brought his body over mine. Hovering over me he reached his hand up and brushed a strand of hair off my face. "You are so beautiful, Libby." He whispered as he lowered his face to me. He brushed his lips gently against mine, before pulling back slightly and gazing into my eyes. I closed the distance between us and captured his lips again, his soft kiss turning more insistent. My eyes closed as he gently bit down on my bottom lip, my mouth instinctively opening for him. His tongue invaded my mouth, and I heard myself moan as I felt his tongue brush against mine. He pulled away slightly and peppered tiny kisses down my neck, tracing his way back to my mouth with his lips. He kissed me again, and I reached up threading my fingers through his hair, needing to touch him. I pulled him closer to me as I got lost in him. I'd never been kissed like this; he was consuming me, and my whole body felt on fire.

I never wanted him to stop, and I whimpered as he pulled away. He rested his forehead on mine staring into my eyes. "Wow," I whispered.

"I might just need to try that again." He said smiling as he found my mouth again, kissing me hungrily. I found myself arching up into his body trying to get closer to him. He fisted his hand in my hair and began kissing down my neck. He suddenly pulled away, both of us panting heavily. "We need to stop sweetheart…" He said breathlessly.

I felt my face flush, and I dropped my eyes from his, I didn't know what had come over me. No one had ever made me feel like Mason did, he made me lose control, and I felt like I needed to be as close to him as possible. "Libby, look at me." He asked gently, pausing until I lifted my eyes to his. "Don't ever feel embarrassed when you're with me. I want you to feel comfortable with me and be able to tell me anything. Okay, sweetheart?" He brushed the back of his hand down my cheek and kissed my forehead.

"Okay," I whispered. He rolled off me and lay down pulling me into his chest and wrapping his arms around me.

"Let's get some sleep." He smiled down at me. "Night darlin'."

"Night Mason." I reached up and pecked his lips, pulling away before we both got carried away again. I snuggled into his chest and closed my eyes, quickly falling asleep listening to the rhythm of his heart.

Chapter Thirteen

I stretched my arms above my head and turned onto my side. My eyes flew open, suddenly remembering where I was and what had happened last night. Mason was asleep next to me, his face level with mine. I took the opportunity to look at him, he really was beautiful, his dark hair messy and falling over his forehead, his long dark eyelashes resting on his cheeks. I reached forward and brushed his hair out of his eyes. My eyes fell to his bare chest; he must have removed his t-shirt at some point during the night as I'd fallen asleep with him still wearing it. I could see his tattoo in full from the way he was lying. It was a black and white tribal design, wrapping around his arm, over his shoulder, and onto his chest. It looked incredible. I watched his chest rise and fall and noticed his breathing quicken, I looked up to his face, his eyes still closed but his mouth lifting into a small smile.

"Enjoying the view?" He teased, opening his arms to me. I buried my head in his chest laughing.

"I thought you were asleep," I told him, my voice muffled against his chest. He lifted me up and looked me in the eye.

"Morning darlin'." He reached up and kissed my lips, I pulled away quickly conscious that I hadn't brushed my teeth. "What's wrong? You're not regretting your decision are you Lib?" He asked me looking worried.

"Of course not! I... I just haven't brushed my teeth yet." I told him sitting up. "Can I use your bathroom?" I asked him blushing.

"Yes." He said, pulling me down on top of him. "But I want you to say good morning properly first. Kiss me, Libby." He demanded.

"Bossy!" I told him, laughing as I pressed my lips to his. The kiss quickly turned heated, and I straddled his lap. He ran his hands up my thighs and rested them on my waist. He sat up still kissing me, and I wrapped my arms around him, running my fingers through the hair at the base of his neck. I pulled my mouth away from his, breaking the kiss before I lost control. "Bathroom," I said my heart pounding in my chest.

"Bathroom." He said laughing. I climbed off the bed turning to look at him, he was watching me, his arms behind his head and a huge grin on his face. I smiled back shyly at him.

"Be right back." I murmured, padding across the bedroom and down the wooden staircase.

Once in the tiny bathroom, I used the toilet and washed my hands, splashing cold water on my face. I looked up into the small round mirror above the sink, my hair was all over the place, and my eyes were red and puffy from crying. I was a mess! My lips were swollen from Mason's kisses, and I reached my fingers up to trace where he'd last kissed me. Still not believing that he had actually kissed me. I squirted some toothpaste onto my finger and began cleaning my teeth the best I could. There was a knock on the door, and I heard Mason ask if I was okay. I mumbled yes, with a mouthful of toothpaste before rinsing my mouth and opening the door.

"I've put the coffee on, help yourself, sweetheart." He said brushing my lips with his as he passed me and entered the bathroom.

I suddenly realised that no one at the house would know where I was. I looked around for a clock to see what time it was, but I couldn't find one. "Mason," I shouted. "Do you know what time it is?"

"Not sure, my cell is on the bedside table if you want to grab it." Came the reply from the bathroom.

I ran upstairs into his bedroom, spying his phone I picked it up and pushed the button to illuminate the screen. It was 8.20 am, I'd just have to hope that Aunt Claire was either having a lie in or had already left for the day. I couldn't help but see that Mason had an unread message on his phone.

Amber: Hey baby. You fancy a repeat of...

A repeat of what I wasn't sure, his phone only displayed the first line and there was no way I was going to read his message. My stomach bubbled with jealousy. He'd already told me he'd been with a lot of women; this was obviously one of them. I didn't really know where we stood after last night, he'd said that he wanted to see what this connection between us was, but did that mean he would still see other people. I had no idea. I put the phone back, grabbed my flip flops and headed back downstairs.

Mason stood in the kitchen drinking coffee. He looked over to me his eyes dropping to the flip flops in my hand. "Are you leaving?" He asked me frowning.

"Yeah, I'd better go, everyone will wonder where I am. I didn't bring my phone, so I can't text Savannah."

"Use my cell, I've got Savannah's number. Didn't you bring it down?" He asked looking at my hands. "I'll go and fetch it." He walked passed me towards the stairs.

"No Mason it's fine. I need to get back anyway..." I started to say, but Mason was halfway to his room before I could finish. I made my way to the door, not wanting to be here when he read that message, he would know that I'd seen it. I opened the door and went out onto the porch. "Libby wait." I heard Mason shout from inside. I stopped not turning around. He came outside and stood in front of me. My eyes were on my bare feet.

"I'm guessing you saw this message on my phone, and that's why you're desperate to leave." He sighed. "Look at me, Libby."

I raised my eyes to his. "I didn't read it Mason; I just saw it when I checked the time. It's nothing to do with me anyway. It's not like we're exclusive." I told him shrugging my shoulders.

He took my hand and led me to the bench next to the door, pushing gently on my shoulder until I sat down. I watched him as he knelt in front of me still holding my hand. "Libby, sweetheart, we are most definitely exclusive. I won't share you with anyone."

"Neither will I Mason."

"You won't have to. I'm not interested in anyone else Libby." He stood up and sat next to me on the bench. "That text you saw, Amber is someone that I used to see from time to time. I won't be seeing her again; it was just sex. She didn't mean anything to me."

I swallowed nervously unable to look at him. What was I even doing here? I couldn't compete with the likes of Amber; I'd only kissed one or two guys never mind done anything else. He was obviously used to dating girls who knew their way around in the bedroom. I chewed on my bottom lip, not sure what to say to him.

Mason must have noticed my nervousness. "Libby, I don't want to come on too strong, I know you want to take things slowly, and we'll go as slowly as you want, but you need to know that kissing you last night, I've never felt like that with anyone before. I haven't been able to stop thinking about you since the first time we met." His eyes dropped to my mouth, and he reached up and gently pulled on my chin, freeing my bottom lip from my teeth. He rubbed his thumb across my lip trying to sooth the part I'd been chewing on. "I've got a past, and I've done things I'm not proud of, there are things I need to tell you, and we can talk about them. I'll tell you everything. But talk to me if something is worrying you, okay sweetheart?"

I let out a shaky breath. "I can't stop thinking about you either Mason, but I can't compete with girls like Amber. I'm not like them. I've never even…" I trailed off feeling my face flush. I'd almost blurted out that I was a virgin, he was used to sleeping with handfuls of women and here I was having only kissed two people!

"Libby… are you a virgin?" He asked me, shock evident in his voice.

"Yes," I said quietly dropping my eyes to my lap.

"But you're absolutely gorgeous, surely you've dated?" My face flushed again at his compliment, and he chuckled at my reaction.

"I suppose I've just never met the right person. I didn't see the point in dating someone if that spark wasn't there and I guess I've never felt it… until now." I lifted my eyes to Mason and saw his face break out into a breath-taking smile.

"Sweetheart there is enough of a spark between us to burn the stables down." He winked at me, and I laughed.

"So, it's not a… a problem for you then?" I asked nervously.

"No baby, no problem. We'll take things as slow as you want, as long as I get to kiss you whenever I want, then I'm happy. Oh, and just so you know, what you said a minute ago, about not being able to compete. You were right, you can't compete, you're already the winner, hands-down."

My stomach erupted with butterflies, and my heart pounded. I thought I liked it when he called me sweetheart, but when he called me baby, I melted. This man definitely knew all the right things to say. I just prayed my heart was safe with him, he was already holding it in the palm of his hand, and I hoped he knew that he had the power to crush it.

He pulled me to my feet, wrapping me up in his arms. "We okay?" He asked me, kissing my hair.

"Yes, we're okay. Maybe we could have that talk you mentioned tomorrow night? If you're not busy of course?" I asked him.

"I'm not busy sweetheart. I think that's a great idea. We could go down to the lake again and watch the sunset?"

"I'd like that." I reached up and looped my arms around his neck. Standing on my tiptoes, I pressed my mouth to his and kissed him. He quickly responded and kissed me back, pulling me closer to him.

"Mason, sorry to interrupt you and your latest conquest but I can't find Libby. I'm worried about her." I heard Savannah say. I pulled my lips from Mason's and rested my forehead on his chest. Savannah couldn't see me as I was totally hidden from her view by Mason's body. I took a deep breath and moved out of Mason's hold, he immediately reached for my hand squeezing it in support. Her mouth dropped open when she saw me, her eyes dropping to our joined hands. "Oh my god!! Libby!!" She squealed, jumping up and down. "You spent the night here, with Mason. I knew you liked him!" She turned to Mason before I could answer her, hitting him on the shoulder. "I was going to kick your ass when I saw you kissing someone. I knew you liked Libby, I thought you were kissing some skank!" Mason chuckled putting his arm around me and pulling me to his side.

"Savannah, I didn't spend the night with Mason, well I did spend the night, but nothing happened." I rushed out.

She laughed. "Libby I don't care what happened, I'm just glad you finally admitted you like him." She said winking at Mason. "You make such a cute couple! You are a couple now, aren't you?" She asked, looking between us.

I rolled my eyes, smiling at her, we'd barely decided ourselves what was going on, she was like an excited child. Before I could respond to her, I heard Mason say. "Yes, we're a couple, as of last night." My eyes flew to his and before I could say anything he was kissing me again. I lost myself in his kiss only being pulled back to reality by Savannah coughing loudly.

"As adorable as you two are, I don't really want to watch my cousin and my friend making out, so Mason, put her down." She joked. Mason took no notice and continued kissing me. I hungrily kissed him back, his kisses were addictive, and I could have stayed here like this all day. "Eww, come on guys." She moaned at us.

Mason reluctantly pulled away from me, turning to Savannah. "No one's asking you to watch Sav." He told her, laughing.

Savannah stuck her tongue out at Mason. "We should really be heading back Lib, Mom's out, so she doesn't know you've been here, but Jack will be wondering where you are."

"Okay," I told Savannah, glad that Aunt Claire was out and I wouldn't have to tell her about Mason and me. From her comments the other day I knew she thought that Mason was too old for me. I wasn't worried about telling Jack, he was the one encouraging me to let someone in. I reluctantly peeled myself out of Mason's embrace. "I'll see you later?" I asked him.

"Yep, I'll pick you up just before 1.30. I've arranged for everyone to meet at the house. Savannah's got my number, get her to give it to you and then text me, so I've got yours."

I nodded. "I'd better go then." I reached up and kissed him, now that I'd tasted his kisses I couldn't get enough. He kissed me back, pulling away before it got too heated again. I turned towards Savannah, and as I walked away, I felt him swat me on my bottom.

"Bye baby. See you later." He called after me. I turned back and flashed him a wide smile before linking my arm with Savannah's and heading back to the house.

As soon as we were out of earshot of Mason's cabin the questions from Savannah started.

"How did you end up at his cabin? You have to tell me everything. Is he a good kisser? What made you change your mind about him? Do you think Jack will be okay with it?"

"Whoa, Savannah! Let me get showered and some food inside me and I'll fill you in on everything. One thing I will tell you, oh my god can that man kiss!" I told her laughing, fanning my face with my hand.

I headed into the house with Savannah squealing behind me. I just prayed that I'd made the right decision and that he wouldn't hurt me.

Chapter Fourteen

W e were still laughing as we walked into the kitchen. Jack was sat at the breakfast bar drinking a cup of coffee. I flopped down on the seat next to him.

"You found her then?" Jack asked Savannah.

"Yes, and you'll never guess where." She said smirking at me.

"Savannah!" I protested, glancing from her to Jack.

"Half naked on Mason's porch, kissing the hell out of him, that's where!" She exclaimed, grinning from ear to ear.

"Hey! I was not half naked; I was wearing what I'm wearing now!" I cried, looking down at my shorts and top.

"You're not leaving much to the imagination though Lib," Jack said laughing. "I bet Mason thought it was his lucky day!" I felt my face flush, and I stood up to leave. "Wait Libby don't go, I'm sorry, I'll stop teasing you I promise," Jack said, reaching over and grasping my arm. "What's going on with you two anyway?"

I sat back down shrugging my shoulders. "I'm not really sure, I guess we're just seeing where things go," I told him shyly.

"Well I'm glad, he seems like a good guy. I'll have to have the big brother chat with him of course, ask him what his intentions are towards you." He said smirking at me.

"Don't you dare Jack!" I warned him. He stood up winking at

me. Just then there was a knock at the door. Savannah jumped up and went to answer it.

"Look who I've found on the doorstep, seems he can't keep away." She said when she came back. I looked past her to see Mason following her into the kitchen.

"Hey," I said standing up and walking over to him. "Everything okay?"

"Yeah, you just left your kindle at my place, and I know how attached to it you are." He held the kindle up and winked at me.

"Thank you," I told him, taking it from him.

"No problem sweetheart." He bent down and brushed his lips against mine. Jack cleared his throat behind me. "That's my baby sister Mason, I don't need the visual." He said playfully. Mason pecked my lips once more before pulling away. "Morning Jack." He said smiling at me.

"Morning Mason," Jack said a smile in his voice. I knew Jack liked Mason and was just winding him up.

"I'd better go; I've got a few things to do before we go out later." He said to me.

"I'll walk you out." I took his hand, pulling him towards the door.

"Catch you later guys." He said to Jack and Savannah, lifting his hand in a wave as we left the kitchen.

"Bye." They called out behind us.

We walked the short distance to the door in silence, his hand clasped in mine. I bit my lip, suddenly feeling nervous around him. He glanced over to me his eyes dropping to my lips. Before I knew what was happening he'd spun me around and gently pushed me up against the front door. He cupped my face with one of his hands and lowered his face to mine. My heart was racing, and my breathing was ragged as he pressed his lips firmly against mine. I kissed him back urgently, the kiss quickly intensifying. He fisted his hand in my hair, dropping his lips from mine and kissing down my neck. "God Libby, what are you doing to me?" He whispered into my neck, his breath making me shiver. "I can't control myself around you." He dragged the tip of his nose up my neck and found my lips again, kissing me softly this time. He pulled back and smiled at me. "Sorry, I got a bit carried away." He said sheepishly, taking my hand in his again.

"Don't apologise. I like it when you kiss me." I blurted out, blushing.

"I like it when you blush and I love that I'm the reason for it." He chuckled, reaching up to stroke my pink cheeks. "I really had better go, though."

"Thanks again for bringing my kindle over."

He smiled at me and pecked me on the lips. "I'll see you in a few hours baby."

I grinned back at him. "Can't wait," I told him.

I went upstairs after he'd left and jumped in the shower, I washed and blow dried my hair, leaving it loose down my back. I wanted to look nice for when I saw him later. I looked through my wardrobe and settled on a short flowery dress to wear which I thought would look good with my boots. I made my way downstairs finding Jack and Savannah in the lounge.

"You look gorgeous Lib," Savannah told me as I walked in.

"Thanks," I replied glancing down at my dress.

"Come on let's give Jack a quick guided tour of the ranch before it's time to go."

"Sounds good to me," Jack said, jumping out of his chair. "Looks like a lot has changed since we were last here."

I linked my arm with his and we made our way outside. We spent an hour or so showing Jack what was new on the ranch, from the new log cabins to the extra horses in the stables. We bumped into Brody in the stables. I'd kept an eye out for Mason but never saw him. I asked Brody if he knew where Mason was, he told me that he wasn't scheduled to work today. Apparently, he'd asked if he could borrow one of the trucks for an hour or so and had headed out. Maybe he was getting something for the rodeo this afternoon.

After showing Jack around and catching up a bit with him, we made our way back to the house to eat lunch before Mason was due to pick us up. Brody came back with us so that he could shower and change. We found Josh waiting for us on the porch swing and he wasn't alone.

"Hey man," Brody said to him, pulling him into a one-armed hug.

"Hey, Brode." He greeted him back. He turned to the girl standing next to him. "This is Averi, Averi this is Brody, his sister Savannah and their cousins Libby and Jack." He gestured with his one hand to each of us, his eyes lingering a fraction longer on Savannah than everyone else. His other hand was wrapped around Averi's waist.

"Nice to meet you." I heard Brody say.

I looked over to Savannah who was as white as a sheet, her eyes fixed on Josh. I said a quick hello to Averi and Josh and then turned to Savannah. "Hey Sav, can you help me with something inside?" I grabbed her hand and pulled her into the house leaving everyone else still on the porch. I led her straight upstairs and into my room. "Savannah, are you okay?" I asked her concerned.

"Why would he bring a girl with him." She whispered, tears tumbling down her cheeks. "She's gorgeous as well."

I couldn't deny that Averi was beautiful, she looked a lot like Savannah, long brown hair and green eyes. Why would he date someone who looked like Savannah but not be interested in her? I pulled her into my arms and let her cry. "She's not as beautiful as you Sav," I told her truthfully. "Josh is an idiot. I can't believe he's brought someone when he knows how you feel about him. Especially someone who looks like you. Please don't cry."

"I just don't understand him. He goes all caveman on me last week in the bar just because I was dancing with a guy, then brings some girl to flaunt in front of me. God, I wish I could hate him right now!"

"We're still going to have a great time," I told her, passing her a tissue to wipe her eyes with. "Once we get there, we can leave them and do our own thing."

She laughed. "Libby that's kind of you, but Mason will be pissed if I drag you away from him."

As much as I wanted to spend time with Mason, Savannah needed me, and I wasn't going to see her hurt and upset just so that I could be with Mason. We'd arranged a date for tomorrow night, and we'd be alone then, pissed or not, he'd have to deal with it. "Mason will be fine Sav," I told her waving my arm.

"Mason's going to want to know why we aren't staying together as a group, I really don't want him to know. I can deal with Josh and Averi. Maybe I'll find myself a rodeo cowboy." She winked at me, a small smile on her lips. She wasn't fooling me, though. I knew she was hurting.

She wiped her eyes just as a knock sounded on my door, Brody poked his head in. "Jack's making some sandwiches if you want to eat before we go?" He asked, looking between Savannah and me.

"Is everything okay? Have you been crying, Savannah?" His brow furrowed in concern.

"Everything's fine Brody. Come on let's eat, I'm starving." She said to him, smiling widely. Brody looked at me, shrugged his shoulder and followed her out.

After eating lunch, we headed out onto the porch to wait for Mason. Savannah ignored Josh as much as possible, which was probably a good thing as Averi was all over him. I didn't want to judge her, as I didn't really know her and I'd made that mistake with Mason, but I was struggling to like her. She'd only just met us, but thought it was appropriate to straddle Josh on the bench and shove her tongue down his throat while we all watched! Josh was an idiot for bringing her. Savannah was in a different class completely to this girl.

A horn sounded from the driveway, and I looked up to see Mason parking the minivan. He jumped out and made his way up to the porch. He slapped Brody on the back as he passed him and shook Jack's hand, his eyes fixed on me. He looked as gorgeous as ever, messy hair, jeans that fit like a glove and a crisp white t-shirt stretched tight across his chest. I smiled at him as he approached me, my heart beating out of my chest.

"Hi, sweetheart." His eyes scanning down my body. "You look beautiful." He bent his head and caught my lips with his.

"Thank you," I said quietly, my stomach fluttering with nerves. He pulled his lips from mine and curled his arm around my waist pulling me close to him.

"Am I missing something?" Brody asked, looking at Mason and then at me. "When did you two become an item?" He looked over at Savannah. "Did you know about this?" He asked her.

Before Savannah could respond, I heard Mason say. "We're dating Brody, it's pretty new. She took some convincing, but we're giving things a go."

"I like you Mason, but you'll have me to deal with if you hurt her. She's been through a lot." Brody warned.

"I know what she's been through and I don't plan on hurting her. I'm glad you're looking out for her, though, I wouldn't want it any other way." He pulled me even closer into his side, and I felt him kiss me softly on my head.

"That's enough macho behaviour," Savannah exclaimed. "Let's go!"

"Everyone ready?" Mason asked. There was a chorus of yes's, and we made our way to the minivan. "My girl's up front with me." He announced, as he held the door open for me and I climbed in, smiling gratefully at him.

Everyone else climbed in, and I noticed that Josh and Averi went for the back seats, no doubt to carry on what they'd started on the porch swing. Savannah, Jack, and Brody sat on the seats behind Mason and me. I turned and caught Savannah's eye, she gave me a small smile before focusing her attention on the view from her window. My heart broke for her; surely Josh knew that bringing Averi would upset her. I felt Mason reach across and take my hand, pulling me from my thoughts.

"You okay?" He asked, his brows furrowed with concern. "You look like you're miles away. Are you worrying about the drive up to Burnet?" He spoke quietly to me, making sure that no one else could hear our conversation.

"I'm okay, a bit nervous. I think I'll be alright if you'd hold my hand again…that really helped me last time." I smiled shyly at him. I didn't want to betray Savannah's confidence by telling him about her feelings for Josh, and I wasn't lying, I was nervous about the drive.

"Of course, I was planning on it anyway darlin'." He winked at me. "Right." He said loud

enough for everyone to hear. "Ready to go?" There was another chorus of yeses, and we headed down the long driveway to the main road. I focused on my breathing and the feeling of Mason's hand in mine, his thumb was stroking the back of my hand, and while I felt apprehensive, I knew I wasn't going to have a panic attack. Mason somehow knew to leave me alone and not talk to me, only asking occasionally if I was okay, to which I nodded my head. It was only about a twenty-minute drive to Burnet, and we were there before I knew it.

Mason parked the minivan into a field adjacent to where the fair and rodeo was being held. We all piled out and headed over to the kiosk to pay the entry fee. I dug around in my bag for my purse, but Mason put his hand on mine stopping me. "I'm paying sweetheart." He told me bending down and kissing me on the nose.

"No Mason, I should be paying for you, you drove everyone," I told him.

"I pay for my girl when we're out." He said, not taking no for an answer and quickly handing the money over. I saw the girl in the kiosk do a double take when she looked up to take his money, she was looking at him like she wanted to devour him. She tried to engage him in conversation, but he stepped back and wrapped his arm around my waist. This, however, didn't stop her and she continued to flirt and give him the eye, I might as well have been invisible. Mason ignored her advances while still managing to be polite. I, however, wanted to scratch her eyes out! We moved away letting Savannah and the others pay.

"Does that happen a lot?" I asked him.

He looked at me puzzled. "Does what happen a lot?"

"That girl at the kiosk, I think she'd have dropped her knickers right there and then if you'd asked her to!"

He turned back towards the kiosk, and the girl gave him a wave. He ignored her and turned back to face me. "Libby, are you jealous?" He asked, a cocky grin forming on his lips.

I folded my arms across my chest, willing my face not to flush with embarrassment. "No! She was just… overbearing that's all." I pouted, dropping my eyes from his.

He laughed. "I never even noticed her Lib. I'm not interested in anyone except you." He lifted my chin with his finger. "I love that you were jealous, though, but trust me you have nothing to worry about baby." He stroked my face with his fingers.

"I love it when you call me baby," I whispered, my eyes widening as I realised that I'd voiced my thoughts out loud. My cheeks flushed again, and I dropped my head to his chest, mortified.

He chuckled "I'll have to remember that baby." He said, emphasising the word baby and circling his arms around me. I inhaled deeply, taking in his scent. It was his usual smell of soap and aftershave, but it was addictive.

"Put her down Mason." I heard Jack shout from behind us. I rolled my eyes and pulled out of Mason's embrace. "Come on, let's get in there," Jack said leading the way. Mason laughed and grabbed my hand pulling me along to follow the others.

Once inside I stood and looked around, there were three arenas, two of which were open and hosting various animal shows with the third, the much larger of the three, enclosed with tiered seating all around. Posters advertised monster truck racing at various times throughout the day, along with the rodeo that would be happening tonight. Surrounding the arenas were rows and rows of stalls, selling food, drink, clothing and everything in between. There was a stage off to the left where a band was playing live music, and behind the arenas, I could make out some fairground rides and a large Ferris wheel. "What shall we do first?" I asked excitedly. "What about the rides? Sav, what do you want to do?"

"The rides look good to me. Come on." She grabbed the hand that Mason wasn't holding and pulled me from his grip. I looked over my shoulder as she pulled me towards the rides, Mason was laughing, and he nodded for me to go with Savannah. "Don't worry, lover boy's coming," Savannah said rolling her eyes.

"Save the Ferris wheel for me, sweetheart," Mason called out. I waved my free hand his way and flashed him a grin.

When Savannah finally stopped pulling me along, we were far enough away from our group to not be heard. "You okay Sav?" I asked her.

"Yeah, I'm okay."

"Liar."

She gave me a short laugh. "You know me too well. There's nothing I can do about it. I've just got to get on with it and get over him."

"If it's any consolation, it won't last. She's not right for him."

"Doesn't matter Lib, if it's not Averi it will be someone else. Just not me, unfortunately." She shrugged her shoulders in defeat. I linked my arm through hers and pulled her towards me.

"I'm sorry Sav."

"Me too Lib." She took a deep breath as if pulling herself together. "I'm not going to let him ruin today, come on, what shall we go on first?"

She obviously wanted to change the subject, and I couldn't blame her. "That one," I said excitedly, pointing to a huge ride lit up with hundreds of white lights. We stood and watched it, listening to its riders screams as it threw them upside down and round and round.

I felt someone come up behind me. "You're not going on that, are you?" Mason breathed in my ear, his lips brushing my neck. I leaned back against him, still watching the ride.

"Not scared are you Mason?" I teased him. "A big strong cowboy, afraid of a fairground ride." I turned and smirked up at him.

"I'm not the one trembling baby." He whispered against my lips.

"I'm not trembling because of the ride," I whispered back, my eyes never leaving his.

"I know Lib." It was his turn now to smirk at me. He knew exactly how my body reacted to him when he was close to me. He kissed me gently before pulling back. "Enjoy the ride sweetheart." He pushed me gently towards Savannah who was chuckling at us.

"How does he manage to do that?" I asked her, shaking my head.

"Do what Lib?"

"Make me forget my own name, just by whispering in my ear!"

She smiled sadly, glancing over towards Josh. "I wish I knew." She paused. "Come on."

We queued for the ride with Brody and Jack, and I screamed the whole way around. I loved it! We went on three more similar rides afterward, and my throat actually hurt from all the screaming. After the last ride, we went to find Mason and the others, there were crowds of people, and we had some trouble finding them. Brody was just about to call Josh on his phone when Jack shouted that he'd found Mason. I turned to look where he was pointing and stopped dead in my tracks, Savannah ploughed into the back of me, just like the first time I'd seen him. This time was different, though, this time there was a gorgeous leggy blonde with her arms draped around his neck, he was standing with his back to me, hands on his hips. We were about ten feet away from them, and the girl looked over, she narrowed her eyes at me and smirked before bringing her face closer to his as if she was going to kiss him. I turned around, stumbling into Savannah who caught me.

I'd let my guard down and let him in, and now my already damaged heart was breaking all over again.

Chapter Fifteen

I heard a gasp come from Savannah and she grabbed my hand. Unable to stop myself I looked back over my shoulder, Mason chose that moment to turn around, his eyes finding mine over the crowds. As he looked at me, my stomach rolled, and I thought I was going to be sick. He quickly removed her arms from around his neck and pushed her away, anger evident on his face. He started to make his way through the crowds towards us. "Get me out of here Savannah." I pleaded, tears threatening to fall. She silently pulled me into the crowd, and I followed her blindly, trusting her to not let me fall, my vision blurred from the tears that were now falling down my face.

"Libby wait!!" I heard Mason shout frantically. I felt Savannah increase her pace and I stumbled behind her. "Libby, stop. Please." His voice sounding desperate. I wanted to turn around and look at him, but I couldn't make myself do it.

"I'm heading for the maze; we can hide in there for a bit," Savannah told me. I nodded even though she couldn't see me. I saw her turn and look behind me. "I think we've lost him for now." She said slowing down her pace.

There was a maze of maize behind the Ferris wheel, and we slipped inside without anyone from our group seeing us.

"Savannah, do you know who that girl was with Mason?" I asked her quietly as we stopped just out of view of the entrance. I wiped my eyes as I waited for her to answer me.

She sighed. "Yes, that was Amber."

"Amber? There was a text this morning on Mason's phone from an Amber. Do you know her?"

"Only by her reputation. She's tried getting it on with nearly all of the men in Marble Falls, most of which have let her, according to Brody. She's the same age as him, and they went to school together."

"And Mason was one who didn't say no?" I asked, already knowing the answer.

"Yes... but Lib, Amber is known for trying to get her claws in, I think you should speak to Mason, what you saw, there might be an innocent explanation."

I looked at her, in disbelief. "You're taking his side?"

"Of course not Libby, but I've seen the way he looks at you, the way you look at him. There is something real between the two of you, anyone can see that. All I'm saying is, save judgement until you've spoken to him."

"I like him Sav, I like him a lot. I've never felt this way about anyone before, it scares me." I paused, my eyes dropping to the ground. "My heart broke when I found out Mia had died; I can't go through that again. I know I've only known Mason a short time, but I'm falling fast... and they looked pretty cosy. He was hardly pushing her away."

"Lib I'd give anything for Josh to look at me the way Mason looks at you. I know what you saw looked bad, I'll be the first to admit that. But don't throw away what you could have with Mason before you know what happened. Speak to him, please. I'll be the first to kick his ass if he's up to anything with that skank, believe me." She reached into her bag and pulled out her phone, she held it up to me. "It's on silent, but I've got 13 missed calls, all from Mason." As she held it the display lit up, his name flashing across the screen.

I took in a shaky breath. "Answer it," I told her. "I'll speak to him. It's not like I can ignore him all day."

She answered the phone, telling him where we were. I could hear him, he sounded frantic. Maybe Savannah was right, and there was an innocent explanation. God, I hoped so. Savannah gave me a few minutes to pull myself together, hugging me tightly before she linked my arm and we made our way out of the maze. Mason was waiting for me by the entrance. Savannah squeezed my arm. "I'll leave you two to it, I'll go and find Brody." She said disappearing into the crowd.

"Sweetheart." Mason began, reaching for me. I took a step back, his hand dropping in front of him. "Libby, what you saw, it's not what it looked like."

"Tell me what it was then Mason," I replied seemingly calm, although on the inside I was a nervous wreck waiting to hear what he would say.

"The girl you saw was Amber. We've been…together a few times over the past couple of months, she wanted more, I never did. After she text this morning, I went to see her."

I gasped, dropping my eyes from his. "That's where you were this morning" I whispered, hurt evident in my voice. "You went to her after I spent the night with you?" I felt a lump form in my throat and bit on the inside of my mouth to try and stop the tears that were building. He reached for my hand again, and this time I wasn't quick enough to pull back.

"Yes, but to tell her that I wouldn't be seeing her again." He rushed out. "I knew she wouldn't take any notice of a text, so I arranged to meet her at the coffee shop in Marble Falls." He paused. "Look at me Libby, please." I slowly raised my eyes to meet his. "I told her that I'd met someone and that I only wanted to be with her."

"So, what was that?" I gestured with my hand to the other side of the fair where I'd seen her draped all over him.

He dragged his hand through his hair and sighed. "She was upset, she told me I'd led her on and that she loved me. I swear to you Libby, I never led her on. I told her the first time I took her out that I wasn't looking for a relationship, she told me she wasn't either. She started getting clingy a few weeks ago, so I cooled things with her, but a couple of weeks before I met you..." He trailed off, taking a deep breath and letting it out slowly. "I slept with her again, and now she's pissed at me. What you saw was her hugging me, she caught me off guard. I'm so sorry." He reached up and stroked my face under my eyes. "I hate that I'm the reason you've been crying. I never want to be the reason you cry again." Without me realising he had somehow edged closer as we'd been talking, he was now standing right in front of me. I could feel his breath on my skin as he spoke and I closed my eyes and lowered my face, resting my forehead on his chest. He wrapped his arms around me, and I felt him kiss the top of my head. We stood there, neither of us saying anything for a few minutes, my head spinning. "Say something sweetheart." He pleaded.

I looked up into his eyes, did I listen to my head or my heart? My heart believed him, my head was telling me to run. I'd judged him wrongly before, and I wanted to believe what he'd told me. I decided that I needed to be honest with him. "Mason I really like you." Embarrassed I dropped my eyes to the floor. "I've never felt like this before; it scares me how quickly I'm falling for you. I don't want to get hurt." I whispered, looking up at him.

"It scares me too baby, but I won't hurt you, I promise." He said, his eyes sincere.

"You can't promise me that Mason."

He paused. "I would never intentionally hurt you, Libby."

"I guess I panicked. When I saw her all over you, I felt like someone had kicked me the stomach. It's ridiculous I know; we've only known each other a week. That's what's so scary."

"Lib, it's not ridiculous, if I'd seen you in the arms of some guy, I'd have ripped his head off. I'm falling just as fast sweetheart." He bent his head and tentatively brushed his lips against mine. "Is this okay?" He whispered against my lips. I threaded my arms around his neck, digging my fingers into his hair. I pulled his mouth to mine and kissed him hungrily, brushing my tongue against his. He moaned into my mouth and pulled me closer to him. "I'll take that as a yes!" He smiled as he pulled away. "You owe me a ride on the Ferris wheel, come on."

The Ferris wheel was amazing, you could see for miles, although I didn't spend a lot of time looking at the view, I was preoccupied with the gorgeous cowboy next to me. His arm was around my shoulder, and I was pulled tightly into his side, my new favourite place to be. "Mia would have loved it here," I told him quietly. "She'd have loved you too. We never argued over men, but I'm sure I'd have had a fight on my hands if she'd met you!" I laughed. "She was man mad!" I really missed her, but I found that I was able to think about her without my chest hurting quite as much as it did.

"I would have loved to have met her sweetheart, it sounds like she was a real character. I can't wait to hear more about her when you're ready to tell me."

"She was; we were complete opposites, but I loved her to pieces." I gave him a small smile, and he pulled me tighter to him, kissing me on the forehead.

Once the ride ended Mason called Brody, and we arranged to meet everyone by the food stalls. We made our way over hand in hand, catching sight of Josh and Averi all over one another again,

Savannah thankfully had her back to them, and she was talking to Jack. "Josh is such an idiot." I heard Mason say.

"Why do you say that?" I asked him, curious as to what he meant.

"Bringing Averi with him and letting her paw him while Savannah watches. When he finally gets his head out of his ass and admits to himself that he likes her, he's going to hate himself for hurting her like he's doing. Unless of course it's too late and she's moved on with someone else, then he'll hate himself even more!"

I turned and looked at him in amazement. "You know that Savannah likes him?" I asked.

"Yes, it's written all over her face. He likes her too, although right now he's got a funny way of showing it." He said, frowning as he looked over to Josh and Averi.

"Has he told you he likes her? God, does Brody know?"

"Not in so many words but he's hinted at it when he's been drunk, and his reaction to her dancing with that guy in the bar last week speaks volumes." He grinned down at me, obviously thinking about his similar behaviour at the bar. "Brody hasn't a clue, though. I don't know why Josh won't tell them how he feels. I've tried to talk to him, but he won't listen."

"I hate to see Savannah hurting but they've got to sort it out themselves, something is obviously holding Josh back. I just wish they would talk to each other." Mason nodded his head in agreement. "I hope they can work it out before it's too late."

"I see you two have worked things out. Are you okay Lib?" Jack asked as he walked over to us, the concern evident in his voice.

I looked up to Mason, who squeezed my hand. "I'm fine Jack, just a misunderstanding."

"Good. Let's eat I'm starving." He exclaimed rubbing his hands together.

As if on cue my stomach rumbled. Mason laughed. "I think my

girl's hungry too!" He led me towards the stalls. Looking around, there was every sort of food you could imagine, burgers, hot dogs, jacket potatoes with various fillings, chips, and nachos. The list was endless. What did catch my eye was one stall selling cookies by the bucket full. They were filling small buckets to the brim with cookies for $10. I was definitely getting one of those to take back to the ranch!

After we had chosen a cheeseburger and chips each, we headed to sit in the picnic area behind the food stalls, the others following with their food. Savannah sat down beside me with a huff. "Urgh! If I have to watch Averi grope Josh once more, I'm going to throw up! That girl has no shame." I gave her a sympathetic smile and squeezed her hand. "Enough about my sad excuse for a love life! Are you and Mason really okay? What happened?" She asked me in a hushed tone so that no one else could hear her.

I looked across to Mason who was chatting with Brody. "We're okay," I said, turning back to face her. "Amber reckons she's in love with Mason, so she didn't take too kindly to him telling her he'd met me. He said she was upset and hugged him, which is when I saw them." Savannah's eyes widened in surprise.

"She's in love with him?"

"Apparently. Mason said they'd only been together a few times, but she'd started to get clingy so he'd cooled things with her."

"God, she sounds like a real catch! What was he thinking?" Savannah said, rolling her eyes.

"He wasn't thinking, but he definitely won't be making that mistake again." Mason breathed into my ear, kissing my neck. I shivered under his touch, he'd obviously heard my conversation with Savannah.

"Well, I hope we've seen the last of her," Savannah exclaimed.

I looked at her in surprise. "You think she might cause trouble?" I asked.

"No, No Lib. I'm sure she won't, I was just thinking out loud."

"Don't worry sweetheart, I made it perfectly clear I didn't want anything to do with her. She won't be back." Mason said confidently. I smiled at him, hoping he was right.

After eating we spent another hour or so around the fair, I managed to persuade Mason to have a go on a couple of the faster rides with me. I took pity on him after the second ride that threw him upside down, though, as he came off looking a pale shade of green. At around 7 pm we made our way over to the rodeo arena to get some seats. The light was starting to fade, but huge floodlights lit the arena. We managed to find some seats near the front, as we sat down the announcer began running through the order of events. There was everything from calf roping, bareback horse riding and bull riding, saddle bronc riding, and barrel racing. I didn't know what half of the events were, but I couldn't wait to find out.

The arena was packed, and it seemed like nearly everyone had a cowboy hat on. "Where's your hat, cowboy?" I asked Mason, grinning at him.

"I left it at home, why?" He returned my smile before leaning over to kiss me on my nose.

"Everyone here seems to have one." I paused. "They're hot..."

"You like my hat?" He smirked at me.

"Do you have any idea how sexy you look in it?" I asked him.

"Why don't you tell me, baby?"

"Why don't I show you?" I leaned over to him and snaked my arms around his neck. I lightly brushed my lips against his, pulling away to look into his eyes. I watched his eyes drop to my lips, and I pulled him closer to me, kissing him firmly, his tongue snaked into my mouth, and I let out a moan.

He pulled back, breaking the kiss. "Wow, sweetheart, I think I'll be wearing my hat all the time if it means you kiss me like that." He whispered against my lips. I smiled.

"I think I'd like that," I told him. A pool of lust settled low in my stomach and I almost forgot we weren't alone. We were interrupted by a huge cheer erupting from the crowd. The first event was starting; I forced myself to move away from him, but he kept a strong grip on my hand, rubbing his thumb lightly over the pulse point on my wrist. He must have been able to feel the effect he was having on my body, as my heart was racing under his touch.

The rodeo was incredible! My heart was in my mouth for the bareback bull riding and the saddle bronc riding. I had no idea how the riders managed to stay on, I was watching behind one hand while the other grasped Mason's hand tightly. Every time it looked like a rider might be thrown, I squeezed his hand, and I could hear him chuckling by the side of me. I shot him a couple of dirty looks when I could bring myself to tear my eyes away from the arena, this just made him laugh more.

The next event was the calf roping, I didn't really know what this was, but I quickly discovered that I didn't like it! It was basically a cowboy on horseback, throwing a rope over a fleeing calf, jumping down from the horse and throwing the poor thing on the ground and tying its legs up with the rope. This was all timed, and the winner was the rider who could do it in the quickest time. It all seemed a bit cruel to me, the calf must have been terrified. "God this is brutal, the poor calf," I said to Mason turning away from the arena. I looked along the row of seats to see that Jack looked equally horrified.

"It is pretty vicious. Do you want to go outside?" Mason asked me, concerned.

"I'm going to find the toilet; I'll be back in a minute."

"I'll come with you," Mason said starting to get up.

"Don't be daft, I'll be fine," I told him putting my hand on his leg. "I'll only be five minutes." He nodded and kissed my hand as I passed him.

I made my way outside and around to the back of the arena where there was a line of portable toilets. I joined the small queue suddenly feeling uncomfortable, I pulled my arms tight around my body, I had the strangest feeling that I was being watched. I felt the hairs stand up on the back of my neck and I shivered, I looked around but couldn't see anything out of the ordinary. I was at the front of the queue, and when a toilet became free, I made for the door, glancing over my shoulder as I went. After using the facilities, I quickly washed my hands and unlocked the door, as I opened it Amber was stood in the doorway, her face like thunder. "Can I help you?" I asked her, sounding more confident than I felt.

"So, you're Mason's latest lay then?" She spat at me, her hands on her hips. "It won't last you know. Me and him, we have something special, once he gets tired of you, he'll come back to me. He always does."

"Excuse me," I said, ignoring her comments. "I need to get back." I moved towards her, trying to get past but she didn't budge, her hands firmly on her hips.

"I know that you saw him with me earlier, he was going to kiss me you know, and then you showed up." She sneered at me. "He doesn't want a little girl like you, he wants a real woman who knows what she's doing."

I'd heard enough. I pushed her out of the way, and she stumbled backward. "Stay away from Mason, he's mine. You're seriously deluded if you think he'd go anywhere near you again. Now if you don't mind I need to be getting back to my boyfriend." I walked away, my whole body shaking. I'd never confronted anyone like that before, I don't know what had come over me.

"Watch your back little girl. I always get what I want." She screamed after me. I saw people turning around to see what the commotion was and I lowered my head, hurrying towards the entrance of the arena.

My heart was pounding, and tears were threatening to fall as I walked into the arena. I wasn't looking where I was going and slammed into a hard body, I felt arms around my waist, and I started to panic until my senses were overloaded by the familiar smell of Mason. "Mason." I croaked, throwing my arms around him. He pulled me into him, hugging me tightly.

"Libby, what's wrong? What's happened?" He asked concerned. He pushed me away from him slightly, frantically checking me over to see if I was hurt.

"Amber." I murmured.

"What about Amber?" He lifted my chin, so I was looking at him. "What did she do?" His voice full of anger.

I took a deep breath, letting it out slowly. "She was waiting for me when I came out of the toilet, she said you'd get bored of me and that you'd end up going back to her like you always do." I saw his eyes flash with anger and he pulled me closer to him, kissing me on the head.

"Did she say anything else sweetheart?"

"Erm, no... not really..." I trailed off biting on my bottom lip.

"Tell me, Libby." He demanded, leaning back so he could see my face.

I sighed. "She just said that you were going to kiss her earlier, before I showed up, and... and that you wouldn't want a little girl like me, that you'd want a woman who knew what she was doing." I saw his jaw clench in anger. "She told me to watch my back, and that she always gets what she wants."

"God, that bitch is crazy. I'm so sorry sweetheart. Did she touch you?" I knew he was angry, but his eyes softened as they looked at me.

"No. I'm fine," I whispered.

"I won't have anyone speaking to my girl like that. I'm going to take you back to Jack and Brody, where I know you're safe, then I'm going to find her and tell her to stay the hell away from us." He took my hand and started pulling me towards our seats.

"No Mason!" I pulled back on his arm. He stopped, turning to look at me. "Please don't, can we just forget about her," I begged him.

He sighed. "Okay sweetheart, if that's what you want, we can forget about her for tonight, but I will be speaking to her, and soon." He paused and lifted my chin so I was looking into his eyes. "Nothing she said is true baby, you know that right?" I nodded my head. "I'm crazy about you Lib."

I smiled up at him. "I'm crazy about you too," I whispered, going up on my tip toes to kiss him. It wasn't long before the kiss turned heated. Mason pulled away and rested his forehead on mine.

"Stay with me tonight?" He asked.

I bit down on my bottom lip. I wasn't ready to sleep with him; would he be expecting that if I said yes? As if reading my mind, he whispered. "I'm not expecting you to do anything you're not ready to do Lib. If you'd rather not, I understand." He moved back to see my face.

"No, I want to." I rushed out, not wanting him to think I didn't want to be with him. "I'm just not ready to…" I trailed off, looking down at my feet.

"I know baby; I would never make you do anything that you're not comfortable with." He reassured me, reaching up and tucking a piece of hair behind my ear. "Come on, let's head home, things are winding down here now anyway."

Mason called Brody, and we met everyone by the minivan. Savannah could tell that something was wrong, but I shook my head at her indicating that I didn't want to talk about it. I would tell her what had happened, but I didn't want everyone to know, especially Jack, he would only be angry. I was too busy thinking about what Amber had said to me to worry about the journey home. I sat in the front again with Mason, who held my hand the whole way. I was uneasy on the way back to the ranch, the more I thought about the confrontation with Amber the more I thought that today wouldn't be the last we heard from her.

Chapter Sixteen

I woke up the next morning pressed tightly into Mason's side, my head on his chest and his arms wrapped around me. Once I'd managed to turn my mind off from everything that had happened yesterday, I'd slept really well. After returning from the rodeo, I'd gone back to my bedroom to wait until everyone was asleep before heading over to Mason's cabin. Savannah had come into my room to check that I was okay, I'd told her what had happened at the rodeo, and she was livid at what Amber had said to me. She wanted to tell Jack and Brody but I begged her not to, and she'd reluctantly agreed.

Once the house had fallen silent, I'd crept downstairs and out to the stables where Mason was waiting for me. He'd spun me around whispering that he'd missed me. I'd missed him too, even though we'd only been apart for an hour or so, these feelings I had for him were crazy and intense.

We'd gone back to his cabin, and thankfully Mason hadn't mentioned Amber, I think he knew I was done talking about her for the night. After a pretty heated make out session he'd pulled me into his arms and he fell asleep. He'd never pushed me to go any further, letting me take the lead on how far we went, which I was grateful for. I knew the other girls he'd been with were more experienced than me, and that he wasn't used to waiting. I knew he wouldn't wait forever, but for now, he seemed happy to. I'd watched him while he slept, snaking my fingers up and down his chest, circling around his tattoo. I'd eventually fallen asleep, waking up encased in his arms.

Mason was still sleeping when I woke up, and slowly I wriggled out of his grasp, somehow managing not to wake him. I lay my head on my pillow so that my face was level with his, I just lay there for a few minutes watching him, I could stare at his gorgeous face for hours. I'd no idea what he saw in me, he was way out of my league.

"You're staring again Lib; this is becoming a bit of a habit." He chuckled, his eyes still closed. I was grateful he couldn't see me, as I felt my face get warm with embarrassment. "And I'm betting that beautiful face of yours is all pink, I'm right aren't I?" He asked me, finally opening his eyes. I met his eyes for a split second before turning my head and burying my face into his pillow, I heard him laughing. "Show me, baby." He demanded. I slowly lifted my head and looked over to him, his hand reached out and stroked my face. "Just as I thought." He whispered. "Stunning." His compliment making me blush even more.

He pulled me into his chest, and I looped my arms around his neck, he lowered his head and kissed me hungrily, rolling me so that I was underneath him, pinned to the bed. His tongue stroked my bottom lip, and I opened my mouth to him, his tongue duelling with mine, pulling away he peppered light kisses around my jaw and down my neck. My breathing accelerated as I felt his hand slip under the t-shirt that I was wearing, his fingers stroking lightly on my skin. I let out a gasp when his hand travelled up my side, and his fingers brushed the underside of my breast. He lifted his head and rested his forehead on mine.

"Is this okay Lib? He asked me, his voice breathless.

I nodded. "Please don't stop," I whispered.

He smiled at me. "I won't." He promised, kissing me again and stealing my breath. I felt his erection pressing against me as he pulled me even closer to his body, as he broke the kiss he reached for the bottom of my t-shirt and pulled it up over my head, leaving me in just my knickers. I felt my face flush, and instinctively I moved my hands to cover my breasts, never having been this exposed in front of someone before. Mason saw what I was doing and reached for my hands.

"Don't baby. Don't ever feel self-conscious in front of me." He said, dropping his eyes from mine and looking at my exposed body. "You are so beautiful, Libby." He murmured, his hands cupping my breasts as he kissed me, his tongue swirling with mine. My back arched, pushing my breasts further into his hands, I let out a moan as his thumbs brushed my nipples. His fingers continued to play, his kisses spilling down my neck, I began fidgeting underneath him, needing something more. Mason ground his hips against mine, his erection hitting me exactly where I needed it, the thin fabric of our underwear the only thing separating us. I felt a sensation building low in my stomach, my heart was pounding, and my breathing was ragged. As if knowing what I needed Mason brought his mouth to my nipple and as he did the sensation in my stomach intensified. I threaded my fingers through his hair holding his head to my chest, I lifted my hips to meet his, needing to be even closer to him. Suddenly my body erupted, and I pulled sharply on his hair, a small moan escaping my lips. His mouth released my nipple, and he kissed up my neck his mouth finding mine in a tender kiss.

"Oh my god Mason." I gasped as he pulled his lips away.

"Was that your first orgasm sweetheart." He asked quietly. I nodded, squirming underneath him. "Don't be embarrassed, I'm glad it was me, that no other man has ever touched you like that. I loved watching you fall apart from my touch, knowing that no one else has ever seen that." I smiled shyly at him. As I squirmed, I could still feel his erection pressing against me.

"Mason, you haven't…erm…" I trailed off not sure of how to put it, instead gesturing with my eyes towards his boxers.

"It's fine sweetheart, I wanted this to be about you. I can wait. I'll take a cold shower." He said laughing. He reached over the side of the bed and grabbed the t-shirt he'd taken off before falling asleep last night, he pulled it over my head, his smell invading my senses. He kissed my forehead and headed downstairs to the bathroom. I flopped back on the bed smiling widely, I closed my eyes and pulled his t-shirt up over my nose, inhaling deeply. I was falling hard and fast for Mason, and I could easily see myself falling in love with him. I was sure that I was already half way there.

I headed downstairs deciding to make us some breakfast while he showered. I made myself at home in his kitchen, pulling eggs, ham, and cheese out of the fridge and putting the coffee on to brew, it didn't take me long to find everything I needed in the tiny kitchen. I cracked the eggs into a bowl and whisked them up, adding a dash of milk and some black pepper, I chopped up the ham and cheese and added these to the egg mixture. There was a small two burner hob on the worktop, and I turned it on to heat up. I found a frying pan in one of the cupboards and poured the mixture in. I heard a low whistle come from behind me, and I looked over my shoulder to see Mason standing there with just a small white towel wrapped around his waist. My mouth went dry at the sight of him my eyes focusing on his bare chest and the perfect v that disappeared beneath his towel.

"God, my clothes look good on you baby." He said pulling me from my drooling session. I looked up to his face to see his eyes tracking up and down my body.

"You're staring Mason." I teased him, throwing his earlier words back at him.

"Yes, I am. I'm looking at what's mine" He said, a cocky smile on his face.

I turned back to the omelette, smiling at the realisation that I really was his. I think I had been from the moment I saw him, regardless of how much I'd tried to fight it. I felt him come up behind me, circling his arms around my waist and pulling me back slightly so that I was resting against his bare chest.

"That looks good sweetheart." He said, eyeing the frying pan in my hand. He moved my hair off my shoulder, placing small kisses on the side of my neck, I sagged against him and closed my eyes, loving the feel of his lips on me. "I'll just throw some clothes on, I'll be back." He breathed against my neck.

Mason returned a few minutes later, dressed in jeans and a t-shirt. "I feel a little underdressed." I laughed, reaching to tug his t-shirt further down my thighs.

"You look absolutely perfect baby."

"You're looking pretty perfect yourself cowboy." I told him, raking my eyes up and down his body."

"You need to stop looking at me like that sweetheart, otherwise that t-shirt of mine, it'll end up back on my bedroom floor." He muttered, looking at me through hooded eyes, his words creating a stirring in the pit of my stomach.

I tore my eyes away from him and plated up breakfast. Walking to the sofa, I sat down. "So," I began, in an attempt to change the subject before I jumped on him, I had no idea where this side of me came from when I was around him, but I was starting to like it! "Are we still on for tonight?" I asked him, devouring my omelette.

He smiled at me obviously aware of what I was doing. "Definitely darlin'. I've got to work for a few hours today, but I can pick you up later." He hesitated, the smile fading slightly from his face. "Lib, I want you to know that I called Amber after we got back last night. I'm sorry if that upsets you, but I needed to make it clear that she needs to stay away from you. I won't have her speaking to you like she did."

"What did you say to her?" I asked quietly.

He took my plate along with his and placed it on the coffee table in front of us, turning on the sofa to face me, he took my hands in his. "That you were my girlfriend and that it was serious between us, that you weren't just someone I was messing around with. I told her to stay away from us and to move on, that I could never be with her the way she wanted me to be."

My eyes widened in shock at what he'd said to her. "It's serious between us?" I whispered.

"Yes, sweetheart, about as serious as it gets. I know you feel it too." I stared at him, not able to respond. I knew I was falling in love with him, which made no sense to me at all. I hardly knew him, but being with him felt right. I couldn't tell him how I felt, though, he said it was serious between us, that didn't mean he was in love with me.

"I feel it too," I told him. "It's crazy though Mason, I hardly know anything about you."

He sighed. "I know Lib, I was going to wait until tonight to talk to you, but as we're here now...," He trailed off, a worried look crossing his face. My stomach erupted with nervous butterflies at his words. "About eighteen months ago, I was engaged to a girl called Emmerson, we'd been together since high school, and we were due to get married. In the weeks running up to the wedding, Emmie started acting strangely, disappearing for hours and being quiet around me. I questioned her about it, but she assured me that it was just pre-wedding jitters, turns out I was right to be worried." He paused, taking in a deep breath. "The week before the wedding I found her in bed with my older brother Dylan, I went mad and started hitting him. Emmerson was screaming for me to stop and yelling that she'd fallen in love with him and wanted to be with him, that she didn't love me anymore. Turns out they'd been messing around behind my back for nearly a year."

"I'm so sorry Mason, I can't believe your brother would do that to you," I told him squeezing on his hands.

"I was so angry Lib, I couldn't stop hitting him, I hit him over and over again." He dropped one of my hands and ran it through his hair, his face a picture of pain. "It was only when my Dad came into the room and pulled me off him that I stopped. He was unconscious, and I still didn't stop." He shook his head. "He was in the hospital for three days recovering. I was arrested and charged with aggravated assault and served nine months in jail. I got off lightly in my opinion." He paused, dropping his eyes from mine but still holding on tightly to my one hand, as if it was his lifeline. "I need you to know Lib, that while I haven't always been perfectly behaved, I got into a fair bit of trouble when I was younger, I'd never hit anyone before that night, and I've never hit anyone since. I had a lot of time to think in jail, and while I loved Emmie, I know now that I wasn't in love with her. Things hadn't been right for a while, but I just couldn't see it at the time, we were high school sweethearts and marriage seemed the next logical step. In reality, we'd fallen out of love a long time before I caught her in bed with my brother. I will always regret how I handled things, I just hope what I've told you won't change how you look at me."

He looked up at me, and I saw a vulnerability in his eyes that I'd never seen before. I squeezed his hands again to reassure him. "What happened to Emmerson and your brother?" I asked him.

"They got married while I was in jail. Turns out they really did love each other, they are still together as far as I know."

"You don't speak to your family anymore?" I asked, frowning.

"No. As I said I wasn't exactly the model son growing up, but

Dylan was, he could do no wrong. Although my parents didn't agree with Dylan and Emmerson sneaking around behind my back, they couldn't forgive me for hurting him. We haven't spoken since my first week in jail. Claire and Ryan were kind enough to offer me a job and a place to stay when I was released, and I grabbed the opportunity with both hands."

"I'm so sorry that you had to go through all that Mason, I can't believe that your parents turned their back on you. I'm not saying that I agree with you beating up Dylan, but I can see why it happened and for them to just take his side... I'd like to think that when I eventually have children, I'd be there for them no matter what, even if I didn't agree with the things they did."

He looked up at me in surprise. "So, my past doesn't scare you?"

"No Mason." I leaned over, kissing him softly. "My instinct is telling me you're a good man and I trust my instinct. Have you ever tried contacting your family?" I asked him.

His relieved eyes met mine, and he took a deep breath, letting it out slowly. "After about three months in jail, after I'd had plenty of time to think things through, I wrote to Emmerson, Dylan and my parents. Emmerson replied, telling me how sorry she was that things had turned out the way they had, and that she had never meant to hurt me. I didn't know if Dylan was aware that she had written to me, but I guessed he didn't as neither he nor my parents ever wrote back."

My heart broke for him; yes, he was in the wrong for what happened with Dylan, but he'd gone from having everything to nothing in the blink of an eye, without any sort of support from his family. His parents seemed to have overlooked the fact that his brother had betrayed him in the worst possible way.

"Well, I'm still crazy about you cowboy," I whispered to him, wrapping my arms around him in a hug. I felt him let out a shaky breath, his body sagging against mine.

"I was worried you'd look at me differently once you knew what I'd done, I was dreading telling you." He murmured into my neck. I squeezed him even harder in an attempt to try and show him how much I cared about him, how much he meant to me. I couldn't believe that anyone would cheat on him, he was incredible.

I leaned back and brushed my lips against his. He pulled me onto his lap, and I rested my head on his shoulder. After a few minutes, I realised that we hadn't finished talking about what had happened earlier. "Mason, what did Amber say when you told her we were serious?" I asked him, anxious to find out what she'd said.

"She didn't say much, she got angry and hung up on me, don't worry though baby I don't think she'll be bothering us again."

I breathed a sigh of relief hoping he was right.

"Sweetheart, as much as I'd love to stay here with you all day, I've got to get to work. Do you want to stay here for a bit or shall I walk you back to the house?" Mason asked me, his fingers running up and down my bare thighs.

I shivered under his touch, goose bumps erupting on my legs where he was touching me. "I'll head back." I sighed. "Spend some time with Jack. I might see if he wants to go to our lake for a swim."

"Our lake?" Mason teased, tickling me. "I'm pretty sure it's Claire and Ryan's lake." He laughed, moving my body so that I was lying down underneath him on the sofa.

I squirmed beneath him, laughing out loud as he continued to tickle me. "Mason stop!" I squealed. "Stop."

He stopped suddenly and lowered his face to mine, kissing me gently on my nose. "I shouldn't tease you, I love that you call it *our* lake." He whispered against my lips before capturing them with his own.

"Well, it was where we had our first date," I said breathlessly when he pulled out of the kiss.

"I thought you said it wasn't a date?" He asked me, a smile forming on his lips.

"I changed my mind," I said, winking at him. "No one, other than my parents, has ever gone to that much trouble for me."

"You're worth it sweetheart." He jumped up and pulled me up off the sofa. "Get some clothes on that cute butt of yours, and I'll walk you home." He gently pushed me towards the stairs, swatting my bum as I passed him.

I came down five minutes later, dressed and hair thrown up in a bobble. Mason was sat on the sofa waiting for me. "Ready to go Lib." He asked me, standing up and reaching for my hand. I nodded, and we headed hand in hand towards the house. We walked in comfortable silence past the stables and up the garden path. As we climbed the stairs of the porch the front door opened and Aunt Claire walked out. I saw her eyes widen in shock as she looked down at our joined hands. I felt Mason tug on my hand pulling me into his side.

"Hi, Claire, nice to see you," Mason said to her, wrapping his arm around my waist.

"Libby, what's going on? Have you spent the night at Mason's?" She asked me with a frown.

"Erm... yes, I spent the night there," I said dropping my eyes from hers.

"Is there a problem?" Mason asked, looking confused. He looked between Claire and me waiting for one of us to say something.

"Mason, you do know that Libby is only nineteen and that she's here with us because she's been through something horrific at home?"

"Aunt Claire!" I exclaimed.

"I know how old she is Claire, I also know about Mia and the reason she's here at the ranch, she's told me everything." Mason pulled me closer into his side and kissed me on the side of my head.

Aunt Claire looked at me in surprise, her eyebrows raised in question. I nodded my head at her, letting her know that what Mason said was true.

"I think your niece is amazing Claire, I really care for her, and I think she cares for me. I won't hurt her; you have my word."

Aunt Claire sighed. "And you feel the same, Libby?" She asked me.

I nodded. "I do. I'm sorry I didn't tell you, I know you think Mason's too old for me, but I really like him. He's really helping me." She looked between the two of us obviously trying to decide what to say.

"Okay, but no more sneaking out of the house at night, you might be an adult, but your parents are trusting me to look after you, to do that I need to know where you are."

"Thank you, Aunt Claire." I stepped away from Mason to pull her into a hug. She hugged me back tightly.

"Look after her Mason, she's special." Aunt Claire told him over my shoulder.

"She certainly is." I heard him tell her.

"I'd better get going, I'll see you both later." She said, waving as she made her way to the stables.

"That went better than I thought," I said, relieved.

"You never told me she thought I was too old for you? When did you talk about me, baby?" His cocky grin returning.

I smirked back at him. "After you went all psycho in the bar last week, not letting me dance with that guy."

"I did not go psycho!" He exclaimed. "There was no way I was watching some random guy put his hands all over you. I'd never felt so jealous as I did that night, we'd only just met, but I knew I wanted you for myself." He laughed. "You were so mad when I pulled you out of his arms, you look absolutely beautiful when you're angry baby."

"I was angry, but you impressed me too. I kind of liked how possessive you were, even if I didn't show it at the time," I reached up and kissed him. "You'd better go, don't want you in trouble with the boss!" I joked.

He laughed. "Come to my place about six tonight." He kissed me again, stealing my breath, before making his way down the porch steps.

"Oh, and Mason…" I watched him turn around as he walked backward towards the gate. "I might wear my new bikini to the lake this afternoon, if you find yourself anywhere near there, come and say hi."

I heard him groan. "Sweetheart I'll make sure I'm nearby!"

"Looking forward to it," I shouted to him, smiling to myself as I made my way inside.

Chapter Seventeen

After showering and changing into my bikini, throwing a floaty dress over the top, I headed to the stables with Jack and Savannah. I'd suggested visiting the lake for a swim, and they'd both thought that it was a good idea. It was another hot day and cooling off in the lake sounded perfect, plus I would get the chance to wear one of my new bikinis. We had decided to ride the horses rather than take the truck, so we saddled them up and had a steady ride out to the lake.

The horses were tied up in the shade once we arrived, and Jack spread out a blanket that he'd brought with him. I flopped down onto my back, using my arm to shade my eyes from the sun.

"So, Lib, how's it going with lover boy?" Savannah asked me, a smirk on her face.

I laughed. "Very good thanks."

"Is that it? Is that all I'm getting out of you? I want details girl!" She pouted, sitting down next to me.

"God, I'm going for a swim; I don't want to hear details of my little sister's love life!" Jack said with a grimace. He pulled his t-shirt off and waded into the lake. "Bloody hell! It's freezing!" He shouted.

"Come on then, now Jack's out of earshot, spill!" Savannah demanded, bouncing on her knees with excitement.

"Mason's amazing, I'm falling hard for him Sav. It scares me just how quickly I'm falling for him."

"Well I'm sure Mason feels the same way about you, it's written all over his face. I can't believe that bitch Amber, has he spoken to her yet?"

"Yeah, he called her last night and told her to leave us alone. I just hope she listens."

"I don't know what he ever saw in her!"

"I'm guessing it was the long blonde hair and the model like body," I said sarcastically, rolling my eyes.

"Libby you're gorgeous and an incredible person, you've got the whole package, and Mason obviously thinks so too." She raised her eyebrows at me. "So, is he a good kisser then?"

I shook my head at her and jumped up. "I don't kiss and tell Savannah," I told her, laughing. I pulled my dress over my head and threw it at her, running towards the lake.

"Hey!" I heard her shout. "Wait for me!"

I ran into the lake, squealing as the cold water hit my body, Savannah followed me in, squealing even louder. It didn't take long to get used to the temperature, though, and we spent a while splashing around and talking. Jack had another two days at the ranch, and then he was meeting up with his friends in Austin.

"Brody and I are heading to a bar tonight, are you two coming?" Jack asked, splashing us both with water.

"Jack!" I scolded, splashing him back.

"Lib's got a date with lover boy," Savannah told him, smirking at me. "But count me in."

I stuck my tongue out at her and turned to speak to Jack. "We're coming here to watch the sunset, I'm sure we could meet up with you later. It will be fun to all hang out before you have to leave. I'll speak to Mason." As much as I wanted to spend time with Mason, if Jack was leaving in a couple of days, I wanted to see as much of him as possible. It was likely that after this week it would be a few months before I saw him again.

We spent the next hour or so lying in the sun on the bank of the lake. Jack was telling us where he and his friends were planning on going next, when we heard the hum of an engine in the distance. As we sat up, we saw Mason's truck come into view.

"It's lover boy," Savannah announced. "He's going to freak when he sees you wearing that bikini." She wiggled her eyebrows at me.

I rolled my eyes at her, jumping up from the blanket to go and meet him. He stopped the truck and got out, walking over to me, his eyes scanning my body.

"God Lib, you look incredible." He rubbed his hands up and down my bare arms before pulling me into his chest, his head dropped to my neck where he placed small kisses, making my body shiver in his arms. "I want to take you back to my bed and peel that bikini off you." He whispered in my ear, his warm breath tickling my skin. His words created a stirring low in my stomach and a tingling between my legs. His mouth found mine and I sagged in his arms, he pulled me closer to him, his hands digging into my hips. As the kiss became more heated, I heard someone clear their throat behind me. I pulled out of the kiss and dropped my head to Mason's chest, I was so caught up in him I'd forgotten that we weren't alone and I felt my face flush. I could hear Mason chuckling as he wrapped me in his arms.

"Hey Jack, how you doing?" Mason asked him over my head.

I heard Jack let out a small laugh. "I'm good, although I wish you'd stop kissing my sister in front of me, I don't need to keep seeing that."

"Jack!" I exclaimed, turning to face him. Mason wrapped his arms around me from behind and pulled me back against his chest.

"Relax Lib, I'm joking, sort of. It's obvious that he makes you happy, and with everything you've been through you deserve some happiness."

I smiled gratefully at him and felt Mason tighten his grip on me, pressing his lips to my head. I grabbed Mason's hand and pulled him towards the blanket. "Can you stay for a while?" I asked, looking over my shoulder at him.

He smiled at me. "I can stay for a bit sweetheart. I've got a riding group to lead this afternoon."

Mason sat down on the blanket with his legs open, I sat in between, scooting closer to him so that my back was resting on his chest. His arm snaked around my waist, and I relaxed against him. "Everyone is heading out for a drink tonight; do you mind if we go after we've had our date?" I turned my head and looked up at Mason. "Jack's leaving in a couple of days, and I'd love to spend some more time with him?"

"Of course we can go sweetheart. I want you to spend time with Jack while he's here." He

bent his head and brushed his lips against mine. Pulling away he turned to Savannah. "Where are you meeting?"

"I'm not sure, I'll have Brody text you the details." She reached for her phone, firing off a text to Brody.

I felt Mason's phone vibrate in his pocket "That was quick!" He said, pulling his phone from his jeans pocket. I turned around kneeling up in between his legs. I watched his eyes flash with anger and his jaw tense as he read the message.

"Mason, what's wrong?" I asked him, concerned. "Is it Brody?" I rested my hands on his thighs, squeezing his leg gently when he didn't answer me.

"Yeah, it's Brody, there's a problem, I need to go. I'm sorry I can't stay longer baby." He reached for me, kissing me on the nose. He looked at his phone as another message flashed up, his hands gripped his phone tightly, his knuckles turning white. "I've really got to go. I'm sorry baby."

"That's okay, I understand that you have to work. Do you need any help?" I asked him, worried about how angry he seemed.

"No, no, you stay here and enjoy yourself. I'll see you at my place later, come over about six." He muttered, distracted by another message on his phone. He kissed me on the cheek and ran to the truck, pulling away quickly leaving a cloud of dust behind him.

"What do you think all that was about?" I asked Savannah, who was lying on the blanket with her eyes closed.

"Who knows." She shrugged, not opening her eyes. "Probably a disgruntled guest, there's always somebody moaning about something."

I looked over to where Mason had sped off in his truck, he seemed angry for it just to be a disgruntled guest, but what did I know. "Yeah maybe." I murmured, not convinced.

The afternoon passed quickly, Jack rode to the house and brought us back some lunch which we ate under the shade of a large oak tree. We spent the time, chatting, swimming and sunbathing before deciding to head back to the house. Savannah and Jack were competitive on the horses and decided to race back, galloping off I could hear them laughing in the distance. I wasn't an overly confident rider, so I stuck to a steady trot, arriving back at the stables a good five minutes after them. Jack was waiting for me.

"I thought you'd got lost." He mocked, laughing at his own joke.

"Ha ha! Not everything has to be a race, Jack." I smacked him in the stomach, before making my way into the house. I laughed as I heard him groaning behind me.

After showering, I chose a dress to wear for my date with Mason, hanging it on the bathroom door ready to put on just before I went to meet him. I still had an hour to kill before that, so I reached for my phone, texting my parents to say hello and to let them know that I was okay. I didn't expect a reply back as they would be asleep, so I grabbed my kindle and read for a while. After I had finished my book, I started to get ready, curling my hair in loose waves down my back and applying a bit more makeup than I usually wore. Happy with how I looked, I grabbed my bag and went to find Savannah and Jack to say goodbye. I found Savannah in her room studying.

"Wow Lib, you look amazing," Savannah exclaimed as I entered her room.

I gave her a twirl and laughed. "Thanks, Sav. I'm heading to Mason's now, but I'll see you later at the bar." I bit my lip. "Is Josh going tonight?" I asked cautiously, not wanting to upset her.

"Urgh! No idea, I haven't asked Brody. He usually comes if Brody goes out, let's just hope if he comes he leaves Averi and her grabby hands at home!" She gave me a small smile before jumping off her bed and coming over to hug me. "Have a great time Lib, don't do anything I wouldn't do!" She said with a wink.

I laughed. "I'll try my best, can't make any promises, though," I told her, returning her wink.

I heard her chuckling as I closed the bedroom door behind me and went downstairs in search of Jack. I couldn't find him anywhere, so I guessed that he was somewhere with Brody.

I made the short walk over to Mason's cabin taking in the beautiful surroundings, I inhaled deeply, loving the smell of the country air. As I got closer to the cabin I heard raised voices, one of which I recognised as Mason's, the other was the voice of a woman, a woman whose voice I'd have trouble forgetting. Amber.

"What are you doing here? I thought I told you earlier to stay away." I heard Mason say, his voice full of anger.

I frowned, what did he mean by earlier, was that who was

texting him when we were at the lake? Why didn't he tell me? Why did he say it was Brody?

"I needed to see you, please Mason, we can make this work." Amber cried.

"No!" Mason exclaimed. "I don't want to be with you Amber, why can't you understand that!"

I was stood on the porch now and could clearly hear all of their conversation. I wasn't sure if I should knock and go in, or just go back to the house.

"Amber, what are you doing? Shit! Put your top back on, have you got no self-respect!" Mason shouted.

On hearing that, I flung the door open to see Amber standing topless in Mason's lounge. Mason spun around as he heard the door open, a look of horror on his face when he saw it was me.

"Libby, this isn't what it looks like I promise." He blurted out. "She just turned up at my door five minutes ago, I thought it was you, so I just called out for her to come on in. The next thing I know she's taking her top off!" He looked at me, panic evident on his face.

"It's fine Mason," I told him calmly. I walked past him to where Amber's top was lying on the floor, reaching down I picked it up and threw it at her. "I think you need to leave Amber. Mason has made it very clear he doesn't want you here."

"He's lying, we've been in bed together all afternoon, he text me asking me to come over, said his English girlfriend wasn't giving him what he needed." She smirked at me.

"That's not true!" Mason exclaimed.

I turned to Mason and gave him a reassuring smile, before turning back to Amber, my face like thunder. "I don't believe you, Amber. Unfortunately for you, I trust Mason, plus I heard most of your conversation before I came in. Like Mason says, have a bit of self-respect and stop throwing yourself at a man who clearly isn't interested. Now get out!" I managed to stay calm until the end of my speech before I screamed at her to get out. I saw her eyes widen and she took a small step back from me. She quickly pulled her top on and picked up her bag.

"Just you wait and see, he'll be interested soon enough." She muttered to herself as she strutted past me, running her fingers across Mason's chest as she passed him.

Mason grabbed her hand and pushed it away before guiding her forcefully through the door, slamming it shut behind her.

Mason came to stand in front of me. "Are you okay baby? You're shaking." He reached for me, pulling me into his chest. I went willingly into his arms, inhaling his familiar scent.

After a while, I moved my head to look up at him. "I really hate her Mason; why won't she leave you alone?"

"I wish I knew sweetheart." He said with a sigh. "She won't win though Lib; I won't let her come between us." He bent his head and kissed me, before he could deepen the kiss I pulled back.

"Was it Amber that text you earlier, at the lake?" I whispered, dropping my eyes from his. He lifted my chin with his fingers until I was forced to look at him.

"No baby, it was Brody. He text to tell me that Amber was on the ranch and that she was looking for me."

"Why didn't you tell me?"

Mason took a long, slow breath in before exhaling quickly. "I didn't want you to be upset. I wanted to get rid of her as soon as possible and not have to worry you. I'm sorry Lib."

"So, has she been here with you all afternoon? I thought you said she only knocked on the door five minutes ago?" I asked him, confused.

"When I left you at the lake, she was waiting here for me. I made her leave, I thought that would be the end of it. She was only here for a few minutes, I never thought she'd come back." He hesitated.

"You do believe me don't you Libby? None of what she said was true."

"I know Mason; I do believe you. She's not going to go away, though, is she? She seems pretty determined to get you back." I bit down on my bottom lip, feeling self-conscious.

"I was never with her; I was never hers to try and get back. It was never like that with us. I meant what I said earlier, I won't let her come between us. You mean too much to me."

"What are we even doing Mason? I'm going to be back in England in a few weeks, what's going to happen then. It's not like we can carry on seeing each other, how would that even work?" I removed myself from his arms and took a step back.

"Don't Lib." He reached for me, but I took another step back. "I don't have all the answers but please don't push me away because you're afraid." His eyes were pleading with me to listen to him.

I shut my eyes and sighed. "I am afraid Mason, I'm afraid that I'm falling in love with you, and that I'll be going home with my heart in a worse state than it was when I came here." I opened my eyes to see his face breaking out into a breath-taking smile. I gasped when the realisation of what I'd just admitted to him hit me. He moved towards me, taking my hands in his before I had a chance to stop him.

"You're falling in love with me?" He asked, his eyes dancing with excitement.

"No! No, I just…I just meant that I could see myself falling in love with you. I'm not in love with you now." I rushed out, looking at the ground. "That would be madness, we've only known each other just over a week." I couldn't believe I'd blurted out that I was falling in love with him, it was too fast, too soon!

"I'm not falling in love with you either." I heard him say, my stomach sinking with his admission. He reached for my chin again, lifting it until I was looking at him. "I'm not falling in love with you because I've already fallen baby, head over heels. It might be fast, and as you say, madness, but I love you, Libby."

I stared at him with wide eyes, he couldn't love me, could he? "I don't know what to say Mason, this is crazy." I couldn't tell him I loved him too, not yet. I was too afraid to say it out loud. It somehow made it more real to voice it, and while I felt it, I wasn't ready to admit it yet.

"You don't have to say anything sweetheart, I know you're scared of getting hurt. I don't know what the future holds and how we can be together when you're on the other side of the world, but what I do know is that I love you and we will work through whatever is thrown at us. Please don't push me away."

He made it sound like we could overcome anything, even the 5,000 miles that could soon separate us, maybe, just maybe he was right, and I should take that chance. "Okay," I whispered.

He smiled, his whole face lighting up again. "Just promise me that you'll talk to me if you get freaked out or worried about anything."

"I will, but the same goes for you with Amber, I want to know if she comes around again, even if you think it might upset me."

"Okay, sweetheart." He guided me towards him, capturing my lips with his. His tongue brushed my bottom lip, and I opened my mouth for him, as he deepened the kiss I heard him moan into my mouth. After a few minutes, he broke the kiss, resting his forehead on mine. "I need to stop sweetheart or we'll never make it out tonight. You still want to go and watch the sunset, don't you?" He asked me, looking a little unsure.

"Of course, if we haven't missed it." He took my hand and guided me outside. Walking hand in hand to the truck, he led me to the passenger side, opening the door for me, he helped me climb in.

As he leaned over to fasten my seat belt, he whispered. "You look beautiful tonight baby."

"Thank you." I murmured, smiling shyly at him.

It was only a few minutes' drive to the lake, but Mason held my hand the whole way. Because of the drama with Amber, we only had about ten minutes to watch the sunset, but it was spectacular. Mason had brought a duvet which he lay on the flatbed of his truck, and we sat together with our backs to the cab entwined in each other's arms. "Thank you for bringing me here, it's beautiful," I told him, quietly.

"I thought you'd like it." He replied with a smile. We sat in comfortable silence before he asked me. "Will you tell me about Mia? What was she like?" He must have felt me stiffen in his arms. "You don't have to sweetheart. I didn't mean to upset you."

"You haven't upset me; I'm just not used to talking about her, but I want to." I turned slightly so that I was still in his arms but facing him.

"She was great, a pain in my ass most of the time, but I wouldn't have changed her for the world. She rescued me on the first day of primary school. I was stood alone on the playground, and she ran over to me, telling me we'd be the best of friends. She was the complete opposite of me, loud and outgoing. Everyone loved her. We were like sisters, we did everything together, her parents worked long hours so she spent a lot of time at our house and I always hoped she'd end up with Jack, I'm sure he liked her." I gave him a small smile and snuggled into his chest. "There was never any question that we wouldn't go to the same university, we were studying different subjects but still managed to spend our free time together, and we shared a house with a couple of other girls. We were in our second year of university when the accident happened."

"What were you studying? Are you planning on going back?" Mason asked me.

"Yeah, I guess, eventually. I was studying English Literature. I'll probably stay closer to home rather than go back to Manchester. Too many memories, good and bad." I let out a laugh.

"What's so funny?" Mason asked me, smiling.

"I was just thinking about fresher's week in our first year. Mia was a nightmare that week, she made me go to every party that was on. I had to hold her hair back while she threw up on three separate nights that week!" I sat up on my knees and faced Mason. "Thank you for asking me about Mia, it feels really good to talk about her."

"I would have loved to have met her." He leaned over and kissed me on the lips.

"She would have loved you! She had a thing for cowboys. Actually, she had a thing for boys in general!"

Mason laughed. "And what about you? Do you have a thing for cowboys?" He pushed me back gently so that I was lying on the duvet, his body pressing down on mine. My breathing accelerated, and it felt like a million butterflies were dancing in my stomach.

"Just one cowboy in particular," I told him quietly, reaching my hands up, threading them through his dark hair.

"Anyone, I know?" He teased.

"I think you know him," I whispered, pulling his head down to mine. I kissed him hungrily, and he quickly responded, deepening the kiss, his tongue invading my mouth. He pulled away slightly and kissed down my neck, nipping at my skin with his teeth before soothing it with his kisses. I moaned and arched my back as his fingers brushed my breast on their way down my body. I gasped as his hand traced up my bare leg and under my dress, stopping on the inside of my thigh.

Mason brought his lips to my ear and whispered. "Is this okay Libby?" I nodded, my body was on fire, and I didn't trust myself not to beg him to touch me. His hand moved further up my thigh towards my knickers, his fingers gently brushing across them. His mouth was back on mine, and I moaned against his lips. His fingers slowly began to rub against me, and I felt the same build up low in my stomach as I had last time. His hand slipped inside my knickers, and he gently pushed a finger inside me, his thumb now stroking me.

"You're so wet, baby." He whispered in my ear.

His words turned me on even more, and I writhed beneath him, my heart racing and my breaths coming out in gasps. His other hand came down to my breast and began pinching my nipple through my dress, this pushed me over the edge, and I called out his name as I came.

"You are so beautiful when you come Libby." He murmured, kissing around my jaw before taking my mouth again. I blushed at his words, but thankfully it was dark enough that he couldn't see me.

"I want to touch you, Mason," I whispered, feeling his erection against me.

"As much as I want you to sweetheart." He said, resting his forehead on mine. "We need to go and meet the others. I don't want you to miss seeing Jack."

"I suppose." I pouted, dropping my head back on the duvet. Mason laughed, lying down next to me he pulled me into his arms.

"We have plenty of time sweetheart there's no rush."

I bit down on my bottom lip, suddenly nervous. "Can I stay at yours tonight?"

"I was hoping you would baby." He paused. "Don't be nervous to ask me Lib, I always want you around, just because you're staying over though it doesn't mean I'm expecting anything to happen."

"You're incredible, you know that?" I whispered, leaning over to kiss him.

He sat up, smiling down at me. "I think you're pretty incredible sweetheart." He paused, staring into my eyes. "We'd better go." He sighed, reaching for my hands he pulled me up and I scooted off the back of the truck. He folded up the duvet and held the passenger side door open for me as I climbed in.

We arrived at the bar ten minutes later and spotted Jack, Brody, Josh and Savannah sitting at a table on the other side of the dance floor. Thankfully I didn't see Averi, and I hoped for Savannah's sake that she didn't put in an appearance. Mason led me across the dance floor, his hand encased in mine. No one from our group had seen us arrive and as we made our way over to them, I watched as Josh and Savannah chatted easily with each other, the tension from the rodeo seemingly gone. I would go as far as to say that there was even some flirting going on between the two of them, they were sitting pretty close to each other.

"Look at Sav and Josh, they look like they are getting on well," I whispered in Mason's ear. I saw him glance at the table before nodding at me.

"It's better than seeing them argue," Mason replied.

As we neared the table, I saw Brody look up. "Hey, the love birds have arrived. Finally," He exclaimed. "Nice of you to join us." He joked.

"Leave them alone. They're cute." Savannah said, standing up as we stopped in front of the table. She pulled me into a hug. "You have fun?" She asked into my ear.

I nodded. "Looks like you're having a good time too," I whispered, gesturing with my eyes to Josh who was staring intently at Savannah.

"We're just talking." She shrugged her shoulders, giving me a sad smile.

"It looked like more than that to me. You looked pretty cosy."

"He apologised for bringing Averi to the rodeo and told me he didn't mean to hurt me."

"He likes you Sav, I'm sure of it. Somethings holding him back, you just need to find out what."

"I need to move on Lib, I'm tired of feeling like this, I can't keep hoping he's going to suddenly want to be with me." She paused and glanced over at him, their eyes met for a second before Josh turned away and began speaking to Brody. She turned back to me. "A guy from school has asked me out a few times, I've always said no. Maybe it's time I said yes."

"Maybe it is," I told her. I didn't want to push her into waiting for Josh if she had the chance to be happy with someone else. "Come on, let's get a drink."

The bar was quiet as it was mid-week and we pretty much had the place to ourselves. After a few drinks, we moved to a room at the back of the bar where there were two pool tables. The guys played pool while me and Savannah sat and chatted. Mason would make his way over to us every so often, checking if we needed drinks and to steal a kiss. I noticed Jack watching Mason every time he came over to me, after the last time, Jack pulled Mason to one side. There was no music playing in the pool room, and I concentrated on trying to listen to their conversation.

"You seem serious about my sister," Jack asked him.

"I am Jack. I know we haven't known each other long, but I've never felt this way about anyone before."

I watched as Jack nodded. "She likes you a lot too, I can tell." He paused. "She's been through a lot Mason. I don't know how much she's told you, but I'm not sure she could take being hurt anymore." I smiled to myself, as much as this was an embarrassing conversation to listen to, I couldn't help but feel a rush of love for Jack and his protection of me.

"She's told me everything. I'm not going to hurt her Jack; she means too much to me." I heard Mason say. "You've got nothing to worry about." Jack nodded again and stuck his hand out for Mason to shake. Mason took it and pulled Jack in for a one-armed guy hug. Mason's eyes found mine, and he smiled. "Come here, sweetheart." He called out, holding his hand out for me. "I'll show you how to play pool."

It turned out that I was useless at pool, much to the delight of Mason who seemed to enjoy trying to teach me. Every shot I took he pressed himself against my back as I leaned over the table, his hands covering mine on the pool cue, he'd put me in the correct position before moving his mouth to my ear and asking if I was ready. His breath on my ear, and having him pressed right up behind me was distracting in the best possible way, but it meant I couldn't concentrate on what I was doing. I just wanted to push him against the wall and kiss the hell out of him. He was fully aware of my body's reaction to him as I'd hear him chuckle each time I missed the shot. I could tell that he was getting just as worked up as I was as I could feel his erection pressing against me.

After about five missed shots I'd had enough. "I think you need to take me home Mason." I murmured, his body still pressing me against the pool table.

"And what do you want to do once we get home sweetheart?" He asked, his lips brushing against my neck making me shiver.

"Take me home, and you'll find out," I told him, sounding braver than I felt. He pulled me up and spun me around to face him. He looked at me through hooded eyes before taking my hand and guiding me towards the exit.

"We'll see y'all tomorrow." He shouted to the others. I heard them all laughing behind us as we quickly made our way out of the bar.

Chapter Eighteen

We arrived back at Mason's about fifteen minutes later. Like every other time he had driven me anywhere, he held my hand the whole way home, stroking his thumb across the back of my hand, my body tingling with the anticipation of what was to come. He parked the truck and slowly made his way around to my side, his eyes watching me through the windscreen. Opening the door, he reached into the cab, his hands going around my waist as lifted me from the truck. I instinctively wrapped my legs around him as he lowered his head to kiss me. I heard the slam of the truck door as he carried me towards the cabin, his mouth never leaving mine. He pressed my back against the front door as his tongue snaked into my mouth. I kissed him back eagerly, reaching my hands up to run them through his hair. He fumbled in his pocket for the keys, and after a few minutes, he managed to open the door and carry me inside.

He broke the kiss and gently dropped me to my feet. "Is this too fast Lib? I don't want to rush you." He looked down at me, his eyes full of concern.

I smiled at him shyly. "Well, I thought that we didn't have to do… everything?" I watched his mouth curve into a smile, and he reached for me again pulling me into his chest.

"What did you have in mind sweetheart?" He asked, grinning down as me.

"I think you can work it out." I murmured into his chest.

"I think I can too." He whispered, picking me up again and carrying me up the stairs to his bedroom.

He put me down next to his bed. Standing in front of me, he reached his fingers up to sweep my hair behind my ear, and then traced them around my jaw. My breathing increased as his fingers stroked down my neck, he leant down kissing me softly on the lips, I reached my arms around him and pulled him closer deepening the kiss.

"God Lib, I could spend all day kissing you and never get tired of it." He murmured against my lips, kissing me again while his hand slipped down from my waist to stroke my thigh, my body trembling under his touch. He broke the kiss taking a step back and turning me so that I was facing away from him, he moved my hair over one shoulder and placed soft kisses in the nape of my neck. I felt his fingers reach for the zip of my dress and he pulled gently exposing my back to him, my breathing became laboured as I felt his fingers brush my spine. He spun me around to face him before letting my dress drop to the floor, I stood in front of him in just my bra and kickers.

"I don't know what I've done to deserve you Lib, but I'm never letting you go. You are so beautiful."

I smiled and dropped my eyes from his. "I think you're wearing far too many clothes cowboy," I told him, pulling his t-shirt over his head and dropping it on the floor next to me. I ran my hands up his arms over his shoulders and down his hard chest, stopping at his belt. My hands were shaking, and I fumbled with the buckle. Mason reached down and removed my hands, undoing it himself.

"Breathe sweetheart." He whispered, scooping me up bridal style and placing me on the bed. I sat up on my elbows and watched him as he pushed down his jeans, kicking them off. He stood in front of me wearing only a pair of tight black boxer shorts, my mouth went dry at the sight of him. He was absolutely gorgeous. He saw me watching him, and his mouth curled up into a smile. "You're staring again Lib." He teased.

"Yep! I am! I'm just looking at what's mine." I told him with a smirk, repeating his own words from yesterday.

"I'm all yours baby." He said as he climbed on the bed, lying next to me.

I turned on my side so that we were face to face, I felt his fingers trace up and down my bare thigh as we stared at each other.

"I love you Lib." He whispered as he leaned towards me brushing his lips against mine, my heart stuttering at his words. The kiss started off softly but soon turned heated as our tongues battled together. He rolled me onto my back, lowering his body over mine and pressing me down into the mattress. His hand reached under my knee, and he wrapped my leg around his back. I could feel him hard against me, and he ground his hips against mine, his erection hitting me right where I needed him. I arched my back in an attempt to get closer to him and moaned into his mouth, his other hand reached around my back to undo the clasp on my bra. He slowly peeled the straps down my arms, taking his time as if he were unwrapping a present, he then tossed it over the side of the bed, his eyes focused on my naked chest. His lips left mine, and he brushed small kisses down my neck continuing until his head was level with my breasts, he swirled his tongue around my nipple, and I gasped as pleasure raced through my body settling between my legs.

"God Mason," I muttered, my hands threading through his hair. He released my nipple from his mouth and moved up my body kissing me again, I hungrily kissed him back my body aching for him. After a few minutes, I pulled out of the kiss and pushed Mason onto his back.

"Are you okay?" He asked me, his voice full of concern.

"I'm more than okay Mason," I told him, sounding more confident than I was. I lay down next to him, nerves bubbling in my stomach. I wanted to touch him, but I had no idea what I was doing. I turned my head and kissed him, tracing my fingers over his chest, biting down on my lip I sat up and straddled his waist, his hands found their way to my hips, and he gazed up at me through hooded eyes.

"You look incredible sitting there Lib." He told me, his voice husky.

I leaned down and kissed him again, I could feel his erection pressing against me, and I moved my hips rocking into him. He moaned into my mouth, his fingers gripping my hips tightly. I continued to rock my hips, encouraged by the sounds that Mason was making and finding that it felt good for me too. I sat up, and he moved his hands from my hips to cup my breasts, his thumbs stroking my nipples. I arched my back pushing my breasts further into his hands.

"That feels so good baby." He said breathlessly, moving his hips against mine.

"Mmmm," I replied, my body moving quicker as the I felt the sensations building inside me. Mason reached his hands around my neck and pulled me down so he could kiss me, his teeth biting gently on my bottom lip before his tongue pushed into my mouth. His hands moved back to my hips, and he moved my body against his, finding a rhythm that felt good for both of us.

Breaking the kiss after a couple of minutes, he whispered breathlessly into my ear. "I'm going to come sweetheart." Hearing his words, I felt myself let go, and I shuddered in his arms. I heard him moan out my name and his fingers tightened on my hips as he came. I dropped my face into the crook of his neck breathing heavily. His arms snaked around my body, and he held me close to him. "I haven't come in my underwear since I was a teenager." He murmured into my hair, amusement evident in his voice.

I lifted my head to look at him. "Was it okay?" I asked him nervously.

"Baby, it was incredible, you are incredible. When you're ready, and we do make love, it's going to be explosive." He gently kissed my nose.

"I love it when you do that," I whispered.

"Do what sweetheart?"

"Kiss my nose." I paused and smiled. "Stupid I know," I told him shrugging my shoulders.

"It's not stupid, I love kissing you anywhere." He rolled me onto my back, kissing my nose again. "I need to go and clean up darlin'." He reached on the floor for his t-shirt, motioning for me to sit up he pulled it over my head. "Do you need anything?"

I shook my head at him and pulled the duvet over me, loving the feeling of being wrapped up in him, his scent surrounding me. I was going to have to sneak one of his t-shirts in my bag so that I could wear it to bed when I wasn't sleeping over. I let out a contented sigh and found that my eyes felt heavy, closing them I sank into Mason's mattress quickly falling asleep.

I stirred as I felt Mason pulling me into his arms and kissing me on the head. "Night, sleepyhead." I heard him whisper. "I love you."

"I love you too." I murmured sleepily. Looking up at him I saw a huge smile on his face, closing my eyes I fell back to sleep safely folded up in his arms.

"Libby! Libby wake up!" I heard Mason frantically calling out to me, his hand gently shaking my shoulder. My eyes flew open, and I sat up, my heart racing and my body covered in sweat. "Sweetheart are you okay? You were having a nightmare." He said to me gently, sitting up next to me. I turned to look at Mason and saw his face full of concern.

I closed my eyes in an attempt to calm down, my trembling hands reached for Mason, and he pulled me onto his lap. I nuzzled my face into his neck, breathing in his familiar scent. "I'm okay, I'm sorry I woke you."

"Don't apologise baby. I'm just glad I was here with you; I wish I could take away your pain. Do you want to talk about it?" He stroked my hair, my heart rate calming at his touch.

"What was I doing? Was I screaming?" I asked him quietly, cringing into his neck at the thought that he'd seen me like that.

"Yes." He paused. "And shouting out for Mia. Were you dreaming about the accident?" I nodded my head, and I felt his arms tighten around me.

After a few minutes, I reluctantly pulled my head out of the safety of his neck and looked up at him. "It's always the same dream, the van hitting us and the sound of metal hitting metal, I don't think I'll ever forget that sound. Mia's screaming my name, desperate for me to help her, but I always wake up before I can reach her." I didn't realise I was crying until Mason reached his hand up and wiped my tears away with his thumb. He didn't say anything; he didn't need to, there was nothing to say. He simply lay me down, wrapped me in his arms and stroked his fingers up and down my back until I felt my eyes closing and sleep taking me.

I woke up the next morning stretching my arms above my head, I turned over to find Mason's side of the bed empty. I sat up listening for any sounds that might indicate that he was downstairs, but I was met by silence. My stomach fluttered with nerves, had he changed his mind about us now that he'd seen how messed up I was? I closed my eyes and shook my head, no that couldn't be it, he was so supportive last night, I was just jumping to conclusions, my insecurity taking over. I scooted to the end of the bed and dropped my feet to the floor, looking up I saw a note on the chest of drawers along with a bunch of wildflowers. Picking the note up my nerves disappeared as I began to read.

Morning Sweetheart,

Sorry, I'm not there to kiss you good morning, I had an early fishing trip to lead. You looked so beautiful sleeping in my bed I couldn't bring myself to wake you, and after last night I thought you could do with the rest. Help yourself to anything you want, feel free to take a shower... I'm already imagining you naked and soapy!!

Text me when you wake up.

Love you

Mason xxx

A huge smile came over my face, and I picked up the flowers he'd left me, bringing them to my nose and inhaling deeply. I loved that he'd gone to the trouble of writing me a note and picking me flowers. I found my phone and fired off a message to him.

Me: *Morning babe. Thank you for the flowers I love them xxx*

I made my way downstairs making coffee in the small kitchen before flopping on the sofa to drink it. My phone vibrated on the table, and I reached for it seeing that I had a text from Mason. Grinning like an idiot, I read it.

Mason: Hey baby, glad you liked the flowers, how are you feeling after last night? Xxx

Me: I'm okay, I'm sorry you had to see me like that xxx

Mason: Stop apologizing Lib. I want to be there for you xxx

Me: Well thank you, I'm glad you were xxx

Mason: What are you up to? Are you still at my place? Xxx

Me: Yep, just sat on your sofa drinking coffee. Might have that shower in a minute... xxx

Mason: Arghhh you're killing me, baby! Xxx

I laughed out loud at Mason's last message, I wasn't going to have a shower there, I was going to head back to the ranch house and hang out with Jack. Savannah had a full day at university so it would be just him and me.

Me: Just kidding... heading back to the house in a min to spend the day with Jack. How's the fishing going? Xxx

Mason: Tease!! I'm just supervising, Taylor's in the water with them xxx

Mason: Lib, do you remember everything from last night? Xxx

I frowned at my phone, what did he mean? Was he talking about my nightmare?

Me: Do you mean my nightmare? I think so?? Why? Xxx

Mason: No reason baby. I'd better go, Taylor's calling me. Have a good day with Jack. I'll call you later. Love you xxx

Did I say something I shouldn't have last night? I thought back but couldn't figure out what he meant. I'd have to ask him later. I finished my coffee and picked up the flowers before heading back to the house. Jack was in the kitchen when I got there.

"Hey Lib," Jack said with a smile as I sat down in the seat next to him.

"Morning."

"Have a good night?" Jack asked, wiggling his eyebrows at me.

Blushing I replied. "Yes, thanks."

"My little sister's finally in love." He teased, eyeing the bunch of flowers I'd put down on the table.

"I'm not in love..." He raised his eyebrows at me sceptically. "Okay, okay! I might love him." I sighed. "God Jack what a mess! Why did I have to fall for someone who lives thousands of miles away." I dropped my head on the table in front of me.

"I wish I could tell you it will be okay Lib." He squeezed my shoulder.

"Oh shit!" I suddenly sat up, remembering what I'd said to Mason last night.

"Libby, what's wrong? You've gone really pale." Jack asked me, concerned.

"I think I told Mason that I loved him last night?"

Jack burst out laughing. "What do you mean, you think you told him? How can you not know?"

"I was half asleep, and he told me he loved me, and… oh god! I remember saying I love you too, before falling back to sleep."

"I'm confused, if he loves you, and you love him, then why is telling him such a problem?"

"Because I'm not ready to be in love with him Jack!" I exclaimed. "We've only known each other just over a week, how can I be in love with him!"

"What are you afraid of Lib?" Jack asked me quietly.

I closed my eyes, I couldn't hide from him, he knew me too well. I whispered. "Losing Mia broke me, and now I've allowed myself to fall for Mason, if I lose him too…" I trailed off. "I'm going to have to go home at some point and leave him here." Jack stood up and pulled me up with him, wrapping me up in a hug.

"You have to decide if he's worth taking that risk Lib, but it sounds to me like your heart's already decided for you. Sometimes love hurts, but surely, it's better to have had Mason's love than to never have known it. I know you're scared but what if it all works out? What if Mason's the one to fix your broken heart?"

I looked at him in shock, I'd never heard Jack talk like that, it sounded like he was talking from experience. "Where did all that come from?" I asked him, pulling out of his arms to look at him.

He shrugged his shoulders and dropped his eyes from mine. "I missed my chance with Mia. I stood by and watched while all those idiots she went out with treated her like shit." He sighed and looked at me. "I waited too long, and now it's too late. If Mason makes you happy, and I can see that he does, don't be afraid to love him. You can make it work if it's what you both want."

"Why didn't you tell me how you felt about Mia?"

"You were so lost after she died, you didn't need me adding to your pain."

"Oh, Jack. Why didn't you ever tell Mia?"

"I thought I had time, you were both off at Uni, and I was travelling, I just figured when we were all back in the same place I'd tell her how I felt." He smiled sadly at me.

"I'm so sorry Jack."

"Don't miss your chance Lib, if Mason's who you want, find a way to make it work." He stood up walking over to the sink with his mug. "I'm going to have a shower. Fancy taking the horses out for a bit?" He asked me, changing the subject.

"Yeah, that sounds good," I told him with a smile. "I need to shower too; I'll meet you back here in a bit." He nodded, stopping to kiss me on the head as he went past.

Under the hot spray of the shower, I replayed Jack's words in my head. Although I'd suspected that he had liked Mia, his feelings for her obviously ran deeper than I thought. I had been so swept up in my own grief after she had died, I'd never noticed that he was grieving as well. I felt awful that I hadn't been there for him. I thought about what he'd said about Mason, I desperately wanted it to work, and I was pretty sure Mason felt the same. I decided that I was going to go for it, stop worrying about the future and live in the now. I knew better than most that the future wasn't guaranteed, and that life could be snatched away from you in the blink of an eye.

Chapter Nineteen

Jack's last two days went by far too quickly, and before I knew it, we were saying goodbye. Uncle Ryan was driving him to the airport, but I'd chosen not to go with them opting to say my goodbyes at the house, saving myself the long car ride.

The previous two days we had spent riding and swimming and just spending time together. It was great to spend some time just the two of us, it had been far too long and who knew how long it would be before we would do it again.

His last two nights at the ranch had been spent on a boy's only night that Brody had arranged at a bar in Marble Falls, and then a family meal on his last night. I was really going to miss him. I hadn't seen much of Mason over the last two days, he'd been working both days, and we hadn't had the chance to meet. Aunt Claire and Uncle Ryan had invited him to the family meal, and he'd sat next to me, his hand stroking my leg under the table. He'd asked me to spend the night with him, but I'd decided to stay at the house to spend the morning with Jack before he left.

After a tearful goodbye, I called out to Savannah, who was studying on the porch swing, telling her that I'd decided to take Cookie out for a ride. I fancied reading my kindle by the lake in the sunshine, escaping into my latest book. Savannah had gone inside to fetch me a bottle of water, and as I waited for her, I felt the hairs on the back of my neck stand up. I spun around quickly feeling like I was being watched, but there was no one there when I looked. I shook my head thinking that I was going mad. When Savannah came back, I thanked her for the water and headed over to the stables.

I hadn't been out alone before, but I knew the ranch well enough to find my way around if I didn't venture too far. I made my way to Cookie's stall. "Hi, beautiful," I said to her as I approached, reaching up to stroke her nose. "Fancy a ride?" I made my way into the tack room in search of her saddle, the smell of the leather invading my senses. As I was searching I heard a noise from the stalls, poking my head around the door, I called out. "Hello?" Assuming one of the ranch hands was in there seeing to the horses, but there was no reply. An uneasy feeling came over me, but I pushed it aside and went back to searching for Cookie's saddle. Finding what I needed I quickly saddled her up, leading her outside into the sunshine. I looked over to the house and saw Savannah waving from the porch, I waved back after I'd mounted her and disappeared around the back of the stables towards the lake, setting off in a steady trot.

It was a beautiful day, and I was looking forward to lying by the lake and reading. After ten minutes or so I was feeling comfortable on Cookie, so I pressed my legs against her encouraging her to go faster. As we picked up speed, the saddle began to move, and I started to slip, I pulled back on the reins but it was too late, the saddle worked loose, and I was flung into the air. A scream came from my mouth before my head impacted with the ground, and I was knocked out.

I was surrounded by blackness, my eyes felt heavy, and as hard as I tried, I couldn't force myself to open them. There was a pounding in my head, and my left wrist was throbbing, my other hand was intertwined with someone's, and I could feel them gently stroking a finger over the pulse point on my wrist. I tried to move my fingers but it was as if my body wasn't cooperating with my mind and nothing happened. There was a constant beeping noise coming from the side of me, and I could hear muffled voices talking, I thought I recognised the voices, but I couldn't place them. Suddenly the fog lifted slightly, and I heard a woman say. "The cinch was cleanly cut, it looked like it had been done with a knife, it was only held on by a thread. I'm surprised she made it as far as she did without falling off. This wasn't an accident Mom, someone did this, and I've a pretty good idea who!" I recognised the voice as Savannah's. I desperately tried to open my eyes, but nothing happened.

"What do you mean, who do you think did this?" I heard a different female voice say, one I recognised as Aunt Claire's.

Then I heard Mason, he must have been close to me as his voice was louder than the others. "Amber, someone I was seeing before I met Libby. We've had a couple of run-ins with her, although nothing like this." Anger was evident in his voice. He must have leaned closer towards me, and I felt his breath against my ear as he whispered. "Please wake up sweetheart. I need to know that you're okay. I love you, baby. I'm so sorry this happened." I felt him press his lips to mine in a soft kiss.

"God Mason! Why would she do this? Are you sure it was her?" Aunt Claire asked.

"I wouldn't put it past that psycho bitch!" I heard Savannah say, fire in her tone.

"I really don't know Claire, but I don't know anyone else who would want to hurt Lib. She has this deluded idea that we should be together and hasn't taken too kindly to me dating someone else. Have you managed to get hold of Libby's parents yet?" Mason asked.

"No, I haven't been able to contact them; I'll keep trying, though."

I desperately tried to move my hands or open my eyes, I didn't want my parents to know that I was hurt. They were so far away, and they would be so worried. I felt my eyelashes flutter as they began to open, squinting against the bright lights of the room. "Mason." I croaked, my throat dry and scratchy.

"Libby baby, I'm here, you're going to be okay I promise." He said reassuring me, his voice low and full of love. "She's awake, fetch the Doctor." I heard him say to someone behind him. My eyes were slowly adjusting to the light, and as they began to focus, I could see Mason sat next to me holding my hand. His face was a mask of concern, but he smiled at me when our eyes met. "Thank god sweetheart. You had me scared there for a while." He stood up and gently brushed his lips against mine.

"Where am I? What happened?" I asked him, confused. As he pulled away from me I saw Savannah standing behind him along with Brody and Uncle Ryan, I gave them a small smile before returning my gaze to Mason, waiting for him to respond.

"You fell off the horse and hit your head, you're in the hospital. You've been unconscious for quite a while, and because of your previous head injury the Doctors have been worried." As he said that Aunt Claire came back into the room, followed by a man in a white coat who I assumed was the Doctor.

"Hello Libby, I'm Dr. Carter, how are you feeling?"

"I'm okay, my head hurts, and my arm is sore." I looked down at myself for the first time since I woke up and realised that my arm was in a plaster cast. "Is my arm broken?"

"I'm afraid so, it's a relatively clean break, but you will be in a cast for about six weeks, as for your head, you sustained quite a nasty bump when you were thrown from the horse, and we've had to stitch a small gash in your hairline. You're going to have some bruising from where you fell, and you'll probably find yourself stiff and sore tomorrow. You've been unconscious for about an hour while you've been here but were not sure how long you were on the ground before someone found you. We did a CT scan when you first arrived, and there is no bleeding or swelling to the brain, so that's good news. Do you remember if you were awake at any point after you fell?" He asked me with a kind smile.

"I don't think so, I don't really remember much, one minute I was riding Cookie the next I woke up here."

"Don't worry too much about not being able to remember, it may come back to you." He came over to the side of the bed. "I just need to shine a light in your eyes." He told me flashing a bright white light at me. "It all looks good, try and get some rest. We'd like you to stay overnight as a precaution, but you should be able to go home tomorrow. The nurse will be in shortly to take your vitals. If you've got any questions, the nurses will be happy to page me."

"Thank you," I whispered as he left the room. Mason moved back from my bed so that Aunt Claire could reach me, she came over and pulled me into a hug, taking care not to knock my plaster cast.

"I'm so glad you're okay honey." She said hugging me tightly.

"Have you spoken to my parents?" I asked her as she released me.

"No sweetheart, I haven't been able to contact them. Both of their cell phones are turned off, I'll keep trying, though. I didn't want to leave a message and have them worry."

I grabbed on to her hand. "Please don't tell them, they will be so worried, and they are so far away, plus I'm fine, I'll be back to the ranch tomorrow. Please?" I begged her, my eyes wide.

"Libby, I'm not sure that I can do that. If it were Savannah or Brody, then I'd want to know." She frowned at me, chewing on her bottom lip.

"Please Aunt Claire, I've been such a worry to them over the past few months, I don't want to burden them with anything else. I really am okay, I promise." I heard her sigh, and she turned to look at Uncle Ryan who raised his eyebrows at her and shrugged his shoulders.

"Okay." She reluctantly agreed, shaking her head at me. "But I'm calling them if anything changes. No arguments."

"Thank you." I rushed out, breathing a sigh of relief. If they knew what had happened, they would be on the first flight out here, and I knew that it would be a struggle for them to come.

"We're going to go and grab a coffee now that you're awake, we'll leave you two alone for a bit, we'll be back soon." Aunt Claire said motioning between Mason and me before kissing me on the cheek. Uncle Ryan also came and gave me a hug along with Brody before the three of them left the room. Savannah plonked herself down on the bed next to me and took my hand in hers.

"Bloody hell Libby you scared the crap out of me!" She said dramatically.

"I'm fine. Honestly, just a bit bruised. Tell me what happened." I asked, looking over to Mason. I saw him ever so slightly shake his head at Savannah before coming to sit down on the other side of me. He had obviously decided that he wasn't going to tell me that they thought Amber had tampered with the saddle.

Savannah spoke first. "Well I waved you off from the porch swing, do you remember that?" I nodded at her, and she continued. "About forty-five minutes later Cookie came wondering down to the stables with her saddle hanging off and you nowhere to be found. I called Mason who was out at the river, and he came straight back. I wasn't sure where you'd gone, but Mason said how much you love the lake, so he headed there while I called Mom and Dad." Savannah looked over to Mason.

"I found you not far from the lake, lying on the ground

unconscious, I didn't know if you were dead or alive when I first saw you. I've never been so afraid Libby." He pulled me to him gently so as not to hurt my arm. "When Savannah called me and said that Cookie had come back without you..." He trailed off, shaking his head. "I called the EMT's when I found you, and they brought you here, I came in the ambulance with you, and everyone else followed. Ryan came straight from the airport."

"Does Jack know?" I asked.

"No, Dad had already dropped him off and was on his way back when we called to tell him what had happened." Savannah stood up. "I'm going to leave you two alone for a bit, I'll go and find Mom and Dad. I'm so glad you're okay Lib." She smiled squeezing my hand.

After she'd left the room, I asked Mason if he would lie on the bed with me. I snuggled into him, resting my broken arm on his chest. "Mason, before I opened my eyes I heard you all talking... was it Amber who messed with the saddle?" I felt him take in a deep breath before blowing it out slowly.

"I think so, I haven't seen the saddle yet, but Savannah got a look at it while she was putting Cookie back in her stall. She thinks the cinch was cut with a knife, it was cut just enough so that no one would notice, but any rigorous movements while riding would have caused it to snap completely which is what we think happened."

"What's a cinch?" I asked, not familiar with the terminology.

"It basically the strap section of the saddle, it goes underneath the horse and keeps the saddle in place."

"Could it just have been wear and tear and it worked loose? Maybe I didn't secure it properly?"

"No sweetheart." I heard him sigh. "It wasn't a tear in the leather, it was a clean cut according to Savannah. It wouldn't have been because you didn't fasten it properly."

"I had just started to ride faster, and as we increased the pace I felt the saddle slip, and I was thrown. I tried to pull back on the reins, but it was too late." I closed my eyes at the memory. "If it was Amber, why does she want to hurt me?" I asked him in a whisper.

"I don't know baby. I'm so sorry, this is all my fault."

"It's not your fault Mason, don't blame yourself. If it really was her, then she has some serious problems."

"Did you see anyone hanging around the stables before you went out?" He asked me. I thought back to hearing the noise while I was in the tack room and feeling uneasy.

"Actually, I felt like someone was watching me while I was outside the house, then, when I was in the tack room, I heard a noise out by the stalls but when I checked there was no one there." I paused, an uneasy feeling settling in the pit of my stomach. "It was Amber, wasn't it?" I asked him.

"I think so, sweetheart. But unless someone saw her hanging around, we're going to have trouble proving it." I tilted my head back and looked up at him, my eyes dropping to his lips. "Kiss me, Mason. Please." I begged him, desperate to take my mind off what had happened.

He smiled, his mouth inches from mine. "That I can do." He murmured, his lips capturing mine in a soft and gentle kiss. I could feel how much he loved me as he kissed me and after what had happened to me today, I realised that life is unpredictable and that I should grasp tightly onto him and never let go.

As he broke the kiss, I looked up into his eyes and whispered. "I love you, Mason."

His eyes widened in surprise before his face erupted into a heart-stopping smile. "I love you too Libby. So much." He brushed his lips against mine again before pulling me into his chest.

I must have fallen asleep in his arms, and when I woke up, Aunt

Claire and the others were back, chatting quietly amongst themselves.

"How are you feeling Libby?" Uncle Ryan asked me.

"I'm okay, my head's still hurting but not as much as before."

"The nurse came in and topped up your pain relief while you were asleep sweetheart," Mason told me, kissing me gently on the head. "I bet that's started to kick in."

"I really want to go home." I felt Mason tense at my words, and I realised what I'd said, looking up at him I waited until his eyes met mine before speaking. "By home I mean back to the ranch." I felt his body relax and he kissed my forehead.

"Libby honey, if you're okay we're going to head back?" Aunt Claire asked me. "I'm assuming that Mason is staying here with you?" She looked over to him.

Before he could respond, I said. "No one needs to stay with me, I'll be fine."

"I'm staying," Mason said forcefully.

Savannah laughed. "Thought he might be, come on let's leave the love birds to it." She came over to me, and I moved out of Mason's arms to give her a hug. "Mason give me a call when she's discharged tomorrow, and I'll come and get you both." I smiled gratefully at her.

After a round of hugs from everyone, and the promise that we'd call as soon as I was discharged, we were left alone. I couldn't let myself think about Amber, and what we would do about her. Mason must have felt the same as he didn't mention her either, it would have to be a conversation we had once we were back on the ranch.

I managed to force Mason to go and get himself something to eat, finally persuading him that I would be okay on my own for half an hour. He was only gone for ten minutes or so, returning with two canteen sandwiches, telling me that he would rather eat with me than alone in the hospital restaurant. I couldn't help but fall in love with him a little bit more at how insistent he was at taking care of me.

Throughout the afternoon and early evening, the nurses were in and out taking their observations and making sure I wasn't sleeping for long periods of time. They had warned me that I would need to be woken every two hours through the night because of the head injury, so I knew that I was in for a long night. Mason had managed to charm the nursing staff into letting him stay the night, and I was currently curled up next to him, resting my broken arm on his chest.

"You really don't have to stay you know Mason, you're not going to get much sleep wedged on this tiny bed," I told him.

"Lib, I want to be here with you. I'd get even less sleep if I were at home, I'd only be worrying about you. I'm staying."

"Thank you," I whispered.

"Let's get some sleep sweetheart, it's been a long day." He tightened his arms around me, and I turned my head to kiss him goodnight. "I love you." He murmured against my lips.

"I love you too," I told him, before melting into his kisses. Breaking the kiss, he pulled me closer into his chest and exhausted from the day's events I quickly fell into a deep sleep, feeling safe in his arms.

Chapter Twenty

I woke the next morning to find myself alone in the hospital bed, looking to the side of me I saw that Mason was fast asleep in the chair. Sitting up slowly every inch of my body ached, the full effects of the accident showing themselves on my bruised and battered body. I was exhausted, the nursing staff, like they had said, had woken me every two hours through the night as well as taking my blood pressure and pulse. I was eager to get back to the ranch and back to my bed, I just hoped that I wouldn't have to wait too long to be discharged.

I pulled myself out of bed and slowly made my way to the bathroom, feeling dizzy I grabbed onto the sink before looking up at my reflection, I gasped at what I saw. There was blood matted in my hair from where I had cut my head, and underneath my eye, there was a large bruise starting to form. I traced my fingers over my bruised face, wincing at the pain. I turned and looked at the shower, desperate to feel the hot water on my skin. I was pretty wobbly on my feet and wasn't sure if I could manage to shower alone, maybe I could ask a nurse to help me. A knock on the bathroom door pulled me from my thoughts.

"Sweetheart, are you okay? Can I come in?" I heard Mason ask, his voice full of concern.

"Come in," I called out. I was still clutching onto the sink when he opened the door, he glanced down at my hands gripping the side and rushed over to me.

"Why didn't you wake me, Libby, you shouldn't have gotten out of bed on your own. Are you feeling dizzy?"

I nodded my head. "A little, I'm okay. I'd love a shower though I feel yucky. Could you buzz the nurse to help me?"

"I'll help you baby; you don't need to ask the nurse."

"You'll help me in the shower?" I asked him my face flushing with heat.

"Yes, Lib. I'll go and ask the nurse for a cover for your cast, so it doesn't get wet." He walked out of the bathroom, returning seconds later with a chair. "Sit down there, and I'll help you with your clothes when I come back." He said, guiding me by my elbow into the chair.

"Mason, I'm not sure it's a good idea. I can just ask the nurse." He'd never seen me completely naked before, I wasn't sure I wanted the first time he did to be in a hospital bathroom. "I'm covered in bruises."

"Sweetheart, you are the most beautiful woman I've ever seen, with or without bruises. It's my fault you're hurting, please let me help you."

"Okay," I told him reluctantly. "But Mason, what happened, in no way was it your fault. You couldn't have known that Amber would do what she did."

He shook his head. "If I hadn't been thinking with my dick and slept with her, she wouldn't be in our lives now. I'm the reason she tried to hurt you. I had no idea that she would be capable of doing anything like she has, but I do now, and I don't intend to let her get anywhere near you again." He kneeled down in front of me and gently took my face in his hands, looking deeply into my eyes. "You are the most important thing in my life, and I'll do whatever it takes to keep you safe Lib."

"You don't think she's going to try anything else, do you?" I asked him, panic bubbling in my stomach.

He sighed. "I don't know sweetheart, but I don't think we can rule anything out." He pulled me out of the chair and into his chest, wrapping his arms around me. I winced in pain as his arms squeezed my bruised body. He released me immediately and took a step back. "Libby, did I hurt you?" He asked, concern lacing his voice.

I stepped towards him taking his hand. "I'm just a bit sore, you didn't hurt me," I told him reassuringly.

I saw him breathe a sigh of relief. "Come on, let's get you showered. I'll just run and fetch that cover for your cast."

He disappeared out of the bathroom, and I began to remove the hospital gown that must have been put on me yesterday when I was admitted. I was nervous for Mason to see me naked, but I was desperate for a hot shower, and he seemed determined to help me. I needn't have worried; Mason was the perfect gentleman. He stripped down to his boxers and even though I felt like shit my body came alive at the sight of him. Putting his arm gently around my waist he guided me towards the shower area, reaching out to turn the water on. He held me back until the water was warm and then ushered me under the hot spray, careful to avoid the stitches on my head. I closed my eyes, savouring the feel of the water massaging my bruised body. I felt Mason step up behind me and gently snake his arms around my waist, his front pressed to my back. I dropped my head back against his chest relishing the feeling of being safely wrapped in his arms.

"Let me wash you." He whispered in my ear. I nodded my head, and he reached for the soap, gently lathering up my back. He turned me around and did the same to my front, my face flushing with heat as he carefully washed my breasts, taking extra care around my bruised ribs. "What about your hair baby?" He asked me softly.

"I don't think I can get my stitches wet just yet, so we'll have to leave it."

"Okay, let me clean the blood off your face, I won't get your stitches wet." I nodded at him, and he gently wiped my face with a flannel he found by the sink, his eyes never leaving mine.

After we had both dried off, he helped me to put on a clean hospital gown. I didn't have any clothes to wear as the ones I was wearing when I had the accident were covered in blood and dirt.

"Thank you, I feel so much better after that," I told him.

"You're welcome sweetheart, I'm going to find the Doctor and get you out of here." He kissed me softly on the lips before heading out of the room.

A couple of hours later I was discharged with strict instructions from the Doctor to rest for the next few days. He told Mason that I would need to be woken again through the night, because of my head injury. Savannah had arrived with clean clothes for me to change into and finally, we were on our way back to the ranch. Although I had only been in the hospital overnight, with everything that had happened, it felt like I had been away from the ranch for days.

Aunt Claire was waiting for us on the porch as we pulled up the driveway. "I'm so glad you're home honey." She exclaimed, pulling me into a hug as we climbed the porch steps. "Come on I've made you all some lunch."

After eating lunch, I had a pounding headache and felt exhausted. "I think I'm going to lie down for a bit, I'm exhausted," I announced, standing up and wobbling on my feet.

Mason rushed to my side, taking my arm to steady me. "I'll help you upstairs. Don't get too comfy in that bed, though, I want you staying at my place for the next few nights so that I can look after you."

I looked at him in shock. "You want me to stay at yours?"

"Yes baby, I want you close, I need to know that you're okay."

I smiled up at him as he led me upstairs. "Alright." I murmured.

He helped me into bed and pulled the covers over me, kissing me gently on the forehead he whispered. "Close your eyes sweetheart. I'll stay with you until you fall asleep." I smiled up at him gratefully, struggling to keep my eyes open. Within minutes I was flat out.

I spent most of the afternoon sleeping, being woken once by Savannah to check that I was okay, I quickly fell back to sleep eventually waking late afternoon. My body seemed to ache even more than it had this morning, I guess I would feel achy and sore as the bruising came out. I reached for my phone which was by the side of my bed and sent a text to Mason.

Me: Hi baby, I'm awake. What are you up to? Xxx

I used the bathroom while I was waiting to see if Mason replied, I had no idea if he was working, so I wasn't expecting an immediate response. Looking in the mirror as I washed my hands I grimaced at my reflection, my hair was plastered to my head, and the bruise on my face was turning a dark shade of purple. I couldn't do much about my face, but I was desperate to get my hair washed. I wondered if Savannah was free to help me wash it while avoiding my stitches. I hadn't heard my phone chime with an incoming text, so I headed downstairs to look for Savannah.

I found the house empty when I got downstairs. Thankfully I wasn't feeling nearly as dizzy as I was this morning and I grabbed a bottle of water from the fridge as I passed the kitchen. I made my way outside noticing a police car parked next to Savannah's car, my stomach churned with nerves, and I walked quickly down the porch steps, my eyes searching for everyone, where were they all?

"Libby." I heard Mason call. I turned towards the barn to see him walking towards me. "I've been trying to call you sweetheart, I got your message. Are you okay?"

"Sorry, I've left my phone inside. Why are the police here?" He reached me taking my hand in his.

"Lib, Claire, and Ryan have called the police. We looked at Cookie's saddle while you were asleep, it's definitely been tampered with. The cinch had been cut through with a knife, just like Savannah thought. They are speaking with any staff or guests that might have seen anyone hanging around."

My heart was racing, and I couldn't catch my breath, even though I knew at the hospital that there was a possibility that Amber had cut the cinch, now that the police were involved and they were here on the ranch it suddenly felt more real. Mason must have seen that I was panicking. Standing directly in front of me he took my hand and rested it over his heart.

"Deep breaths Libby." He told me calmly. "Feel my heartbeat, count with me, one two three four, one two three four." Repeating the words, he'd spoken to me last week. Looking into my eyes, he managed to pull me from the brink of a panic attack and I felt my heartbeat begin to settle and my breathing even out.

After a few minutes, I whispered. "Thank you."

"Are you okay baby?"

"Yeah, I'm sorry, just seeing the police here makes it real. I know we talked about Amber messing with the saddle, I guess I just hoped we were wrong." He nodded and pulled me into his chest, his familiar scent enveloping me. "How could Amber have known which horse I would be riding, and saddle I would use?" I asked, desperate for it not to be true.

I heard Mason sigh, "I guess she's been watching you sweetheart, she must have seen you out on Cookie when she was at the ranch the other day. If she had enough time in the tack room she could have found Cookie's saddle and cut the cinch." I shuddered in his arms, hating that she had been watching me.

"What have the police said?" I asked him.

"Not much at this stage, they are talking to as many people as they can. They have suggested that unless we can prove Amber was involved there isn't much they can do." He paused and pulled me back slightly so that he could see my face. "They want to speak to you too Lib. It doesn't have to be today, if you're not feeling up to it I can tell them to come back tomorrow?" He looked down at me his face full of concern.

"No, I'll speak to them, I want to get it over with." I smiled up at him, trying to reassure him that I was okay, although I'm sure after witnessing my near panic attack he knew that I wasn't. "Where are they, I'll speak to them now."

Mason led me into the barn, and I spent the next half an hour going over what had happened with Amber, from her verbal attack at the rodeo to her showing up at Mason's cabin. It turned out that no one had seen Amber or anyone else hanging around the ranch yesterday morning, while the police agreed that the cinch had almost definitely been messed with, without proof there wasn't much that they could do. They did offer to go and speak to Amber about what had happened, and ask her to stay away from us. The best that we could hope for was that the visit from the police would be enough to keep her away from us. Maybe she would finally get the message.

The police left about an hour later, we all went back to the house with Mason insisting that I pack a bag and go back to his. I felt a bit apprehensive telling Aunt Claire and Uncle Ryan, thinking that they would want me to stay with them. I knew that they felt responsible for me while I was here. I needn't have worried, though, Aunt Claire was happy for me to go. As I hugged her goodbye, she whispered in my ear, telling me how happy she was for me that Mason and I had found each other. I hugged her tightly, kissing her on the cheek. I said goodbye to everyone else, promising Savannah that I'd call her tomorrow and we'd arrange to do something.

Mason picked my bag up and held my hand with his free one, we slowly walked over to his cabin, and he insisted that I go and lie down while he made us some food. I tried to protest but when he caught me yawning five minutes later he ushered me upstairs, I had to admit that I was exhausted again after dealing with the police. I just hoped that this would be the end of our problems with Amber. Something in my gut, however, told me that it wouldn't be.

Chapter Twenty One

I spent the next few days with Mason. I hadn't expected him to, but it turned out that he had asked Aunt Claire and Uncle Ryan for some time off work to look after me while I recovered. I did try to tell him that I was fine and just needed to rest for a few days, but he didn't take any notice, waiting on me hand and foot for whatever I needed.

I loved spending time with Mason, we watched movies, cuddled on the sofa and got to know each other, talking for hours. After two days of chilling, we decided to go down to the lake for some fresh air. I wasn't going to be getting on a horse anytime soon, so we took Mason's truck.

He'd packed a picnic, and we lay by the side of the lake soaking up the sun. I was lying against his chest, my eyes closed as he stroked his fingers up and down my arm, my body tingling under his touch. "Lib, can I ask you something?" He murmured, gently kissing my head.

"Of course," I replied.

"Have you considered finishing off university here, rather than back at home?" My eyes flew open, and I sat up. Looking at him, he looked nervous and unsure as he waited for my response.

"I haven't really thought about it, why?"

He sighed. "I'm being selfish I know, but I don't want you to go home..." He paused and sat up to face me. "When I found you, after you'd fallen off your horse, I'd never been so scared Lib. I knew that I loved you before then, but God, seeing you lying on the ground, hurt and bleeding..." He trailed off.

I took his hand in mine. "Mason, I'm fine."

"I know baby, I just don't want to let you go." He smiled sheepishly at me.

"Would I even be able to study in Austin?" I asked him, my interest piqued by his suggestion.

"Well...I did enquire about overseas applications, and you just apply directly to the university, there would be tuition fees to consider, though. We could look into it if you're interested? Maybe Savannah would know who we could speak to. What do you think?" He looked apprehensively at me.

I hadn't even thought about studying here, it had never crossed my mind. Now that Mason had mentioned it; I was beginning to love the idea. I'm not sure how my parents would feel about me staying, I would need to discuss it with them. I'd also need to carry on living at the ranch so Aunt Claire and Uncle Ryan would need to be included in any discussions. I felt excitement building in my stomach, this could be the new start that I was looking for. If I went back home and finished Uni, I would still be surrounded by my memories of Mia, while I didn't want to forget her, I was finding it hard to move on at home. Maybe this would be just what I needed to move forward with my life. It also meant that I would be able to stay with Mason, who I was falling deeper in love with every day.

"Lib, you've been quiet for a really long time. If you hate the idea, I understand. Of course, you're going to want to go back home to your parents and Jack." He dropped his eyes from mine, his fingers playing with the edge of the picnic blanket we were sitting on.

"No! Mason, that's not why I was quiet." I reached down and took his hand. "I was just thinking things through, thinking that this could be the new start that I desperately need. Obviously, there would be a lot to discuss and think about, but I love the idea."

"Really?" He asked, his eyes finding mine again, and a gorgeous smile appearing on his face.

I laughed. "Really." I kneeled up, softly brushing my lips against his. "But like I said, there would be a lot to sort out. Maybe we should start by making an appointment to see someone at the university, to see if it's even possible first, before we get carried away? I'll speak to Savannah after dinner tonight." We had been invited to the house for dinner later. Aunt Claire was making my favourite, and I was looking forward to catching up with everyone.

Mason gently pushed me down on the blanket, his body hovering over mine. His eyes dropped to the bruise on my cheek, and I self-consciously touched my fingers to my face. He carefully pulled my fingers away and bent his head, kissing softly along the bruise. With his lips millimetres from mine, he whispered. "Even with bruises, you're the most beautiful thing I've ever seen." I closed the distance between us and kissed him, snaking my good hand through his hair, his tongue stroked against mine and I moaned into his mouth.

I'd missed him touching me. He'd held back since the accident, afraid that he would hurt me, but now I was aching for him. He scattered kisses along my jaw and down my neck. I was panting underneath him, pleasure pulsing through my body. I pulled his head back up to mine, kissing him hungrily. His hand cupped my breast, and his thumb circled my nipple through my top. I arched my back, pushing my breast further into his hand, his erection pressing against my flimsy shorts.

He pulled back, removing his hand from my breast and resting his forehead on mine. "Lib." He breathed out. "We should stop, I don't want to hurt you."

"Don't stop Mason," I whispered against his lips. "You're not going to hurt me. Please." I was practically begging him, but I didn't care. "I'm ready Mason. I want to be with you." I lifted my head and caught his lips with mine. My hips raised to meet his and I heard him moan as he deepened the kiss, our tongues tangling together.

He pulled back again. "Are you sure baby?" He asked, his eyes fixed on mine. "You know that I'll wait, there's no rush."

"I know, but I'm ready Mason. I love you." I told him.

"I love you too sweetheart." He kissed me gently on the lips, making no attempt to deepen the kiss. I glanced up at him, confused when he pulled away again. He laughed. "It's not happening here darlin', the first time we make love you'll be in my bed, not on a blanket in the middle of a field. I don't want anyone other than me seeing you like that."

I glanced around. "Mason, there's no one else here but us," I said incredulously.

"Right now, we're the only ones here, but Brody and Ryan come this way sometimes, as well as any guests that could be wandering around. I'm not taking that risk baby." He leaned down and kissed my nose. I pouted as he stood up. "It'll happen sweetheart, and soon I promise. Come on let's head back." He held his hand out to me, and I reached up to take it. A smile was tugging at the corner of his lips. "It's a turn on to know you want me so badly baby." He whispered in my ear as he pulled me up and into his chest, wrapping his arms around me. My face flushed and I was grateful that my head was buried in his chest. He chuckled, knowing how my body would have reacted to his words.

An hour later we arrived at the house. Aunt Claire had made Frito pie again, and my stomach rumbled when we walked into the kitchen, the smell hitting my nose.

"That smells amazing!" I exclaimed as I walked over to Aunt Claire, who was stood at the stove. She turned and pulled me into a hug.

"How are you feeling honey?" She asked, releasing me and eyeing my bruised face. "I hope Mason's looking after you?" She raised her eyebrows at Mason and then turned to me, waiting for my response.

"I'm good." Mason had made his way over to me and wound his arm around my waist. Pressing myself against his side, I looked up at him. "Mason's looking after me, I'm not allowed to do anything other than lie on the sofa," I said smirking at him.

"Good, I'm glad." Aunt Claire replied, winking at Mason. "Let's eat!"

Savannah must have heard us arrive and she came bounding into the kitchen, making a beeline for me. "Lib!" She screeched as she linked her arm with mine, pulling me towards the dining room. I glanced over my shoulder at Mason who was laughing and shaking his head.

"So," She whispered. "How is it living with lover boy?" She wiggled her eyebrows at me, and I laughed.

"Amazing Sav. He's amazing." I gushed. She clapped her hands together and shouted. "I knew it!"

"Knew what?" Uncle Ryan asked as he came into the dining room followed by Mason.

I shot Savannah a dirty look. "Nothing Daddy, just girl talk." She winked at Mason who looked at me, a smug smile on his face.

"You're in love with him, aren't you?" She murmured in my ear. I shook my head at her, putting my fingers to my lips to shush her. She burst out laughing as we sat down.

The Frito pie was incredible; it was just the five of us as Brody was out for the night and we chatted easily with Mason and Uncle

Ryan discussing work. After we'd eaten and the dishes had been cleaned away, we all went into the lounge to sit down.

"Lib, we've heard from the police today." Aunt Claire said out of nowhere. I turned to Mason who reached for my hand. "They've been and spoken to Amber, they asked her where she was at the time of the accident. Apparently, she has an alibi, she was shopping with her friend all day and came nowhere near the ranch."

"Well, that's a load of bullshit!" Savannah shouted.

"Language Savannah." Uncle Ryan chastised.

"I'm sorry Daddy, but she's obviously managed to get one of her skanky friends to lie for her! Who else would have wanted to hurt Lib."

I felt Mason squeeze my hand. "You okay sweetheart?" He asked quietly. I nodded my head, my eyes focused on our joined hands.

"Is that it then? The police won't do anything? They just believe what she says?" Savannah asked, her voice thick with anger.

"What can they do Sav? We've no proof that she did anything." I replied.

"I'm sorry if bringing it up upsets you honey, but we thought you'd want to know." Aunt Claire said.

"No, I do want to know, thank you for telling me. It wasn't like she was ever going to admit to it anyway. There is always the chance that it wasn't her. Who knows..." I trailed off.

Savannah, sensing that I needed the subject changed, started talking about school and I gave her a grateful smile. I decided that I would wait until it was just the two of us before I spoke to her about university. There was no big rush, I had no plans to leave the ranch anytime soon.

An hour or so later we said our goodbyes. I arranged with Savannah to head into Marble Falls the next day for a bit of retail therapy. Mason wasn't too happy with me going, but I wanted to spend some time with Savannah, and I was feeling a lot better than earlier in the week. He was back at work tomorrow, and I didn't want to be stuck inside, alone all day.

On the walk back to Mason's, my mind was swirling with thoughts of our earlier conversation at the lake. My stomach churned with nervous excitement at the idea of finally being with him. Mason turned to me, pulling our joined hands up to his mouth and gently brushing his lips against the back of my hand.

"Are you okay sweetheart? You're very quiet."

"I'm okay, just thinking." I bit down nervously on my lip.

"I know what you're thinking about Lib, nothing has to happen tonight baby. I meant what I said about waiting."

"I know, but I'm ready. I'm nervous, but I'm ready." I smiled up at him, and he smiled back.

"I'm nervous too sweetheart."

"Why are you nervous? It's not like you don't know what you're doing." I asked him in disbelief. He'd been with loads of women, why would he be nervous. He stopped walking and turned to face me.

"Because it's you Lib." He reached his hands up and cupped my face. "I've never felt this way about anyone, you're it for me sweetheart. None of the others have meant anywhere near what you mean to me." He lowered his face to mine and kissed me gently.

My heart was pounding in my chest at his words, butterflies taking flight in my stomach. I began to kiss him back eagerly, but he pulled his lips from mine. "Let's get inside baby." He whispered against my lips. I nodded and let him lead me to the cabin and straight upstairs to his bedroom.

He pulled me into his body as we stood at the foot of his bed, his arms wrapping around me, trapping my good arm against his chest. "I love you, Libby." He said kissing me on the nose.

"I love you too Mason."

I could feel his heart pounding underneath my hands as he reached for the cotton sundress I was wearing and pulled it over my head, taking care not to snag it on my cast. He dropped my dress to the floor and took a step back, his eyes taking in every inch of my body. I stood in front of him in just a pale pink bra and matching knickers. A burning need flowed through my body as his eyes continued their perusal. "Absolutely perfect." He muttered.

With nerves swirling in my stomach I took a step towards him, pushing my hand under his t-shirt, my fingers tracing across his skin. I felt him shiver as I touched him, a small smile pulling on my lips, loving that he was affected as much by my touch as I was by his.

I moved my hand up his chest, taking his t-shirt up and over his head as I went. It fell from my hand as he picked me up and gently placed me on his bed, my hair fanning out on his pillow.

His body came over mine, his hands on either side of my head.

"You okay?" He asked me. I nodded and threaded the fingers of my good hand through his hair pulling his face to mine.

"Kiss me." I murmured against his lips. He brushed his mouth against mine, his tongue snaking between my lips. As he deepened the kiss, I heard him moan into my mouth. His hand stroked down my body, cupping my breast through my bra, my nipple pebbling at his touch. His kisses moved across my jaw and down my neck, I moaned loudly as he gently bit my neck before soothing it with his tongue.

His hand reached around my back, and he unhooked my bra tossing it over the side of the bed. He placed a wet trail of kisses down my body until he reached my breast, his tongue circling around my nipple before finally taking it into his mouth. His hand lavished attention on my other nipple, and I squirmed underneath him, his focus on my breasts creating a tingling sensation between my legs.

I shamelessly lifted my hips in an attempt to ease the ache between my legs. Sensing my need, Mason released my breast from his mouth with a pop, his kisses trailing a path down over my stomach towards the edge of my knickers.

By now my body was on fire, and my breaths were coming out in ragged gasps. I felt Mason's fingers under the waistband of my knickers, and he paused, looking up at me, I lifted my hips in a silent permission, and he slowly pulled them down my legs. He sat back on his heels, and I felt my face and neck flush with embarrassment as he took in my naked body.

"You are so beautiful, Libby." He told me running his hands up my body until his face was level with mine. Kissing me, his hand traced back down my body, and I felt his fingers slowly stroking me between my legs. I kissed him back urgently, gasping into his mouth as his fingers began to move faster. My hand tugged on his hair as the need inside me built. After a couple of minutes, I felt him push a finger inside me, and I cried out.

"Are you okay?" He asked, his breath warm on my face.

"Yes. Don't stop." I panted, my head falling to the side as he kissed along my jawline. His thumb continued to stroke me, and his tongue was back to teasing my nipple. He inserted a second finger, suddenly hitting a sensitive spot inside me and I cried out his name as I exploded, my hand gripping his shoulder tightly. "Wow," I muttered, looking down my body at him.

I saw a smile tugging at the corners of his mouth as he released my nipple from his lips. He kissed his way back up my neck, nipping along my jaw with his teeth before finally brushing his lips gently against mine.

He rolled off me and stood at the side of the bed. Reaching for his belt buckle, he undid his jeans and pushed them down his legs, slowly stepping out of them. I bit down on my lip as I watched him standing there in just his boxer shorts. My eyes tracked to the delicious v shape at the bottom of his toned abdomen, following the line of his abs with my eyes until it disappeared into his boxers. I could see the outline of his erection through his underwear, and I swallowed nervously.

Smiling at me, he opened the drawer on the bedside table and pulled out a condom, kicking off his boxer shorts he climbed back onto the bed. I watched as he rolled the condom down his erection, my heart pounding out of my chest as he lowered his body over mine kissing me gently. "You okay?" He asked me again. I nodded my head. "I love you Lib." He murmured against my lips before I felt him gently start to push inside me.

I tensed and closed my eyes tightly as he pushed in further, a burning pain making me inhale sharply. "Relax baby." He whispered kissing me. His tongue brushed against my bottom lip, and I opened my mouth to him, eager to deepen the kiss. His hand snaked down to my breast, and he rolled my nipple between his fingers. As my body relaxed he pushed further inside me, stilling when his hips met mine, he lifted his head up. "You're so tight, sweetheart." He panted, his jaw was tense as if he was trying to hold back. "Are you okay?"

"Yes," I whispered. "Please move Mason," I begged as the pain began to ease. He moved his hips and thrust gently against me. I gasped as the burning returned, but nodded my head for him to carry on. I moved my hips against his, and he continued to kiss me, the pain turning to pleasure as he rocked into me. I moaned against his lips, and I heard him groan as I dug my nails into his back.

His pace increased, and his breathing became laboured, sweat covering both our bodies. I could feel a second orgasm building, and he reached his hand between us, stroking me until I felt myself fall over the edge, trembling in his arms. He thrust his hips twice more before I felt him shudder against me, a moan falling from his lips and his head dropping into the crook of my neck. He placed soft kisses along my neck before lifting his head and kissing me tenderly on the lips.

"That was incredible Libby." He murmured against my lips. He gently pulled out of me, and I whimpered at the sting that was left behind. "Are you okay?" He asked me, concern lacing his voice.

"That's about four times you've asked me if I'm okay. I'm perfect Mason," I told him, grinning. "That was perfect, and you're perfect, thank you."

He pulled me against his chest, and we lay in each other's arms, neither of us saying anything, comfortable with the silence. "I need to get rid of the condom baby," Mason said after a while, climbing out of bed. "I'll be back in a second." He leaned over, kissing me softly on the lips before reaching for the sheet and covering my naked body.

I heard him flush the toilet and lock up the cabin before he climbed back into bed, pulling me against him, his front pressing against my back. "How are you feeling sweetheart? Are you sore?" He asked against my hair.

"A little," I confessed. I felt his arm tighten around my waist pulling me even closer to him.

"I'm sorry I hurt you, baby." He whispered.

"I'm not. It was amazing Mason, I'm so glad I waited. I love you."

"I love you too Libby, so much." He rolled me onto my back, his body pressing down on mine. He kissed me until I was breathless and aching all over again. As if reading my mind, he whispered against my lips. "I want to make love to you again sweetheart, but not tonight, you need to rest."

"Tease," I told him, brushing light kisses all around his face. He was right though, my body ached all over, and I was exhausted, not that I was going to admit that to Mason. I didn't want him refusing to touch me again, insisting that we wait until I was better. After what we'd just done, there was no way I wanted to wait long before we did it again!

He laughed and pulled me into his body, resting my cast on his chest. "Sleep baby." He told me.

I nodded and closed my eyes, a smile on my lips as I nodded off.

Chapter Twenty Two

I woke up the next morning stretching my good arm above my head. Muscles I'd never used before screamed out at me in protest, and as I moved to roll over, I winced, feeling an unfamiliar soreness between my legs. I smiled, thinking about last night and how amazing it had been.

"Morning baby," Mason said, his voice thick with sleep.

I looked over at him, his hair was messy giving him that sexy bed hair that I loved, and his face had lines from where his head had pressed against the pillow. My eyes dropped to his naked chest, taking in his sculpted abdomen. The sheet had dropped below his waist, and I could see the trail of hair starting at his belly button, my eyes tracking it as it disappeared underneath the sheet.

My blatant examination of him didn't go unnoticed, when my eyes met with his they were hooded, and his stare was full of lust. "Sweetheart." He said, pulling me on top of him. "I know you must be sore after last night, but if you keep looking at me like that…" He trailed off, his voice husky.

I lowered my head to his. "I wouldn't be opposed to the idea," I whispered against his lips, feeling his growing erection on my stomach. I brushed my lips against his, nibbling along his bottom lip, he opened his mouth and our tongues collided. As the kiss became more heated, he gently rolled me onto my back, careful not to catch my broken arm.

He pulled his lips from mine, his breaths coming in ragged pants. "You have no idea how much I want to slide inside you Lib, but I have to get to work, and what I want to do to you baby, can't be done quickly." Speechless, my stomach clenched at his words and my heartbeat quickened. He took my lips again, this time in a tender kiss before climbing off the bed. I sat up, watching him as he pulled a pair of shorts on. He made his way to the top of the stairs before turning around. "You are staying here tonight, aren't you?"

I hesitated. "Erm, I was going to…if that's okay with you?"

"Baby, I'd have you stay forever if it was up to me." I looked at him, my eyes wide. Laughing at my expression, he jogged down the stairs. "I'm going to run you a bath, it will help with the soreness." He called out, not giving me a chance to argue.

Mason had reluctantly gone off to work, but not before ensuring that I take a bath by physically putting me in it! I had to admit though, that I felt better for it, the hot water soothing my aching body.

A couple of hours later, Savannah and I were sat in her favourite coffee shop in Marble Falls. Mason had already text twice, checking that I was feeling okay, that I wasn't having headaches or feeling dizzy. I smiled down at my phone, loving that he cared enough to check up on me. The waitress brought our drinks over along with two huge oatmeal raisin cookies.

"So," I said to Savannah, once the waitress had left. "I'm thinking of looking into studying at the University of Texas." I looked down at the coffee in my hand, waiting for her reaction.

"Oh my god!!!" She screeched, I turned around to see everyone in the coffee shop looking at us, and I laughed. "When did you decide that?" She asked, bouncing up and down in her seat.

"It was actually Mason's idea, he mentioned it yesterday. Seems he doesn't want me to go home."

"That man's got it bad!" She exclaimed.

I rolled my eyes at her. "I was hoping you might be able to help me out with how I go about applying?"

"Definitely! I'm going to Uni tomorrow, come with me, and we can talk to the admissions office. I can't believe that you might be staying!" She clapped her hands together in excitement. "You've got it bad too, haven't you?" She teased.

I shook my head at her and laughed. "I'd love to stay Sav, it wasn't something I'd considered before, but the more I think about it, the more I want it. I can't imagine saying goodbye to Mason…" I told her quietly.

She reached across the table and clasped my hand. "Well, hopefully you won't have to. So," She said smirking at me. "Have you bumped uglies yet?"

"Savannah," I whisper shouted at her, glancing around to see if anyone had heard her. "I'm not talking about that here!"

"I'll take that as a yes then!" She said smugly. "I want *all* the details later." She exclaimed. I felt my face flush with heat, and she chuckled. "We need to go." She suddenly said, her voice angry.

"What? Why?" I asked her. "I haven't drunk my coffee yet." I saw her glaring at someone over my shoulder, and I turned to see who she was looking at. As soon as I turned around, I wished I hadn't. Amber was stood in the queue to be served, and she was staring right at me. I quickly turned back around to face Savannah. "Come on, let's go," I told her, anger bubbling in my stomach.

As I stood up to go, I saw Amber making her way over to us. I tried to walk past her, but she blocked my way. "Hello again, Libby." She said, her voice dripping with disdain. "That's quite a bruise you've got on your face, and you've broken your arm too." She said, her eyes dropping to my cast. "Whatever happened to you?"

I felt Savannah standing behind me, and I heard her say. "You know exactly what happened to her, you psycho bitch. Now get out of our way."

She moved to the side to let us through. As I walked past her she reached her hand out, grabbing my arm. "Tell Mason I'll be popping by tonight to see him, there's something we need to discuss."

I yanked my arm out of her grasp and turned my body so that I was standing directly in front of her. I clenched my hand into a fist feeling like I wanted to smack her. "What could you possibly have to discuss with Mason? He wants nothing to do with you, Amber." My voice was low as I tried to control my anger.

"It's not really any of your business." She sneered at me. "I did want to tell Mason first, but you may as well know…" She paused, looking me in the eye. "I'm pregnant and it's Mason's baby."

Her words hit me like a fist to the stomach, and I stumbled backward into Savannah, her hands reaching out to steady me. "What?" I whispered. "That's not possible."

"Oh, I can assure you it's possible." She took a step closer to me. "He couldn't keep his hands off me before you came along and ruined everything."

My head was spinning, and I felt as if I was going to pass out. "You're lying." I heard Savannah say from behind me. "Even if you are pregnant, how do you know it's Mason's? Haven't you slept with half of Marble Falls?" She spat at her.

Amber reached into her bag and pulled out a scan picture, holding it in front of my face. "I'm eight weeks pregnant, and there's the proof. I haven't been with anyone but Mason since we started dating. It's his baby." I lifted my head and looked at the picture, my heart breaking at what I saw. "Do you really want to stop us from being a family? Can you live with yourself knowing that you would be keeping Mason from his child?"

"I've heard enough of this shit!" Savannah exclaimed. "We're leaving, stay the hell away from us." I felt Savannah turn me towards the door and push me gently towards it. "Show your face at the ranch, and I'll call the police," Savannah screamed at her as she propelled me outside.

Savannah steered me down the road to where she had parked the car, bundling me inside. "I'm calling Mason." She exclaimed as she got in the car.

She reached into her bag for her phone, and I snapped out of my daze. "No!" I shouted. Her head flew to look at me, and she frowned. "Please," I begged. "Please don't call him."

"Lib, what's going on? Why can't I call him? Please don't tell me you believe her?" She said shaking her head.

"Savannah, she had an ultrasound scan, it was definitely hers, her name was printed at the top. That's not something you can fake."

"She's the town whore Libby!" She threw her arms up in the air. "If she's pregnant, and as far as I'm concerned that's still a big if, she's slept with so many guys she wouldn't have a clue who the father was!"

"I have a horrible feeling she's telling the truth Sav." Tears threatened to fall from my eyes, and as the first tear rolled down my cheek, I felt Savannah squeeze my hand. "I knew everything with Mason was too good to be true. I don't deserve to be happy." I whispered.

"That's bullshit, Libby. You deserve to be happy more than anyone."

"Amber's right, I shouldn't stand in their way. They deserve a shot at being a family. That child needs both its parents."

"I can't believe I'm listening to this." She turned her body so that she was facing me. "Okay, let's assume she's telling the truth and she is pregnant with Mason's baby. He's in love with you, there is no way he would want to play happy families with psycho Amber! Just because he's having a baby with her, doesn't mean he can't be with you. He can still be a part of the child's life."

"Don't you get it, Savannah, that would mean Amber would always be in our lives, she'd never go away. She would eventually come between us. I don't think I can deal with that." I looked at her, desperately trying to make her understand.

"So, you're saying Mason isn't worth it?"

"No! I'm not saying that at all. I love Mason, more than anything. I'm saying I'm not strong enough to deal with all of this. Can you take me back to the ranch please?" I begged her. "I want to go home."

She threw her hands up in the air again. "Fine I'll take you back to the ranch, but you're going to have to face Mason at some point."

"Not if I'm back in England," I whispered, looking away from Savannah and out of the car window.

"You want to go home to England?" She screeched. "I thought you meant home to the ranch. Don't you think you should at least talk to Mason?"

"If I see Mason I'm going to want to stay. It's better this way Sav. I can't stay and watch him have a baby with that woman." My voice shook, and I burst into tears. Savannah reached across and pulled me into her arms.

"God, you mean it, don't you? You're going to leave?" I nodded my head against her shoulder. "Mason's going to be so pissed."

"I need you on my side, Savannah, I'm going to need your help. Please don't hate me." I said, between sobs.

She pulled away from me. "Lib, I could never hate you. I don't agree with what you're doing, and for the record, I think you're making a mistake, but if this is what you want, then I'll support you." I smiled gratefully at her through my tears. "Let's get back." She said, starting the car and pulling out of the parking space.

We were quiet on the way home, neither of us knowing what to say. I couldn't stay and watch Mason have a baby with someone else, especially Amber. It was going to kill me to leave him without saying goodbye, but I knew that if I saw him, he'd convince me to stay. As much as I hated to admit it Amber was right, if I stayed, I would stop them from trying to be a family. I had to go, and it had to be today.

Once we were back at the house, I went to my bedroom and quickly packed my clothes. I had a few things at Mason's, but I couldn't risk going to get them and running into him. When everything was packed, I reached for my phone and called my parents. It was early evening back home, and I was praying that they would be home. The phone rang for a long time, and I began to panic, thinking that they wouldn't answer when I heard my Dad. "Hello." He sounded out of breath, as if he'd just ran for the phone.

"Daddy," I whispered, holding back the tears.

"Libby, sweetheart. What's happened?" He asked, sensing from my voice that something was wrong.

"I need to come home, Daddy," I told him, the tears spilling down my cheeks.

"Why? What's happened? Libby, are you crying." He asked, concern lacing his voice. I could hear my Mum in the background asking my Dad for the phone.

"Libby, honey what's wrong? Are you hurt?" My Mum asked me, panic in her voice.

I hated that I was causing them to worry all over again. "I'm not hurt I promise, but I need to come home. Can you book me the next available flight?"

"Sweetheart, you need to tell us what's going on. Is Aunt Claire there?"

I closed my eyes and took a deep breath. "I can't explain now. I know I'm asking a lot, but I need you to trust me. I'll explain everything when I get home. Please, can you just book me a flight? I'm leaving for the airport now with Savannah."

I heard my Mum take a deep breath. "Okay honey, as long as you're sure you're not hurt? We'll have a look now and call you back." I could hear the reluctance in her voice.

"Thank you," I whispered hanging up the phone.

Half an hour later on the way to the airport my phone buzzed with a message, thinking it was from my parents, I reached for my phone only to see a text from Mason. My heart was in my throat as I opened the message.

Mason: *Hey baby, how are you feeling? Brody and Josh are heading to a bar tonight, do you and Savannah fancy going? Love you xxx*

I burst into tears as I read his message, doubt creeping into my mind, was I was doing the right thing? Mason was going to hate me when he realised that I'd just upped and left. I bit down on my lip as I reread his message.

"Is that Mason?" Savannah asked me with a sad smile. I nodded my head, not trusting myself to speak. "It's not too late Lib, I can turn back."

I shook my head. "No, this is for the best."

"The best for who." She muttered.

I glared at her. "The best for Mason. The best for me! I thought you were going to support my decision."

"I don't think Mason would agree that this was what's best for him. I know I said I'd support you, and I am, I'm driving you to the airport, aren't I? But I think you're panicking and running away from the problem." She looked over at me, her eyebrows raised in question.

"So what if I am?" I replied, crossing my arms over my chest. "I was wary about getting involved with Mason in the first place, maybe this is fate telling me I was right." I took in a deep breath, letting it out slowly. "I know you don't agree with me Sav, and maybe I am making a huge mistake, but I can't keep letting myself get hurt. I know I'm hurting Mason too and that kills me."

Savannah reached across the car and patted my knee. "I know you're scared Lib, I just wish you'd talk to him."

I looked out the window, there were so many things running through my mind, I hadn't even had a chance to get nervous about the journey, that was the least of my problems. My phone rang in my hand, and I jumped at the noise, my heart beating wildly in my chest at the thought that it could be Mason. Looking down I saw that it was my parent's number. "Hello," I said as I answered the phone.

"Honey its Mum, we've booked you onto the 3 pm flight to O'Hare International, and then you're booked on a flight from there to Manchester. We couldn't get you on a direct flight to Heathrow until the morning. Is that okay?"

"That's great, thank you, Mum," I said quietly.

"I really wish you'd tell me what's happened, sweetheart. You're worrying me."

"I'm okay Mum, I'll fill you in when I'm back."

I heard her sigh. "Okay. I'll text you the flight information, we'll be waiting at the airport for you when you land. We love you, Libby."

"I love you both too. Bye." I whispered, pushing the button and ending the call.

We arrived at the airport and Savannah linked her arm with mine as we walked to the check in desks. "I'm going to miss you Lib," Savannah said quietly.

"I'm going to miss you too." I stopped to pull her into a hug.

"I don't know how long I can keep from telling Mason where you are, he's going to freak. Just promise me that once you're back home, you'll call him and explain."

I nodded, I couldn't promise her that I would, I knew that if I heard Mason's voice, I'd crumble and want to rush back into his arms.

After checking in, I said a tearful goodbye to Savannah and went through to departures. Mason had text again, and I ended up turning my phone off. I hated myself knowing that I was hurting him. If I stayed and fell even more in love with him, if that were even possible, the hurt would be ten times worse for both of us further down the line. It was better to leave now, even though it felt like my heart was breaking.

It was just over a two-and-a-half-hour flight to O'Hare International Airport, and I had an hour layover before catching the flight to Manchester. I realised pretty quickly that I'd left my kindle at Mason's in my rush to leave. I don't think I could have read anyway as my head was all over the place. I just stared blankly out of the plane window, lost in memories of Mason, my heart breaking a little bit more each time I thought of him. Tears tracked down my face, and I let them, not attempting to wipe them away.

After we had landed, I made the mistake of turning my phone on. I had twenty-three text messages, twenty-two of which were from Mason and eight voicemail messages. There was a text from Savannah and I opened that one first.

Savannah: *Mason knows, and he's beside himself Lib. Please call him x*

I closed my eyes and dropped my head back against the chair I was sitting in. The pain in my chest at knowing I'd hurt him was unbearable. I reached my hand up, rubbing over my heart in an attempt to ease the ache. I opened the last of Mason's messages, my heart pounding in my chest.

Mason: Libby sweetheart, I know you'll be on a plane right now but as soon as you get this, call me, please. IF Amber is carrying my child, I still want to be with you. I will support the child, but I don't want to be with Amber. I love you. Please call me xxx

Once again tears streamed down my face, and I couldn't read anymore, I knew if I did I'd be boarding the next plane back to him. I reluctantly turned my phone off and sat silently waiting to be called for my next flight.

I didn't have to wait long, and before I knew it, I was on my way home. I'd only been in Texas for two weeks, but they had been the best two weeks of my life. Meeting Mason had shown me that there was life after Mia, and I would be eternally grateful to him for that. He was starting a new chapter of his life with a baby on the way, and now somehow, I had to restart my life, I just had to learn to do it without him by my side.

I only hoped that I could.

Chapter Twenty Three

After what felt like the longest night of my life, I finally touched down in a wet and cold Manchester. My parents were waiting for me when I came through arrivals. I threw myself into my Mum's waiting arms and broke down crying.

"Libby sweetheart, whatever's wrong? What happened to your face, and your arm?" My Mum asked in a panic, her arms tightening around me.

"Oh, Mum." I sobbed against her shoulder. "Everything is such a mess."

She gently pushed me away from her, her fingers reaching out to trace the bruise on my face. "What happened Libby?" Her eyes bore into mine, pleading with me to tell her.

"I fell off a horse and broke my arm," I told her through my tears, lifting my cast to show her. "The rest are just bruises. I was only in hospital overnight, I'm fine."

"Hospital!" She shouted. "Why didn't you ring us? Why didn't Claire ring us?"

"Don't be mad at Aunt Claire, I begged her not to tell you. I didn't want to worry you."

"Libby, you should have told us. Is that why you've come home?" She asked.

"No, yes, partly…" I muttered, shaking my head. My Dad pulled me in for a hug and kissed me gently on the head.

"Come on, let's get you home, you can tell us in the car what's been going on." My Dad said, taking my suitcase off me with one hand and wrapping the other around my shoulder, guiding me out of the airport.

I was quiet for the first half of the car ride home, staring out of the window, watching the countryside go by. It would be the middle of the night back at the ranch, I wondered if Mason was sleeping, hoping that he didn't hate me. My Mum's voice broke into my thoughts.

"Please tell us what happened Libby, my mind is thinking all sorts of things."

I sighed, taking one last look out of the window before dropping my eyes to my hands, my fingers picking at the plaster cast on my arm. Starting at the beginning, I told them everything, how I'd met Mason and reluctantly fallen in love with him, how Amber had confronted me at the rodeo, screaming at me that she belonged with Mason and then about the saddle strap being cut and me falling off the horse. Both of them stayed quiet, letting me get it all out until I mentioned the accident, and I saw out of the corner of my eye my Dad gripping the steering wheel tightly, his knuckles turning white.

"So, are you saying that this girl, Amber, cut through the saddle strap on purpose, hoping that you'd fall off and hurt yourself?" My Dad asked through gritted teeth. His head turned to me, and I nodded slowly.

"Bloody hell Libby, you could have been killed!" He cried. "What did the police say?"

"They spoke to her, but we had no proof, and she denied she'd done it, so…" I trailed off. I saw him shake his head.

"So, that's why you came home? Why the rush? What aren't you telling us Lib?" My Mum asked quietly from the back seat.

"That's not why I left. Savannah and I were at a coffee shop in Marble Falls yesterday, and Amber turned up. Turns out she's pregnant with Mason's baby, she had a scan picture and everything." I reached my hand up and wiped away the tears that were rolling down my face. "I couldn't stay knowing he was having a baby with her. I had to leave to give them a chance to be a family." I whispered. I felt my Dad's hand reaching for mine, and I held on to his hand tightly.

"Does this boy love you, Libby." My Dad asked me, squeezing my hand.

"I think so, yes," I said turning to look at him.

"And you love him."

I nodded. "More than anything."

"And what does he think about you coming home?" I dropped my eyes from his and bit my bottom lip. "He doesn't know, does he?" My Dad said gently.

"No" I murmured.

"Why haven't you spoken to him, sweetheart?" My Mum asked from behind me.

"Because if I had, he would have convinced me not to go. I couldn't stay and watch him have a baby with Amber. I hate her Mum."

"I understand Lib, but you need to talk to him. If he loves you like you love him, he must be worried sick."

"I will, just not yet." All I wanted was to get in my own bed, I was beyond exhausted. I was hoping that I would go to sleep and find that when I woke up, it had all been a horrible dream.

Thirty minutes later I was home and wrapped up in my duvet. I'd taken one of Mason's t-shirts from the first time I'd slept over at his place, and I'd put that on, his smell enveloping me. I pulled the neck of his t-shirt over my nose and inhaled, breathing in his scent. If I closed my eyes, I could imagine his arms around me and his lips on my neck. Tears rolled down my cheeks, and I pulled my arms around my body, eventually crying myself to sleep.

I woke up drenched in sweat, a scream escaping my lips. Sitting up, I put my hand over my racing heart and took in a deep breath. My mind wandered back to the dream, and I shook my head, it had been about the accident again, but this time it was Mason sitting in the front seat instead of Mia.

Swinging my legs over the side of the bed I forced myself to get up. Reaching into my bag, I dug out my phone, apprehensive as I turned it on. Looking in the mirror I took in my reflection, my hair was sticking up, and my eyes were red-rimmed as if I'd been crying for hours, which I guess I had been. As I turned away my phone started going crazy with incoming messages. I sighed and looked down, ten voicemails and eighteen text messages, not all from Mason, though. A couple from Savannah and one from Aunt Claire.

Reading the messages from them made me feel like shit. Aunt Claire seemed mad that I'd just upped and left, I couldn't really blame her, and Savannah was begging me to contact Mason. I threw my phone on the bed leaving it there while I went downstairs. I couldn't deal with it.

I'd slept for a few hours, and it was early afternoon, the house was empty which explained why no one had come into my room when I woke up screaming. I found a note on the kitchen table from my parents, my Dad had gone to work, and my Mum was at the supermarket. I was relieved to be on my own so that I could wallow in self-pity.

The home phone rang, I picked it up without thinking that it might be someone I didn't want to talk to. "Hello," I said as I reached into the fridge for the orange juice.

"Libby it's me, Savannah." She rushed out.

"Savannah," I said in surprise. "Hey."

"Why aren't you answering your cell?"

I took a deep breath, she sounded pissed, and I learned from a young age that pissing off Savannah wasn't a wise thing to do. "I've only just woken up; my phone's been switched off since I landed. Sorry."

I heard her huff down the line. "I'm glad you've managed to sleep." I heard her mutter under her breath. "Libby, Mason's a mess. He's not slept a wink all night. None of us have. Don't you care what you've done to him?" She asked, exasperated.

"Don't you dare Savannah. Of course, I care, it's because I care that I've left. I'm doing what's right." I shouted down the phone.

"Bullshit! You never even gave him a chance before you ran." She shouted back. "You ran because you're scared Lib." Her voice softer. "And I get that, I do, but you can't run every time you think you might get hurt. At some point you have to take a chance, risk your heart, and have faith that it will all work out, that's part of loving someone."

"I took a chance Sav, I let Mason in after my heart was crushed when Mia died, and this is what happened. You know what Amber is like, if I'd stayed she would be making our lives hell. The last thing I wanted was for Mason to have to choose between his child and me. I would never ask him to do that, and that's the reason I've left."

"Can you live without him though Lib?" She asked quietly.

"I'll have to. I don't have a choice." I said sadly. "I have to go. There's someone knocking on the door." I lied, desperate to get off the phone.

"Okay, but please just text him, so he knows you alright, he's going out of his mind."

"Okay...bye Savannah." I whispered, putting the phone down. It killed me to think that I was hurting him as much as Savannah said, but I just couldn't see a way around it. She was right though I needed to contact him.

I made myself a sandwich but couldn't bring myself to eat it. My stomach was churning, and I'm sure had I tried to eat it I would have thrown it back up.

Knowing that I had to contact Mason, I made my way upstairs to find my laptop. I had too much to say to him to send him a text message, I thought an email would be better. Grabbing my phone, I fired off a quick message to Savannah, asking her if she knew his email address. I didn't have to wait long for a reply from her with his address. I opened my laptop and began what was probably the hardest thing I'd ever had to write.

To: Mason Walker
  Subject: Sorry
  From: Libby Davis

Mason

I'm so sorry.

I'm sorry I left without saying goodbye, I knew that if I saw you, I wouldn't be able to leave you. After I'd seen Amber and she'd told me her news, I knew that I couldn't stay. She would forever be in our lives, trying to tear us apart. I would never want you to have to choose between your child and me. I would never ask you to do that, but I can't stay and watch you have a baby with her.

I love you, but maybe we were just never meant to be together. The distance and now Amber and the baby have come between us, it's better that I left when I did, than down the line when more feelings are involved.

I want you to know that these past two weeks have been some of the best weeks of my life. You showed me that I was capable of loving again after losing Mia, I can't thank you enough for that.

You're going to make an amazing Dad, and maybe one day we'll meet again.

Please don't hate me. I never intended to hurt you.

Love
  Libby x

I hovered my finger over the send button, tears falling from my eyes. It was the final goodbye, and I needed a minute before I could push the button. The pain in my chest made me feel like someone was stabbing through my heart with a knife. With a deep breath, I clicked send and broke down sobbing on my bed.

I must have fallen back to sleep, and when I woke up, it was dark. My body clock was all over the place, and I guess that after sleeping until now, I would be awake all night. I checked my phone and saw that it was 10.30pm. The house was quiet, so my parents must have already gone to bed. My stomach rumbled, and I realised that I hadn't eaten anything in about twenty-four hours.

After fixing myself a sandwich I brought it back upstairs, sitting on my bed to eat it. My laptop was lying next to me, and I turned it on, wondering if Mason had received my message. A huge part of me was hoping for a reply. I couldn't help it; I was still madly in love with him and needed to know that he didn't hate me. Clicking on my emails, I saw that I had a message from him. With nerves fluttering in my stomach I opened the message.

To: Libby Davis
  Subject: Re. Sorry
  From: Mason Walker

Libby. Thank god, you're okay. I've been so worried baby. I could never hate you. I love you.

Please don't do this, don't end us, I'm begging you. I love you so much, Libby.

Savannah's told me that you think I should make a go of things with Amber for the baby's sake. That will never happen Lib. I will take care of my child, but I want nothing to do with Amber. She's driven away the woman that I love, and I will never forgive her for that.

I won't let her come between us. Please come back to me. We can make this work, I know we can.

Please call me, I need to hear your voice baby. I miss you so much.

Always remember I love you. I'm not giving up on us.

Mason
  xxx

I read his message over and over again, not knowing how to respond. I wasn't going back, I couldn't, not with Amber hanging around. I considered not replying, but I needed to let him know that this message would be my last. It was too hard to hear how much he loved me, when all I wanted to do was run back into his arms. Clicking the reply button, I began my response back.

To: Mason Walker
  Subject: *Re. Sorry*
  From: *Libby Davis*

Mason

This is too hard. I physically ache at being away from you, but I can't come back. I'm sorry. I hate that I'm hurting you. We both need to move

233

on somehow, the only way I can even attempt to do that is to break
contact.

I wish things could have been different.

I'm sorry.

Bye Mason

Love
  Libby x

I closed the laptop and lay down staring at the ceiling. I was all out of tears, all I had left was a pain in my chest, a pain like nothing I'd ever felt before, not even when I knew Mia had died. I felt physically sick at the thought of never seeing Mason again. He would move on and meet someone else, and I would become a distant memory. My stomach rolled at the thought, and I jumped off the bed rushing to the bathroom. I made it just in time, throwing up into the toilet.

Sitting on the floor, I leaned back against the bath and closed my eyes, my breathing erratic. My heart was racing, and my fingers were tingling, I knew that a panic attack was coming. I desperately tried to calm my breathing down and count my breaths. My hand went over my heart, and I started to count the beats like Mason had done with me. I thought of his voice and his touch, and after a few minutes my fingers stopped tingling, and my breathing had calmed down.

Mason had helped me more than he knew in those few weeks that I knew him. Was I making a terrible mistake? One that I would regret forever. My heart screamed yes, but my head was undecided. I guess only time would tell.

Chapter Twenty Four

The next week dragged by, Mason had sent more emails, but I'd deleted them, unread, not able to face what he had to say. I knew my parents were worried about me as I was living in my bedroom, only coming out to shower and I could barely be bothered to do that.

I'd cleared my phone of old texts and voicemails, but Mason still text me first thing in the morning and again every night. I read those messages, and they made me cry. He told me how much he loved me and that he wanted his words to be the first thing I read in the morning and the last thing I read at night. I was beginning to look forward to his messages even though I knew I'd get upset. I never replied to him, but my lack of response didn't seem to stop him.

I know I needed to snap out of my funk, but I just couldn't. My parents had suggested that I ring Sarah and see about going back to work. I promised them that I would, but I hadn't found the energy to do it yet. I wasn't sleeping much, I would fall asleep in the day, an hour here or there and just lie awake all night, unable to switch my mind off.

Savannah had kept in touch, and we had skyped a couple of times. I'd asked her not to talk about Mason, but Savannah being

Savannah had taken no notice. She'd told me that Amber was hanging around the ranch, and had even tried to move some of her stuff into Mason's cabin while he was out working one day. Apparently, Mason had gotten mad at her and physically escorted her off the ranch himself. She was obviously trying to establish herself in his life now that I was no longer in the picture.

I'd been at home just over a week when I woke up from a fitful night's sleep, feeling like I needed to see Mia. I threw some clothes on and grabbed my phone, noticing that I hadn't had my usual evening or morning texts from Mason. My heart clenched at the thought that he'd probably had enough of being ignored, and had given up. I couldn't blame him; I knew this day would come.

I padded downstairs finding my Mum in the kitchen. "Hey Mum," I said, reaching in the fridge for some juice.

"Morning sweetheart." She said, trying but failing to hide the shock on her face at seeing me up and dressed. "How are you feeling?"

My parents had tried numerous times to talk to me since I'd come home, but I'd brushed them off, telling them that I didn't want to talk about it. "I'm okay. I'm going to visit Mia's grave. I'll be back in a bit." I said, finishing off my juice and putting my glass in the sink.

"Okay honey, I'll see you later then." She replied with an encouraging smile. I gave her a small smile back before leaving the kitchen and heading for the front door.

It was a short walk to the cemetery, and when I got to Mia's grave, I sat down in front of her headstone, brushing some dirt off with my good hand. I sat in silence for a while staring at the letters that made up her name. "God Mia, I've so much to tell you. I wish you were here. I miss you." I said, my words being carried away on the wind.

I spent the next hour or so pouring my heart out to her. I felt close to her here, and I had hoped to feel better after talking to her, but I didn't. Wiping the tears from my eyes I stood up, tracing my fingers along her name, something I had taken to doing every time I visited. As I turned to leave, I noticed Mia's Mum, Mrs Green, sitting on the bench across the cemetery. When she saw that I was leaving, she stood up and started to make her way over to me.

My heart pounded in my chest, I hadn't seen her since she visited me in hospital. I had avoided her, knowing that she blamed me for Mia's death. Now she was standing right in front of me, and I had no idea what to say to her.

"Libby honey, how are you?" She asked, throwing her arms around me. I was taken aback by her greeting, and it took me a few seconds to hug her back.

"Hello, Mrs Green," I said shyly, dropping my eyes to the ground when she pulled out of the hug.

"I saw you talking to Mia, and I didn't want to interrupt, I sat on the bench until you'd finished."

I lifted my eyes to hers. "Oh, I'm sorry, I didn't realise you were waiting or else I would have gone sooner." I rushed out, my cheeks flushing.

I saw her frown, and she reached for my hand, holding it in her own. "No Libby, I want you to spend as much time as you want with Mia. I know how much you've struggled since she died. I didn't mean that I wanted you to hurry up your visit. You're welcome here anytime you want. Mia loved you, and I love you too."

I looked at her in surprise. "You do?" I asked her.

"Of course I do, why would you think otherwise?" She asked me, frowning again.

"I just thought…" I trailed off, not knowing how to say what I meant.

"You thought what honey?" She prompted.

I took a deep breath. "I thought when you visited me in the hospital, that you blamed me for the accident, that you wished it was me who had died instead of Mia," I whispered.

I heard her breath in sharply, and her hand came up to cover her mouth. "Oh Libby, is that why you've been avoiding us all this time?" She asked. I nodded my head. "I am so sorry that we gave you that impression, that is definitely not the case sweetheart. We were grieving and distraught, but we would never have wished that you had died instead of Mia." She pulled me in for another hug and held me tightly. "We just wanted to know that you were okay. I'm so sorry." She said again.

"It's okay," I told her. "I should have talked to you, it's my fault."

"It's no one's fault honey, just a misunderstanding." She paused before changing the subject. "Your Mum told me you'd gone to your Aunt's ranch in Texas. Did you have a good time?" She asked me with a smile.

I attempted a smile back and nodded my head, not wanting to talk about it. "I'd better go, I'll leave you to talk to Mia," I told her, turning to leave.

"Libby, don't be a stranger, me and Mia's Dad would love to see you, if there is ever anything you need, you know where we are." She hugged me again before I left. It was a relief to know that Mia's parents didn't blame me for her death. I'd spent the last five months avoiding them, afraid to see the pain etched on their faces when they looked at me, when in reality it had all been in my head.

I walked back slowly, I was in no rush to go home, it wasn't like I had anything to do when I got there. I needed to decide what I was going to do with my life, back at the ranch I was considering Uni, maybe I should look into finishing my degree here.

As I closed the front door, I could hear muffled voices coming from the kitchen. Not feeling up to making conversation, I crept past the closed door and started up the stairs. When I was nearly at the top, I heard my Mum call out. "Libby honey, is that you? Can you come in here for a minute?" I closed my eyes and let out a sigh. I slowly turned around and came back down the stairs.

I put my head around the kitchen door, hoping that I could just say hello and escape up to my room. My Mum was standing with her back to me making a drink. "Did you want me, Mum?" I asked her.

"There's someone here to see you, Libby." She said, turning to face me. She gestured with her hand to the kitchen table.

Looking over towards the table my eyes widened in surprise. "Mason." I gasped. "What are you doing here?"

He pushed his chair back and walked the short distance to me. "You left this sweetheart." He said, holding up my kindle. He stepped closer towards me so that there were only inches separating us. My heart pounded, and butterflies swarmed in my stomach.

"You came all this way to bring me my kindle?" I whispered in disbelief.

He reached his hand up and brushed his fingers over my cheek, I closed my eyes, my body trembling under his touch. "I knew you couldn't live without it..." He trailed off. "Open your eyes Lib." I did as he asked, raising my eyes to his. "And I can't live without you. I've tried, but I can't do it."

"I'm going to leave you two to talk. I'll be back later." I heard my Mum say as she slipped out of the kitchen. I didn't acknowledge her; I couldn't tear my eyes away from Mason's.

"What about the baby, and Amber? I can't watch you have a baby with her Mason, I just can't. It would be unbearable." I said quickly, moving to take a step back from him. He dropped his hands to my waist, holding me in place. "Don't Mason, please," I begged, knowing if he pulled me into his arms I wouldn't have the strength to stop him.

"There is no baby Libby. There never was." He said softly.

"But…but I saw the scan?"

"Amber's friend works at an Ob/Gyn clinic in Marble Falls, they paid off a sonographer to put her name on someone else's scan." He squeezed my waist gently. "She made the whole thing up sweetheart."

"How did you find out?" I asked him, dazed by what he'd just told me.

"She tried to move all her shit into my place while I was at work one day. When I got home and found her there, I decided that I'd had enough. I was never convinced that she was pregnant in the first place, I always used a condom and I always checked them after…"

I dropped my head and stared at the floor as he was talking, he lifted my chin with his finger. "I know this is hard to hear, but look at me, baby." He whispered. I met his eyes as he continued. "I told her I wanted to go and see the Doctor with her, she started to make excuses, and when I wouldn't back down, she eventually confessed that there was no baby. She thought if you were out of the picture we would somehow be together." He looked directly into my eyes, and I could see the sincerity in them. "Libby that would never have happened. I would never have wanted anything romantic with Amber, even if the baby had turned out to be real. I need you to know that."

Still reeling from what he had told me, I asked him. "What was she going to do in seven months' time, when no baby arrived?"

"I've no idea, I don't think even she knew." One of his hands released my waist, and he dragged it through his hair. "Come back with me Lib." He begged. "Amber's gone, she won't be bothering us again."

"Gone? Gone where?"

"She's moved away. Florida, I think. I don't really care where she's gone as long as she's gone."

I looked at him, my eyebrows knitted together in a frown. "What did you do Mason?"

He sighed "I gave her $20,000 to leave us alone. Turns out there's not much she won't do for money."

I gasped, I couldn't believe he'd done that. I was still processing Amber never being pregnant, and now he was telling me she was gone. "I can't believe you gave her $20,000!"

"Lib, I'd have given her everything I had if it meant her leaving us alone and you coming back to me. I've been a mess this week without you, I'm not ashamed to admit it."

"I've been such an idiot." I muttered "If I'd just talked to you instead of running. I'm so sorry Mason." I flung my arms around his neck and buried my face in his shoulder. His arms quickly came around me, and he held me tightly to him.

"I love you, baby." He murmured into my hair.

"I love you too."

"Can I kiss you Lib?" He asked quietly. I lifted my head off his shoulder and nodded. He lowered his mouth to mine and kissed me, softly at first before nibbling on my bottom lip, my mouth opening to him. As I felt his tongue brush against mine, I moaned into his mouth and his arms tightened around me. God, I'd missed him, I'd missed how he held me, how he kissed me, how he loved me. I'd missed everything about him.

Breaking the kiss, he rested his forehead on mine. "So, you'll come back with me?" He asked, still sounding a little unsure.

I nodded. "As it turns out, I haven't been doing too great without you either. I need to speak to my parents though, about attending the University of Texas. I really want to finish my degree."

He looked at me sheepishly. "Actually Lib, they may already know."

"What do you mean? How could they know?"

"Don't get mad, but when you wouldn't talk to me, I made Savannah give me your parent's email address, we've been talking, and I may have mentioned it. I was going out of my mind baby, I needed to know that you were okay. I asked them for your address, telling them I wanted to write to you. They had no idea I was going to show up here."

I wasn't mad at him, or my parents, I couldn't be. I knew that they both loved me and wanted what was best for me. "I'm not mad. What did they think?" I asked him, worried that they wouldn't want me to go.

"They think it's a great idea, that it's just the fresh start you need. Obviously, they'll miss you, but they just want you to be happy." I heard my Dad say from behind me. I spun around, not realising that he was standing in the doorway. I rushed to him wrapping my arms around him.

"Thank you," I whispered.

"Anything to see you happy honey." He released his hold on me and turned to face Mason. "Nice to finally meet you son." He extended his hand out in front of him for Mason to shake.

"Nice to meet you too Mr. Davis," Mason said, shaking his hand.

"Mason, how did you manage to talk Savannah into giving you my parent's email address?" I asked him, puzzled. I knew Savannah hadn't agreed with my decision to leave, but I didn't think she would just give Mason their details without a fight.

He smiled awkwardly at me. "Well, I was desperate to know you were okay, I'd asked her, and she wasn't very forthcoming, so...I threatened to tell Brody that she was in love with Josh if she didn't give me the information. I'm not proud of what I did, but I'd do it ten times over if it got me to this point."

I burst out laughing. "I bet you're not her favourite person at the moment! I'd watch your back if I were you, I'd hate to be in Savannah's bad books." I saw a worried look pass across his face before he quickly brushed it off.

"Nah, she'll be fine." He said, waving his hand.

I laughed again. "We'll see!"

My Dad sat at the kitchen table with us while we chatted about university and what course I was hoping to do. My Mum arrived back about thirty minutes later, looking relieved that Mason and I had sorted things out.

We'd decided on takeaway for tea and Mason and my Dad had gone out to pick it up. I turned to my Mum who was sat next to me on the sofa. "Are you sure you're okay with me studying in America, Mum?" I asked her.

"I just want you to be happy sweetheart, it's been a long time since I've seen you smile like you have since Mason arrived. If studying in America and being with Mason is what you want, then your Dad and I support you 100%."

Tears welled up in my eyes. "Thank you, Mum," I told her, a tear slipping down my cheek. "I know I haven't known Mason long, but I really love him, he makes me happy."

"He loves you too Libby, I can see it in his eyes when he looks at you. Not everyone gets to experience a love like you two have, you should grab it with both hands and never let go." The tears were rolling down both of our cheeks, and we laughed when we realised, quickly wiping our eyes.

"I intend to hold on tight and never let go," I whispered. I'd let Mason go once, thinking I was doing what was best for both of us, but he was mine. Being without him made me realise that he had always been worth taking chances for, I just had to be brave enough to let him love me.

Chapter Twenty Five

My parents had invited Mason to stay with us until we flew back to Texas, they were pretty old fashioned though and wouldn't let him stay in my bedroom. They had said they couldn't control what I did when I was away from home, but under their roof there were rules. Instead, he was sleeping in the spare room which was right next to mine. I snuck into him on the first night, but after a brief kiss and a cuddle, he made me go back to my room, saying that he liked my parents and wanted to respect their wishes while he was here. Part of me loved him for it, but it was a small part, the bigger part of me couldn't wait to get my hands on him.

The day after Mason arrived I took him to Mia's grave, I wanted him to meet her, and unfortunately, this would be as close as he got. We stopped at the florist in the village and bought a bouquet of flowers to take with us. Mason grasped my hand tightly as we walked in silence through the cemetery. Dropping my hand, he stood back a little as we came to Mia's grave and I reached forward tracing my fingers over her name.

"Hey Mia, I've brought someone to meet you." I turned around and reached my hand out for him to take. He stepped towards me. "Mia, this is Mason, the guy I told you about. Turns out he came after me." I smiled up at him. "He's a keeper, right?"

Smiling at me, he turned to Mia's headstone. "Hi Mia, Libby's told me a lot about you, all good I promise." He said, winking at me.

Mason sat on the grass with his legs open, and I scooted between them, his chest to my back. "I've nabbed myself a cowboy, Mia," I told her with a small smile. "You'd love him." I felt Mason wrap his arms around me, squeezing me gently.

We sat for a while in silence, I was lost in thoughts of Mia, while Mason seemed happy to just hold me. After a while, I pulled myself out of his embrace and kneeled in front of Mia's headstone. "I guess this is goodbye for a while," I told her, my fingers picking at the grass to the side of me. "I'm going back to Texas with Mason; I'm going to finish my degree there. It's so hard to be here without you Mia, I miss you so much. I'll be back though, I promise." I reached up one last time and brushed my fingers across her name before turning to Mason who pulled me into his chest, kissing me softly on the head.

"Ready sweetheart?" He asked me quietly.

I nodded, turning in his arms. "Bye Mia," I whispered as we walked away, my eyes brimming with tears.

The next few days were nonstop, I gave Mason the grand tour of where I'd grown up, which didn't take long. I showed him the park where Mia and I had spent so much time and the primary school where we'd met. I also took him to the bakery and introduced him to Sarah and Leo. I had been a little apprehensive telling Sarah that I wouldn't be working for her again, I didn't like to let her down. Sarah understood completely though, saying that I couldn't pass up the opportunity of a lifetime.

I'd submitted the online application forms for the University of Texas, and someone from the admissions office there had called to speak to me. They told me that it looked promising that I would be offered a place, and I would find out officially in a few weeks' time.

I'd called Aunt Claire and told her of my plans to study at the

University of Texas, she had been so excited and insisted that I stay with them. I was so grateful to them for taking me in. I had considered looking for accommodation on campus as I didn't want to impose, but Aunt Claire wouldn't hear of it, saying I belonged with them. I thanked her three or four times, telling her that I'd see her soon.

Before I knew it, it was time to say goodbye. Emotions were running high, and plenty of tears were shed. Saying goodbye to my parents for a holiday, like I had last time, felt completely different to saying goodbye and not knowing when I would see them again. They had said that they would try to visit in the summer, before I started university, but that still seemed a long time away.

Fifteen hours later we were back in Austin and waiting outside arrivals for Savannah, who had agreed to pick us up. I was exhausted, the flight back had been bumpy, to say the least, and I couldn't relax enough to sleep. Savannah was late, and I was desperate to crawl into bed. "Where is she, Mason?" I moaned, sitting down heavily on my suitcase.

"Here she is grumpy." Mason teased. I stuck my tongue out at him and he laughed.

"Sorry, I'm late!" Savannah cried as she jumped out of the truck she'd borrowed to pick us up. She flung her arms around me. "I'm so glad you've sorted things out." She said, squeezing me tightly.

Mason had loaded our luggage and jumped in the back while I was sitting up front with Savannah. "I hope you didn't mind me giving Mason your parents email details?" She asked me, biting down on her lip. "It wasn't like I had much choice." She turned and glared at Mason. "Your boyfriend can be quite persuasive when he wants to be."

I burst out laughing. "Told you she'd be pissed," I said to Mason smugly.

"Hey." He said, holding his hands up in defense. "I got my girl back, that's all I care about. Sorry Sav, but I'd do it all over again if I had to."

"Well after that little speech I guess I can forgive you. You brought her back, that's the main thing." She said smiling. "Let's get you home, you look like shit."

"Thanks a lot!" I told her, as she burst out laughing.

An hour later and I was in Mason's bed, his arms wrapped around me. "God I've missed you, baby." He whispered in my ear.

"I've missed you too. Thank you for not giving up on me."

"I could never give up on you Libby. We're meant to be together." I turned my head, brushing my lips against his. He rolled me onto my back, his body pressing me down into the mattress. As he deepened the kiss, I moaned into his mouth and he ground his hips against me. After a few minutes, he pulled away, kissing me tenderly on the nose. "If I don't stop now, I won't be able to. As much as I'm desperate to make love to you sweetheart, you need to sleep."

"Sleep's overrated." I told him, reaching up to pull his mouth back down to mine. I felt him smile against my lips as I kissed him.

"We've got forever to be together baby." He told me quietly. "There's no rush." He rolled off me and pulled me into his body my broken arm resting across his chest.

"Tease," I whispered, my eyes getting heavy. Feeling safe, I succumbed to sleep, wrapped up in him.

Mason woke me up the next morning with breakfast in bed. "You do realise that I'm going to expect this every time I stay over?" I teased, grabbing a piece of toast off the tray.

"That's fine by me sweetheart." He bent over me and kissed me gently. "I need to go and check on a few things around the ranch. I'm taking you out for lunch though, so I'll be back later. Make yourself at home." He winked at me over his shoulder as he made his way downstairs.

"Will do," I called out. "Bye."

"Bye baby."

I forced myself to get up, heading downstairs I jumped in the shower, covering my broken arm with the waterproof protector the hospital had given me. As I was attempting to wash my hair one handed, I heard the door to the bathroom open, screaming, I tried to pull the shower curtain around my body.

"Baby it's me. I'm sorry I scared you." Mason said, walking closer to the bath. "I forgot my cell..." He trailed off, his eyes roaming over my body, the shower curtain failing to cover me. I felt my face flush under his gaze.

"Sorry. I thought you'd left, I thought..."

"You thought it was Amber, didn't you?" I nodded. "She's gone Lib, you don't have to worry about her." He pulled his t-shirt over his head and started to unbuckle his jeans.

"Mason, what are you doing?"

He looked up at me, his eyes hooded. "I can't go to work knowing you're here, wet and naked in my shower. It's been a long week without you baby." He climbed into the bath and gently pushed me against the tiles. I gasped as the cold hit my skin.

He brought his head down to mine and kissed me slowly, his teeth nipping my bottom lip. I opened my mouth, and his tongue swirled with mine. He pulled away, kissing around to my ear. "I've missed you so much, Lib." He whispered, his breath tickling my skin. I moaned, unable to form any words. He kissed me again as his hand found my breast, his fingers rolling and teasing my nipple. My head fell back against the tiles as his fingers continued their sweet torture, creating a pulsing sensation between my legs.

"Mason..." I moaned against his lips, needing more from him. I felt his hand move from my breast, caressing down my stomach. As he reached between my legs he pushed a finger inside, using his thumb to stroke me.

"Does that feel good sweetheart?" He breathed in my ear.

"Mmmhmmm." I murmured, pulling his mouth to mine and kissing him urgently.

"I need to get a condom Lib." He muttered as he pulled out of the kiss. "Don't go anywhere."

He turned to get out of the shower, and I reached for his hand to stop him. "Mason, wait," I said, pulling him back to me. "I'm on the pill…" Hesitating, I bit down on my lip.

"Are you sure? I was checked after Amber, I'm clean baby." I nodded my head and pulled his wet body back into mine. He picked me up, pushing me back against the tiles and I wrapped my legs around him. Positioning his erection, he slowly eased himself inside me, I gasped at the sting and the feeling of being stretched. The pain soon turned into pleasure as his thrusts increased, a familiar sensation building between my legs.

"You feel so good Lib." He moaned, kissing my neck.

Using the wall to hold me up, he moved one of his hands and brought it back to my breast, rolling my nipple between his fingers. His breathing quickened as his thrusts became more frantic. My whole body was on fire and sensing that I was close, he bent his head and whispered in my ear. "Come for me baby."

His words pushed me over the edge and I cried out his name, my orgasm triggering his own and I felt him jerk against me a couple of times, his breathing laboured against my neck. He brushed his lips against mine. "It just keeps getting better sweetheart." He murmured, shaking his head.

"I love you," I told him, not breaking eye contact.

"I love you too."

He smiled and gently dropped my legs so that I could stand up. I reached my good hand out to the wall to steady myself, my legs feeling like jelly. "Let me wash you Lib, it can't be easy with your cast." I smiled gratefully at him as he reached for the shower gel, inhaling deeply as he washed my body. I smiled, loving that I was going to smell like him all day. I heard him chuckle as he watched me.

"What?" I protested. "You smell good!" He shook his head and carried on washing me. "I hope I haven't made you late?" I asked him, worried he would get into trouble, especially after having to take time off to follow me home.

"You've definitely made me late, but baby I don't care. You're worth it." He kissed my nose and reached around me, turning the shower off. "Let's get you dry."

He dried every inch of me, wrapping me up in the towel. I then stood and watched him dry himself, his toned body on full display. I swallowed and pulled my eyes away, knowing he'd be even later than he already was if he caught me looking at him like I wanted to devour him. "I really need to go baby; I'll pick you up from the house at lunchtime." He pulled me towards him, kissing me softly on the lips.

I nodded. "Okay... thank you for helping me." I said shyly. He winked at me as he left the bathroom.

I spent the rest of the morning sunbathing in the garden with Savannah, she'd organised a shopping trip for uni supplies and a girl's night out within ten minutes of me arriving. She was convinced that I needed a whole new wardrobe for uni. That girl definitely loved to shop!

Savannah had grilled me, asking to know everything that had happened with Mason while we were in England. I hadn't asked her what had happened with Amber while I was away, I trusted what Mason had told me, and as long as Amber was gone for good, I didn't need to know anything else.

Mason arrived not long after we'd finished talking and dropped down into the seat next to me. "Hey, baby." He said, kissing me.

"Hey," I replied, smiling at him.

"You ready to go?"

"Yep. Where are we going?"

"You'll see, come on." He said, pulling me up from my chair. I turned to wave to Savannah who was grinning at me.

"You know where I'm going, don't you?" I asked her.

"Yep! My lips are sealed, though, enjoy!" She told me, skipping past me into the house.

Mason grabbed my hand and led me around the side of the house and towards the stables. I pulled back on his hand, slowing him down. "Mason, were not going on the horses, are we?" I asked him, nerves prickling in my stomach.

He stopped and turned to face me. "Do you trust me Lib?"

"Yes," I answered, without having to think about it.

"Then know that I would never put you in any danger. Just trust me, okay."

"Okay," I whispered.

Once we were inside the stables, he stopped in front of Titan's stall. "We're both going to ride Titan. He's used to having two riders, and he's big enough to cope with it."

"Mason." I started.

"You can't be on the ranch and avoid the horses Lib, I know how much you loved to ride before you got hurt, this is the start of getting you back in the saddle."

I sighed, I knew logically that the only reason I fell was because Amber had tampered with the saddle, but I still couldn't help feeling nervous about getting back on a horse.

"It'll be okay. I promise." He told me. I nodded and watched him in silence as he walked to the tack room, returning with a double saddle. He led Titan out of the stall and spent time fixing the saddle, ensuring that it was secure. "Happy sweetheart." He asked me, gesturing to the saddle.

"I'll tell you when I'm up there." I half joked. He mounted Titan and reached his hand out to me. Taking a deep breath, I gave him my shaking hand, and he pulled me up. Once I was in the saddle my arms flew around his waist, and I pressed my body tightly against his back.

"Ready?" He asked, his hand coming down to cover mine.

I nodded my head and he tapped his feet, encouraging Titan to move. I squeezed my eyes shut as we rode away from the stables. Once I'd calmed down, and my heart had stopped pounding I opened my eyes, recognising instantly where we were headed. "Are we going to the lake?" I asked him, my lips tickling his neck.

He shivered. "Yes, baby."

I loved it at the lake, it had fast become my favourite place, mainly because it was where I realised my true feelings for him, even if I had pushed him away on our first trip here. "I love the lake," I told him.

"I know baby." He reached his hand back and squeezed my leg. I was amazed at how relaxed I had become on Titan, I was guessing that it was because I had my arms wrapped around Mason and my body pressed tightly to his.

Before long we arrived at the lake and I dismounted Titan, followed by Mason. He reached for my hand again, and we walked to the water's edge where a picnic blanket was laid out. I turned to him and smiled.

"I thought we could have another first date. After everything that's happened..." He hesitated, sounding unsure.

"That's a great idea," I told him, going up on my tip toes to kiss him.

Pulling me down to sit on the blanket, he reached for the picnic basket that was waiting for us, as he opened it he started taking out everything that he'd brought for our first picnic.

I smiled. "You remembered what we had to eat?" I asked incredulously.

"I remember everything about that day Lib." He said sheepishly.

I smiled at him, biting into one of the pulled pork sandwiches, finding them as delicious as before.

After we'd eaten and packed everything back into the basket, we lay down on the blanket, my head resting on his chest. After a few minutes lying there in a comfortable silence, Mason said. "Lib, I did have an ulterior motive for bringing you here."

I pushed myself up on his chest so that I could see his face. "Really?" I asked wiggling my eyebrows.

"Not that." He laughed. "You've got a dirty mind baby, where's my innocent Libby gone?" He joked

"She's been corrupted," I replied with a cocky grin. "Why did you bring me here then?" I asked him.

"I wanted to ask you something." He sat up, and I sat up with him. "Move in with me Lib, I want to fall asleep with you in my arms and wake up with you in my arms. I want to make you breakfast in bed every morning and make love to you every night. What do you say?"

He looked nervous, he didn't need to be. A few weeks ago, I would have worried that it was too soon, that we didn't know each other well enough, that it might not work out and I might get hurt. Now I didn't even have to think about my answer. "Yes. I'll move in with you." I told him, smiling widely.

"Really?"

"Really," I told him, laughing. "You're stuck with me now cowboy."

"I'm never letting you go, baby." He murmured, pulling me into his arms.

I'd moved halfway around the world to be with him, I didn't

know what the future held for Mason and me, but I knew I wasn't afraid to find out. Losing Mia had taught me that nothing was guaranteed in life, sometimes you just had to be brave enough to take chances.

Mason
Six months later

I paced up and down the cabin, nervously waiting for Libby to get ready. I patted my pocket for what felt like the millionth time, feeling the outline of the ring under my fingers. Hearing Libby coming down the stairs, I quickly dropped my hand. "You look beautiful, sweetheart," I told her, as she stood in front of me in a short skirt and cowboy boots, my hands itching to touch her bare thighs. I watched her cheeks flush as I complimented her, six months into our relationship and my words could still make her blush. My dick twitched in my pants as my eyes tracked up and down her body, she was so beautiful, and I intended to show her just how beautiful I thought she was later. I'd show her now, but unfortunately, that would make us late.

"Come on let's go, everyone will be waiting." I reached for her hand, leading her outside to my truck. We were heading into Marble Falls for a meal, her parents were visiting, and they were meeting us there, along with Claire, Ryan, Savannah and Brody.

We'd been living together for the past six months, and short of sounding like a soppy bastard, they had been the best six months of my life. Everything was falling into place, Libby had been offered a place at the University of Texas to study English Literature and she was loving it. The nightmares from the car accident were, fortunately, getting less frequent, and Amber had heeded my warning and stayed away. Everything was perfect, well almost, it would be by the end of the night if everything went as planned.

I opened the truck door for Libby and helped her in, my hand brushing her thigh. I watched as goose bumps broke out on her leg and her breathing hitched. I smiled to myself, loving how responsive her body was to me.

We drove in a comfortable silence into Marble Falls, my hand tightly clasping hers. She no longer got anxious when travelling in a car, but that didn't stop me from holding her hand, any excuse to touch her. "You're quiet." She said, squeezing my hand. "Everything okay? You're not nervous about dinner with my parents, are you?" She asked laughing.

I smiled. "No baby. Your parents love me." I flashed her a cocky grin, making her laugh even more. I had been nervous to see her parents when they'd first arrived, but only because I needed to ask them for their daughter's hand in marriage. They had been at the ranch for a little over a week, and I'd finally managed to get them alone yesterday, wanting to speak to both of them, thankfully they had happily given their blessing.

I'd had the ring for months; I'd known pretty early on that Libby was it for me. When I'd found out that she'd left me and gone back home, I was devastated. I knew that I had to do whatever it took to get her back; I was always sceptical that Amber had been pregnant with my child, I'd always been careful. I would have fought with everything in me to get Libby back, baby or no baby.

Everyone was aware of my plans as I'd needed their help to set up the surprise that I'd planned for after the meal. Thankfully dinner went off without a hitch, and no one let my secret out. I couldn't eat any of my meal, I was so nervous. Fortunately, Lib had sat chatting with Savannah and hadn't seemed to notice. As the night came to a close, her Mum started to get teary, and I took that as my sign to leave before Lib started to suspect.

We said our goodbyes, and I noticed her Mum and Dad hugging Libby tightly. Having spoken to them yesterday, I knew how happy they were that Libby seemed to be back to her old self. Of course, she would never forget Mia, but she was managing to move on with her life.

As we pulled back into the ranch, I drove straight past our cabin towards the lake, which had become a special place for both of us. I saw Libby look around as she noticed we'd passed the cabin. "Where are we going?" She asked looking over at me.

"Wait and see," I told her with a wink. A few minutes later we were nearly there. "Close your eyes Lib," I asked her.

"What? Why?"

I laughed. "Please, just close them."

"Okay…" She smiled curiously at me.

As I stopped the truck I could see fairy lights twinkling in the tree we always sat under, along with hundreds of rose petals scattered on a blanket that was underneath the tree. Savannah and Libby's Mum had done an amazing job; I'd have to remember to thank them later. "Keep your eyes closed baby, I'll help you out of the truck."

"Okay." She said again, a huge grin on her face. I made my way around to her door and reached my arms around her waist, lifting her out of the truck and lowering her gently to the ground. I kissed her nose and turned her around. "Open your eyes," I whispered in her ear, her body trembling as my breath tickled her neck.

"Oh my god Mason, this is incredible!" She cried, spinning around to face me. "Did you do all this?"

"I may have had a little help," I admitted. "Do you like it?"

"I love it." She stood up on her tiptoes and brushed her lips against mine, I pulled her against me, circling my arms around her. I nibbled on her bottom lip with my teeth and waited for her to open up to me, my tongue plunging into her mouth as she did. Deepening the kiss, I heard her moan and her hands, which were wound around my neck, pulled on the hair at the base. I pulled out of the kiss, not wanting to get carried away just yet. I led her over to the blanket, positioning her so that she was standing surrounded by rose petals. "This is so beautiful." She gushed.

Holding her left hand in mine, my heart pounding, I reached into my pocket pulling out the ring. As I dropped to one knee, I heard her gasp and her other hand came up to cover her mouth. "Libby, the moment I met you I knew that we belonged together, I knew that it was only a matter of time before we got to this point. I promise you that no one will work harder to make you happy, or cherish you more than I do. You make me so happy baby, and if you let me, I'll spend the rest of my life trying to make you as happy. I love you, sweetheart. Will you marry me?" Tears were running down her cheeks as she looked down at me.

"Yes." She whispered, nodding her head. "Yes, I'll marry you." Her face broke out into a breath-taking smile, and I slipped the ring onto her finger. It was a perfect fit. I brushed my lips over it and stood up pulling her into my arms. She threw herself into my body hugging me tightly. "I love you Mason, more than you'll ever know." I leaned back slightly and touched my lips to hers.

We lay down on the blanket, her hand clasped tightly in mine as we stared up at the stars. We'd faced some obstacles to get to where we are now, but there was no doubt in my mind that I had found my soulmate in Libby, and I knew she felt the same. I would spend the rest of my life loving her, never letting her regret that she took a chance on me, a chance on us.

THE END

ABOUT THE AUTHOR

Laura Farr lives in Shropshire with her husband and two children. When she isn't working, or being a Mummy she is pursuing her dream of writing.

She is a romantic at heart and loves nothing more than writing stories with a happy ever after, even if there is the odd chapter of angst thrown in! Her desire to write came from her love of reading and when she isn't writing you will find her attached to her kindle or spending time with her family.

Social media links

Facebook Profile: https://www.facebook.com/laura.farr.547
Facebook Page:
https://www.facebook.com/Laura-Farr-Author-191769224641474/
Instagram:
https://www.instagram.com/laurafarr_author/

Defying Gravity - NOW AVAILABLE

Savannah Parker is miserable.

The reason: Josh Miller, her brother's best friend.

Devastated by the unrequited love she has for Josh, she has no choice but to sit back and watch him play the field, her heart breaking a little more each time she sees him.

In an attempt to forget about Josh and move on, she distances herself from those who love her. Josh is never far from her thoughts though. In a desperate attempt to feel something for someone and fill the void, she makes a reckless choice – one that will change her life forever.

Once her secret is revealed, relationships are threatened, and Savannah stands to lose those closest to her. When she needs someone the most, Josh proves to be her greatest support, and soon the lines of friendship become blurred. When she confronts him about his feelings for her, he reveals a secret of his own – a secret that could destroy them before they've even started.

Can Savannah and Josh make a relationship work? Or are there some secrets that are too hard to overcome?

Made in the USA
Columbia, SC
14 May 2018